Daisies AND *Devotion*

MAYFIELD
FAMILY
SERIES

Daisies AND Devotion

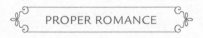

PROPER ROMANCE

JOSI S. KILPACK

SHADOW
MOUNTAIN

Library of Congress Cataloging-in-Publication Data

Names: Kilpack, Josi S., author. | Kilpack, Josi S. Mayfield family ; bk. 2.
Title: Daisies and devotion / Josi S. Kilpack.
Description: Salt Lake City, Utah : Shadow Mountain, [2019] | Series: Mayfield family ; book 2
Identifiers: LCCN 2018039642 | ISBN 9781629725529 (paperbound)
Subjects: | LCGFT: Romance fiction. | Novels.
Classification: LCC PS3611.I45276 D35 2019 | DDC 813/.6—dc23
LC record available at https://lccn.loc.gov/2018039642

Printed in the United States of America
Lake Book Manufacturing, Inc., Melrose Park, IL

10   9   8   7   6   5   4   3   2   1

$\mathcal{D}$aisy

A daisy, despite its simple appearance, is a composite flower; the inner section is called a disc floret, and the outer petal section is called a ray floret. Because daisies are composed of two flowers that blend together so well, they symbolize true love. Daisies come in a variety of colors and sizes, but the traditional flower—yellow center with white petals— continues to be the most popular. The oxeye daisy is traditionally the flower used in the game of "He loves me, he loves me not . . ."

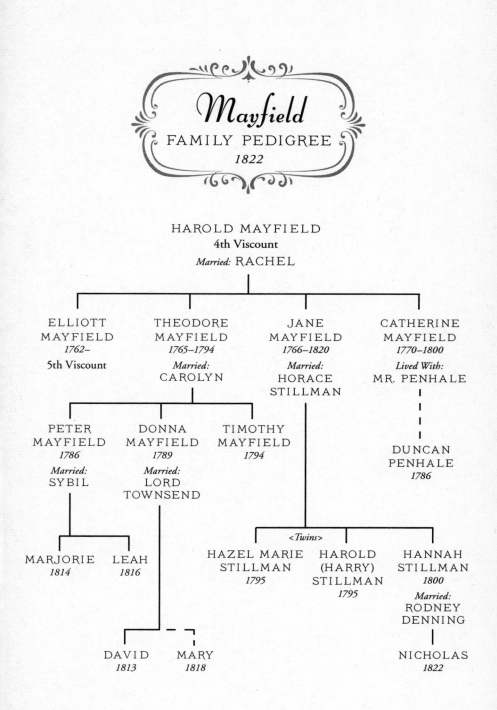

Mayfield
FAMILY PEDIGREE
1822

HAROLD MAYFIELD
4th Viscount
Married: RACHEL

ELLIOTT
MAYFIELD
1762–
5th Viscount

THEODORE
MAYFIELD
1765–1794
Married:
CAROLYN

JANE
MAYFIELD
1766–1820
Married:
HORACE
STILLMAN

CATHERINE
MAYFIELD
1770–1800
Lived With:
MR. PENHALE

PETER
MAYFIELD
1786
Married:
SYBIL

DONNA
MAYFIELD
1789
Married:
LORD
TOWNSEND

TIMOTHY
MAYFIELD
1794

DUNCAN
PENHALE
1786

MARJORIE
1814

LEAH
1816

<Twins>

HAZEL MARIE
STILLMAN
1795

HAROLD
(HARRY)
STILLMAN
1795

HANNAH
STILLMAN
1800
Married:
RODNEY
DENNING

DAVID
1813

MARY
1818

NICHOLAS
1822

Chapter One

April 10, 1822

After two minutes of sitting, Timothy was on his feet, walking the perimeter of the drawing room and looking over each of the excellent paintings on the wall. He'd never been one to sit still very long. Miss Morrington's father, Sir Wayne Morrington, had recently restored this house, so the corners were crisp and the design wonderfully modern. Sir Wayne had invested in gaslights back when other men turned their noses at the idea, and this house had been one of the first homes in London with the innovation. Had it not been the middle of the afternoon, the copper lamp hanging from the ceiling would have kept the lovely room bright. Sir Wayne had done very well for himself, to be sure, and though the *ton* might dismiss men of trade, when those men did as well as Sir Wayne had done, they opened their doors and forgot their prejudice.

Timothy heard movement and turned toward the doorway in time to see Maryann Morrington enter, her maid following behind. Miss Morrington's sister, Deborah, must not be available to attend them today. The maid went straight to the chair in the far corner that Timothy suspected was there specifically for those poor servants who had to attend their charges through visits such as these. His mother had been a maid—a scandal that kept Timothy mindful of the very thin margin that separated him from the serving class.

But life was too short and too beautiful to be spent thinking on the darker corners of things.

Timothy amplified his smile and crossed the room to bow over Miss Morrington's hand. He did not kiss her knuckles, but added a flourish and put his foot forward to exaggerate the bow. The dramatic gesture usually made girls giggle. But not Miss Morrington.

"You look as lovely as the morning, Miss Morrington," he said as he straightened.

She blinked golden-brown eyes and pulled her eyebrows together so that a line showed between them. "The morning is quite gray, Mr. Mayfield."

"Is it?" Timothy glanced out one of the unusually large windows. Lovely windows, truly. The sky was indeed gray! He turned back to her and shrugged good-naturedly. "Well, the temperature is wonderfully mild. I did not even need my greatcoat, though I wore it all the same. Fancy a walk through Hyde Park so that I might prove that even a gray day can be lovely when one has good company?"

Rather than clap her hands and run for her bonnet, Miss Morrington sat on one end of the green-and-yellow-striped settee. *All right then.*

Following her example, he sat in one of the green velvet chairs across from her, a round table between them. The fireplace had been lit which made the temperature of the room very comfortable. "Sadly, I've a head cold and am therefore disinclined to go out."

He sobered. "Ah. I see. It is completely miserable to have a cold in spring. You have my condolences." He refrained from adding that the upside was that she could lie abed and read all day as she recovered. Timothy loved to lie abed and read when he was under the weather. Not everyone appreciated his pointing out such silver linings when they were not feeling well, however.

She smiled, her already round cheeks plumping even more, but it wasn't a happy smile. Poor girl.

"When do you think you might feel better?" Timothy asked when she did not add words to her response.

There came that line between her brows again, and this time with a mild air of exasperation. Gracious, he'd only been in her company a minute and a half, and he was already wearing her thin. That did not bode well for his suit.

"I have no idea when I might feel better, Mr. Mayfield."

Yes, that *was* frustration in her tone. Had he been rude?

She folded her hands in her lap. "I'm afraid the malady did not check in with an expected date of expiration."

Timothy laughed and feigned a parry with an invisible sword. "Touché, Miss Morrington." He assumed an exaggerated frown. "There are few things worse than a lingering illnesses. What might I do to help you feel better?"

Her expression softened, and his spirits lifted in personal victory—Miss Morrington did not smile easily. Perhaps because her mother had died only seven months ago. Or maybe because her father had not come to London with them. She must miss him. But that was all the more reason for her to seek out joy now that she was out of mourning. Besides, coaxing a smile from her was worth twice the victory as that from another debutante because it was so mindfully given.

Suddenly inspired, Timothy jumped to his feet. "I have it,"

he proclaimed, pointing at the ceiling. "I shall act out a scene for you and you might apply your mind to guessing what scene it is. Would you like that, Miss Morrington?"

Her expression froze somewhere between a scowl and a smile. "Act out a scene? What are you talking about, Mr. Mayfield?"

He wagged his eyebrows and surveyed the room for props. He hurried toward a round vase and held it up toward the window, ignoring the slight gasp from the maid in the corner. He would not be distracted. He put his other hand on his chest and began to mouth the words and pantomime the actions associated with Hamlet's soliloquy to poor Yorick's skull. Who did not adore *Hamlet*? Timothy attended plays as often as possible, and he had even acted a part in a production or two when he had been at Cambridge.

When he reached the midpoint of the pantomimed speech, he turned on his heel toward the other side of the room, then fell upon his knees as he silently begged the jester's help in making his lady laugh. In the final moment, Timothy pulled the vase to his chest and bowed his head. He counted to three and then peered up at his audience of one.

Miss Morrington was smiling and shaking her head. "Oh, Mr. Mayfield, you are a jester all your own."

"Jester?" Timothy repeated, putting one hand behind his ear and leaning toward her. "Is that your guess on this scene I have so *expertly* acted out for your benefit?"

She laughed out loud this time, a short, punching laugh, almost like a man's. He only just suppressed a shudder. He'd heard her laugh from afar but never up close. Most unfeminine.

"You are Hamlet addressing Yorick, of course."

"Of course?" He got to his feet, adopting a stiff and offended posture while putting his free hand on his hip as though he were a

fishwife. "Do not damage my pride by insinuating that any number of other suitors have come into this room and dazzled you
with this display of *this* particular scene."

Her smile fell.

He reviewed his words but could not guess where he had mis-
spoken. "Have I said something amiss?" He took his hand from
his hip to better fit the change of mood.

"Suitors?" she repeated.

That was what had drawn her attention? He'd all but stood
on his head like a monkey and what caught her mind was the
word "suitors"? He returned the vase to its place and sat back in
the chair across from her. "That word upsets you?"

"Not necessarily." She shook her head, some girlish insecurity
breaking through her usually confident demeanor.

Timothy did not mind Miss Morrington's advanced age of
twenty-two, but he was still getting used to the difference between her more measured ways and those of the young debutantes so eager to have a man's attention. Those younger girls
simpered and pouted and pranced without restraint—it was all
rather exhausting. Miss Morrington, on the other hand, watched
carefully, spoke slowly, and did not give many hints as to what she
was thinking. She sniffled, and he fetched his handkerchief from
the inside pocket of his coat and offered it to her.

"Thank you," she said as she took the proffered handkerchief
and dabbed at her nose. In the meantime, that flash of insecurity
he'd seen in her expression faded back into politeness. He literally
watched as her back straightened and her chin came up, restoring
her to her regal pose. She fit London and its manners very well
and made those younger girls look rather silly. "Are you a *suitor*,
Mr. Mayfield?"

He felt as though to answer badly would end with a boot in

his backside. Not her boot, of course, but her butler's. In school, Timothy had often been singled out from his classmates after failing to keep quiet through a lecture. The teacher would demand Timothy repeat back the point of the lesson. Which, of course, Timothy had not heard because he had been engaged in a discussion with his neighbor about what games they might play after class.

"Am I *not* a suitor, Miss Morrington?"

She watched him a moment, then looked at his handkerchief in her hand. "I have not been certain whether your intentions were . . . specific or whether we were simply friends."

"Well, we *are* friends." Timothy grinned wider than necessary, hoping to ease her worries. "But as I hear it, friends make the very best of suitors." He winked and was rewarded with the tiniest pink of her full cheeks.

"Are you a suitor because you have learned of my inheritance? I suspect it has been whispered about, despite my family's attempts to keep it from the gossipmongers of the *ton*." She glanced toward her maid, who gave her a sympathetic smile. Apparently, this had been a topic of discussion between the two of them.

Timothy was unsure of the right way to answer. It was gauche to discuss money but rude to ignore a direct question.

When he did not answer, Miss Morrington cocked her head to the side, held him with her golden-brown eyes, and spoke in a soft, but still strong, voice. "If you care for me at all, Mr. Mayfield, I would ask that you be honest. Are you here because of my fortune?"

He would not be any kind of gentleman, or friend, if he did not honor the sincerity of her question. Plus, Timothy was not a dishonest man. Fun-loving, overly optimistic, energetic, engaging, and silly to some, yes—but *not* dishonest. "I am here, first and foremost, because I *am* your friend." He smiled, but she did not. "But I *am* aware of your inheritance."

Her shoulders fell a bit. "From whom did you learn of it? Did Lucas tell you?"

"No." He would not want to cast doubt on his friend's reputation. Not when Lucas was married to Maryann's sister, Deborah, and had been the one to introduce him to Miss Morrington.

"I regret to have to confirm that your inheritance has been quite the topic in town these last two weeks."

She smiled, which he hadn't expected, but then she had been hard to read from the beginning. She would sometimes get irritated when he expected her to laugh, and now she smiled when he thought she'd be upset. Women were mad. Heaven help the men who had to try to make sense of them and were flogged for their attempts. Not actual flogging, of course, metaphorical flogging. Timothy felt sure he'd suffered a couple of lashes already in this conversation, though he'd be hard-pressed to go back and find where he'd earned the punitive measures.

"Thank you for your honest answer," she said, in a tired voice. "I've had half a dozen gentlemen call upon me unexpectedly, and I had wondered if my fortune might be the reason. I asked two others, and they assured me they did not know what I was talking about, but I knew they were hiding something. At least I no longer have to guess at the reasons behind their sudden interest."

Half a dozen? Timothy's mouth went dry at the thought of that much competition. "It would be uncomfortable not to trust the motives of such visits."

She fixed him with those golden-brown eyes again. "Yes, it has been. What, then, should I think of *your* motivation?"

"Your boldness leaves me quite unbalanced, Miss Morrington."

She smiled again, but the expression was not entirely comfortable on her face. As though it covered a more honest expression she did not want to show him. "A woman of known fortune can hardly be blamed for boldness, Mr. Mayfield. Rather she would be a fool to be anything *but* bold. So, is your motivation in calling on me as a suitor the same as the others? Are you in need of making a moneyed match?"

Timothy squirmed in his chair. This was a most unexpected conversation. "You say it as though I have never called on you before. I only learned of your inheritance a fortnight ago, and yet you and I have enjoyed one another's company several times before that."

When Miss Morrington had first arrived in London several weeks ago, she was still in mourning, though she was wearing gray and not black. He'd first sought her company to please Lucas, who wanted his wife's sister to feel welcomed in London. She'd had her coming out in Somerset when she was sixteen, but when her mother fell ill shortly thereafter, she became her mother's companion and caregiver for the next five years. After her mother passed last September, Maryann Morrington could not put off the necessity of a season in London, but she had refused to end her mourning period until a full six months after her mother's death. Though Maryann had attended society events those first weeks, she had not danced or stayed past eleven o'clock. Timothy would seek her out at the events they both attended and found her a good conversationalist and an excellent listener. At the Guthries' ball last week, he had made a point to be the first man to ask her to dance now that she was wearing colors.

And here he was today, calling on her as he'd promised to do that night.

Miss Morrington held his eyes in such a way that he worried

she knew exactly what he was charting out in his mind while she waited for his answer. *Oh, rubbish.* He cleared his throat and reminded himself that his primary goal in pursuing a wife was to not hurt anyone.

"You ask if I am here because of your fortune, and I will tell you the truth." He paused a moment. "I do consider us friends, Miss Morrington, but my more specific attention is indeed partly influenced by the fact that your circumstance could be a boon to my own."

Her eyes widened in surprise, and he continued, not wanting to lose his momentum or his courage.

"I am without security, as I believe is also whispered about amid the *ton*: they track heiresses with the same ferocity as they track penniless men. I have always known I would need to marry a woman with means, and therefore I have kept my formal attentions focused in that way." Her jaw hardened, but he hurried to speak before she could shred him. "However, if I possess no other attribute to offer a woman, let me assure you that I know my own mind and my own heart enough to know that I could never marry only for fortune. I will remain a bachelor all my life if the only other choice is a loveless marriage."

He smiled, wishing she would take some of his energy and put it in her pocket. "I hope to find a woman of means to whom I can also give my heart, and so, while I would never have said so much without your invitation, I implore you to take me at my word and know that I am paying you particular attention in hopes that my heart and your heart might somehow connect and find that they cannot live without one another. If that ends up not to be the case, I hope we will continue as friends as we seek our separate happiness."

Timothy knew he was regarded as a well-known flirt after so

many years in London honing his skills in the business of finding a wife. He loved to make a woman smile, but he was mindful of who he asked to dance, how often he danced with any one individual, and, especially, how he sought out a woman's attention— such as calling on her at her home. His rules kept him from leading women on or becoming too invested in a woman he could not marry. It was wise and fair, but exhausting. He was a man of heart, and yet he could not lead with his in this.

Miss Morrington had watched him closely as he spoke but kept her expression cool. When he finished, silence threatened to flatten the room. Timothy was not very good with silences. He curled his toes toward the floor inside his shoes to give him something to focus on. The big toe on his right foot was rather sore, on account of the too-small boots he'd bought from a distinguished bootmaker. The boots had been commissioned and then returned by a man far wealthier than Timothy because the man felt the buckle too large. Timothy had been able to buy the offendingly-buckled-boots at a deep discount, though it still emptied his clothing budget for the quarter. Timothy had worn them to the ball last night and been suffering ever since.

Do not speak, he told himself while also trying not to tap his foot. *Count to ten forward then backward. Give her some time. She'll fill the silence herself eventually—won't she?*

Finally, she cleared her throat.

Praise the heavens!

"I must say I am completely shocked by your honesty, Mr. Mayfield. I did not expect it."

He grinned, liking that he'd surprised her. "One wonders why you asked, then."

"Because a man is easiest to read when he is lying."

Her quick and confident answer brought him up short.

"When a man is lying to me, I can see it in the way he banks his eyes and in the particular tightness about his ears."

Tight ears? Timothy raised a hand to the side of his head, ever so glad he had not lied.

She continued. "To ask a man hard questions allows me to read straight through him. To have him tell me the truth, however . . ." She leaned back in her chair and cocked her head. Only her soft smile kept him at ease. "Well, I am completely perplexed."

Timothy leaned forward and smiled again. "You are not the first person to tell me I am rather perplexing."

Miss Morrington laughed another brash, unfeminine laugh, then she sobered, though the corners of her mouth stayed up-lifted, which he took as another victory. "With a little luck, and my cook's excellent garlic soup, I hope I shall be feeling better in a few days' time. I hope you *will* call on me again, Mr. Mayfield. A walk in Hyde Park sounds lovely."

Inside, Timothy jumped for joy. *Truth will out!* He was officially tired of the hunt for a wife and was, instead, eager to marry and settle. He was looking forward to trading in the stress of the London seasons in favor of hosting parties and making connections. He hoped that more time with Miss Morrington would confirm their compatibility so he could be through with the marriage mart and on to a family of his own.

"I shall call on you for that walk as soon as I return to London," he said.

"Return?" she asked, raising her eyebrows.

"Oh, did I not mention that? I am leaving for my uncle's estate in Norfolk tomorrow, you see, and shall be gone through the weekend." The invitation had arrived a few days ago with a note saying that Uncle Elliott had something to present to Timothy. Timothy hoped it was a horse. Never mind that he did not have the means to keep a horse; perhaps Uncle Elliott would include a stipend for such consideration. Uncle Elliott had financially supported Timothy all his life, if not in luxury, in comfort and generosity that Timothy did not take lightly. It was not Uncle Elliott's obligation, yet he had taken on the responsibility when Timothy's parents had not planned accordingly.

Timothy smiled at Miss Morrington. "If you are still under heavy skies when I return, I shall act out another scene for you." He turned his head slightly and narrowed his eyes at her in mock reprimand. "Though I will expect applause for a second performance."

She laughed again. He suppressed another wince and reminded himself that a man in need of a fortune could not be *too* particular.

Chapter Two

Timothy arrived at Howardhouse in East Ashlam, Norfolkshire, Thursday afternoon. He and Uncle Elliott dined on a dish that Uncle Elliott had come to love during his years in India. Timothy did not share his uncle's delight in the red sauce over rice—his face felt on fire from the spices. He ate a great deal of the flatbread, instead, and drank too much wine in an effort to keep the flames at bay. Dessert, however, was a pineapple ice that was absolutely delicious and cooled the burning.

On Friday, he rode for miles across the open countryside on one of Uncle Elliott's fine stallions. It had been a long time since he had felt such freedom, and he made the most of it. He stopped at a pub on his way back through Norwich and struck up a friendship with a haberdasher who invited him and Uncle Elliott to dinner. Uncle Elliott was not one for socializing and declined the invitation, but Timothy had a fine time at the hatmaker's dinner party, enjoying the simple meal of beef and potatoes. He and Uncle Elliott went riding together on Saturday, though when they reached the crossroad bridge, Uncle Elliott waved for a stop.

"I haven't your fortitude, Timothy," he said, wiping his brow.

"I think I shall turn back, though I encourage you to take all the time you like."

"I can return with you, Uncle, if you wish."

"I wouldn't think of depriving you of this view," Uncle said, waving his hand to take in the hills and surrounding woods. "Your delight of it is what has brought me this far." His horse, a lovely gray animal with sleek legs and a slightly speckled rump, danced as Uncle Elliott turned toward home. "Do find me in my study when you are returned, however, so that we might discuss the purpose of my invitation."

Timothy had been so entertained during his time in Norfolk that he'd forgotten about the reason behind his visit. *Oh, please, let Uncle be giving me a horse.*

They parted ways, and Timothy enjoyed another hour of the wind in his face and the ground moving at a blur beneath his feet, before cooling temperatures from a gathering storm turned him back to Howardhouse. By the time he reached the estate, his curiosity over his uncle's surprise was getting the better of him and the storm winds were wrestling for his hat.

In the guest room where he always stayed when he visited—the yellow one he found particularly cheery—Timothy straightened his charcoal coat, looked at his profile from both sides, and pronounced himself presentable.

He found the door of his uncle's study partially open, though he still knocked twice before pushing it open the rest of the way. He poked his head inside. "Shall I wait? I don't mean to interrupt."

"No, no," Uncle Elliott said from behind his desk, waving Timothy into the room. "You are the purpose, not the interruption."

Timothy appreciated such a kind comment and entered,

taking one of the red leather chairs across from his uncle. He adjusted his coat and looked about the room. Timothy's father, Theodore Mayfield, had grown up at Howardhouse, the second son and Uncle Elliott's younger brother. He had been the spare, as it were, just as Timothy was the second son of his own parents. Theodore must have sat in this room a time or two, perhaps even in this very chair. Perhaps even when he confessed his affair with the maid that had resulted in Peter's conception, an ill-suited marriage, and—

Timothy pushed aside such unhappy thoughts and looked up at his uncle. It was all so long ago. "I thank you again for this invitation, Uncle. I have had a most enjoyable time here at Howardhouse these last few days. The springtime countryside is so very lush and green."

Uncle leaned back in his chair with a slightly indulgent smile. Timothy was not unfamiliar with such reactions to his optimistic nature.

"I am glad you have enjoyed your time here, Timothy. Your company is always a breath of fresh air. Something I find I am very much in need of this week."

"Is everything all right?" Timothy asked.

Uncle Elliott nodded, though Timothy noted he seemed more subdued than usual. Was Uncle Elliott ill? Dying? Was that the purpose of this visit? A lump formed in Timothy's throat at the thought of losing this man who had been like a father to him.

"Do not worry yourself, Timothy. I'm just an old man battling some old ghosts that have absolutely nothing to do with what I wish to speak to you about." He cleared his throat and folded his hands on his desk. "I'm sure you have wondered at my purpose in luring you away from the city just as the season is filling your calendar. I hope you have not missed anything too sensational."

"Not at all, Uncle," Timothy said. "I am grateful to be able to spend time with you." Were he being completely honest, he would expound on the fact that it *wasn't* that difficult to leave London. Timothy lived year-round in rented rooms in the city, but he wasn't enjoying the season the way he once had. The only thing he was truly looking forward to upon his return to London was his promised walk with Maryann Morrington. She was the best candidate for a wife he'd found thus far. She was steady and smart, well-mannered and bold. She would make a fine wife, and, if the rumors could be trusted, she had enough fortune to establish a very secure future. It had been a relief to have put all their cards on the table before he left London, and he was eager to pursue the connection and see where it might lead. He could love her one day, he was sure.

"I am glad to hear it was not too much of a difficulty for you to come," Uncle Elliott said, drawing Timothy's wandering attention. "And I hope your opinion will not change after our interview."

Timothy's smile froze, and his eyes were drawn to a leather binder squared in the middle of his uncle's desk. He had not noticed it before now, though it suddenly seemed quite prominent. He let his gaze linger, then met his uncle's eyes again. "I hope the same, Uncle."

His uncle took a breath as though preparing himself for something distasteful. Timothy tensed. When one lived on the generosity of others, there was the risk that all could be lost at any time. Without Uncle Elliott's financial support, Timothy would truly have nothing.

"I shall get to the heart of it, then," Uncle Elliott said. He turned the folder around so that it faced Timothy, but he did not push it across the smooth desktop. "I want you to know how much I enjoy spending time with you and what a blessing I consider you to be. You possess the gift of cheerfulness that has been a rarity in my life, and I admire your ability to put people at ease. I find you exceptional."

"Thank you, Uncle. I am humbled by such compliments." *And terrified of where they might be leading.* The words were most definitely a prelude to something of a heavier nature.

Uncle smiled, holding Timothy's gaze. "As you know, I have made it a priority to care for my nieces and nephews. I do not enjoy speaking of our difficult past, but the truth is that my siblings squandered their potential, and as I look upon their children, each of them dear to me, I find myself worried that they may fall into the same fate, either through poor choices or limited opportunity."

Peter, Timothy's older brother, was of exceptional character, but Donna, his older sister, surely fit Uncle Elliott's description and concerns. She had been more like a mother than a sister to Timothy, and yet he hadn't seen Donna for nearly two years, just after her illegitimate daughter was born. He didn't know how to help her except to write every few months.

The only one of his cousins Timothy knew beyond name was Harry, a rake of some reputation, who surely also fell under Uncle Elliott's concern.

"We need not get into the particulars," Uncle Elliott continued, "but I would like to discuss how your situation is affected by the difficulties of past and present generations."

"I do not feel I am overly affected by either, Uncle," Timothy said, hoping to alleviate his uncle's concerns, in regard to himself at least. "Memories are rather short in London, and should the poor choices of others in our family ever rise up, I am quick to prove myself a different man. Some people have connected me with Harry—we share similar features with our blonde hair and blue eyes—but we move in *very* different circles. Thus far, I do not feel I have been terribly misjudged." Timothy did not feel it was his family's reputation that impeded him socially but rather his lack of wealth.

"Peter does not share your optimism. He feels quite burdened by our family history—your parents' especially."

Timothy was surprised to hear that; Peter was as steady as a fence post, always had been. "Anyone would be a fool to allow our parents' choices to overshadow Peter's excellent character." Timothy had admired his brother all of his life and strived to be the same sort of man—with perhaps a bit more ability to laugh and seek enjoyable entertainment. Peter seemed to have received Timothy's portion of seriousness, while Timothy had received his brother's allotment of cheer.

"I agree with you, but I'm afraid your situation *has* been affected. Your father's irresponsible behavior has left you without means."

Timothy shifted in his chair as he felt the conversation deepening even more. In the space of a single tick of the clock that sat on his uncle's desk, he was reminded of his dependence on others to live the life he lived. Why was his uncle bringing this up *now*? "Yes, but your allowance has been generous and sufficient, Uncle. I appreciate it very much." Without his uncle's support, Timothy would have only Peter to rely on, and for all Peter had done to improve the family estate, there was little financial margin for Timothy to draw upon.

"And should the allowance be withdrawn?"

Timothy felt the blood drain from his face. "Wi-withdrawn?" Whatever did he mean by that?

"I am not taking the allowance, Timothy."

Relief flooded Timothy's body, and he let out a rushing breath as he leaned back in his chair.

Uncle Elliott continued. "It is, however, insufficient to support a wife and family. For a time, I had hoped you might go into the church and thus secure your living, but I sense you are not swayed that direction."

Timothy was even more on edge. "I fear I lack the steadiness to perform the work of a clergyman." Wear black all the time and live on the edge of polite society? No, that would never do for Timothy. He liked dancing and card parties and racing carriages through the parks of London early in the morning when no one but his friends were up and about—Harry had an excellent curricle he sometimes let Timothy borrow. Timothy had won fifteen pounds two weeks ago in an early morning race.

"And the military?"

Timothy barely repressed a physical shudder. He could never find satisfaction in brutality and deprivation. "I fear I am even less suited for life as a soldier than I am for a life as a vicar."

To Timothy's relief, Uncle Elliott did not look as though he were going to attempt to convince Timothy in one direction or the other. "So, then, what are your expectations for your future?"

"If you mean to ask if I expect you to support a family, please do not worry. I understand the conditions of my allowance and that there will be no increase upon marriage. I would never think to assume otherwise or push some advantage. I am well aware of your generosity toward me, Uncle, and do not treat it lightly."

"As I have seen," Uncle Elliott said sincerely. "But then what *are* your future plans?"

Timothy took a breath and swallowed his embarrassment. He could not sit still anymore, and, at the risk of appearing rude, he stood and crossed to the window to look out across the estate rolling into the horizon. "I have long known that I will need to marry a woman of fortune." He looked back at his uncle. "I have been about the business of finding such a wife for some three years now."

Uncle's bushy gray eyebrows lifted in surprise. "You only seek out women of means?"

Timothy nodded, refusing to feel shame regarding what was the only course left to him.

"For three years?"

"Well, three seasons," Timothy said. He thought back to the conversation he'd had with Miss Morrington about this very topic and how well his honesty had been received. He hoped his uncle would appreciate it as well. "I do not plan to marry *only* for financial prospects, of course—if that were my goal I could have made a match early on. I have instead kept my serious attentions on those women who I feel could offer me both happiness and security. I do not trifle with anyone's feelings. I have a great many friends of both sexes, but I am sincere and honest in my attentions toward a marriage contract and cautious in giving the wrong impression."

Harry operated very differently in London, and Timothy wanted to make sure that his uncle understood the differences between the two men without specifically disparaging his cousin.

"And you are content with this pursuit?"

Timothy laughed, but without much mirth. "I do not see that I have much choice *but* to be content, Uncle." He shrugged and held up his hands, lace cuffs draping from his wrists.

Donna had made that lace. Selling lace to a vendor in Bath

was how she helped support herself. She'd given Timothy a full twenty inches of it at Christmastime last year, and he'd added it to his favorite shirt. To him it was a reminder that everyone had to do their best with their particular circumstances.

He returned to his chair. "We must play the cards life has dealt us, and I am attempting to play my hand with integrity and practical acceptance. If you have heard reports to the contrary, I would like the chance to defend myself, as any accusations are undeserved." There had been a stolen kiss or two, but that could be said of any young buck in London. This season, especially, Timothy had been a perfect gentleman, determined to make a solid match.

"I've heard no reports," Uncle Elliott said, shaking his head. "And I commend you for your thoughtfulness considering your circumstance." He leaned forward and rested his hands on top of the leather binder on the desk. "What would be different if you had means of your own?"

"I prefer not to indulge in such fantasy. My imagination is such that I can too easily be carried away." More than one woman over the years had unknowingly led him to wonder if somehow love could be enough. He'd corrected his course in each case when reality descended, and regretted that he'd bruised a few hearts, as well as his own, along the way.

"I commend you for that as well," Uncle said, before pushing the leather binder across the desk. "I have taken each of my nieces' and nephews' situations into consideration and created what I believe to be an opportunity to remedy your individual difficulties. In your case, I have formulated the means for you to support a family."

Timothy held the blue leather binder in his lap and read over his name printed in gold in the lower right-hand corner: *Timothy*

Roman Mayfield. He looked up at his uncle, who nodded his permission for Timothy to open the folder.

Timothy felt his eyes widening as he read the words inside. When he finished—barely able to keep his eyes from skipping ahead on the page—he went back to the start and read again with greater focus, nearly forgetting he wasn't alone until he heard the squeak of his uncle's chair. He lifted his eyes without closing the binder. "Is this sincere?" He heard the reverence in his tone. "You mean to gift me . . . all of this?"

Uncle's eyes were soft when he smiled. "I want you to have a good life, Timothy, a happy life, and I would like for your choice of a wife to be made through good sense and genuine affection. I admire the way you have gone about your situation, but I think this"—he nodded toward the folder—"might put you in an even stronger position to make a match that can ensure security and happiness for the next generation of Mayfields."

Timothy turned his attention back to the folder, barely able to breathe through the swirling energy in his chest. "A house in London," he read out loud, then glanced up. "The London house is entailed upon Peter."

"Yes, the Mayfield London house, this estate, and a portion of the tea plantation that I went to India to build up in order to save our family from financial ruin—all those things are entailed upon Peter as heir. But I have personal ownership in the plantation and have used those profits to make my own investments over the years, separate from those of the family. I spent thirty years building my personal wealth alongside the family coffers and those assets belong to me to do with as I see fit. I purchased a house on Montague Street some eight years ago when I came to England for one of my visits and have been letting it ever since. Upon your marriage, it will become yours."

"And land?" Timothy continued, overwhelmed by the details. He would need to study his uncle's offer carefully in order to become familiar with the particulars.

"The one hundred and fifty acres are at present still attached to the lands of a friend I made while I was in India. His brother manages the whole and pays my portion annually. It would merely be a matter of legalities to formalize a division. The proceeds will keep the house on Montague Street and meet the needs of a family for some time, though not in extreme luxury."

"I have no need for extreme luxury," Timothy said. He was good with numbers and knew the income reflected on this page would make him far more comfortable than he was now. A carriage. A horse. A home in London. Land in the country where, perhaps one day, he could build an estate house. Perhaps he could invest in innovations that excited him, maybe even build a mill or purchase a shop to bring in further revenue. He could become the sort of man Peter had become, without needing his wife's fortune to make something of himself. He looked up at his uncle again. "I need only make a match and all of this comes into my ownership?"

"A match of my approval," Elliott clarified. "As I have evaluated our family's situation, I feel that poor marriages have been at least one cause of the disconnect. Bitterness between my siblings and their spouses kept you from knowing your cousins, and enforced isolation kept each family dependent only on each other, and sometimes not even that. I want to remedy those generational disappointments by giving you motivation to establish a whole and responsible life. A woman of good reputation and family, equally prepared for a life with you as you are for a life with her, is an essential element of that future success."

"You will choose my bride?" The offer suddenly lost some color.

"No, no," Elliott said, chuckling. "If you turn the page, you will see the requirements. I only ask that I meet the young lady and have the chance to evaluate for myself that she meets the stipulations I feel necessary for a solid match. I am not trying to extend any prejudice, I have nothing against other classes, however I have seen the difficulties of marriages that are not on an equal plane. I am sure I need not explain the details."

Timothy shook his head, knowing full well that Uncle Elliott was referring to his mother, Carolyn. After Theodore's death, Mother had not known how to function in the world left to her. She had become solitary, raising her children as best she could but rarely venturing into the outside world. She became prone to long, drawn-out periods of sadness where she struggled to care for herself while the children were left to manage the house—without servants. Timothy had never outgrown the feeling that he had failed her all those years ago. If he and Peter and Donna had been able to fill the void their father had left behind, or if they had known how to help her, maybe she would not have lived in such darkness within her own mind.

"I also want to ensure that any young woman you choose is not marrying you only for *your* money—a possibility you should consider as you return to London. You may go public with this information if you like, but be sure you understand the risks."

Timothy turned the page and read through the list of requirements Uncle Elliott set out for the type of woman he would approve: a God-fearing woman of character from a good family or with a fair assessment of their failings; a woman who would be devoted to Timothy, committed to raising a family and upholding the highest of moral standards; moderation in vices, affection, and willingness to adapt to the lifestyle he was able to offer.

Timothy tapped the page. "If I were a more cynical man I would ask about the catch. There is nothing here that I would not seek for myself."

Uncle smiled. "That is precisely what I had hoped. Only, now the woman you decide to court will not need to be wealthy— though she still could be, I suppose."

Timothy read the list a second time to make sure he understood each detail, his spirits lifting higher and higher with every line. Finally, he closed the folder and laid it reverently in his lap. He cleared his throat, thick with the emotion rising from his chest. "Uncle, I have not the words able to express what this means for me." He had to clear his throat again to keep his voice even. "After years of fearing I would have to settle in one way or another, I can now make a choice of my heart, for my heart's sake. Have you any idea how this shall change my entire future?"

A glimmer of sorrow Timothy did not understand entered Uncle Elliott's eyes as he nodded slow and sober. "I think I have some idea of what this means to you, Timothy, and I am very glad to be able to open this door for you. There is nothing more important than family, and I am humbled to be able to help you on your way to finding happiness in your life."

Chapter Three

Maryann completed the final dance of the set, curtsied to her partner, Mr. Andres, accepted his arm, and allowed him to walk her back to her party. He was as stiff and awkward leading her back as he had been when leading her to the floor, which was disappointing as he'd seemed to relax some during the dance.

"Thank you for the p-pleasure, Miss Morrington," he said, releasing her arm and bowing to her like a rusty hinge.

She smiled. "Thank you, Mr. Andres." She gave him a nod, and he shuffled off. She watched him sympathetically. This was his first London season, and he was unaccustomed to the city. Hopefully in a few more weeks, he would not feel so out of place.

Deborah stepped up beside her. "Was the dance as uncomfortable as it looked?" she asked, her voice purposefully light.

"No," Maryann said, taking the cup of punch Deborah offered her and giving her sister a narrowed look. "He is a nice young man, only . . . new to the city, that is all."

"And new to the dance floor, I presume," Deborah continued,

her gaze scanning the ballroom. "I swear I could see his lips counting out the steps."

"Don't be cruel. We all come as we are." Maryann had turned twenty-two on Boxing Day, which made her feel ancient compared to the other debutantes. She hoped the young men would not judge her harshly for her age and thus was inclined to overlook their own weaknesses. Unless their weakness was poverty or debt, then she was unable to give much encouragement because she knew they only pursued her for her fortune.

Deborah shrugged and took a sip of her own drink—wine, not punch. Married women could get away with such things. "All in all, the evening seems to have been a success. This is the first set you have not danced."

"I might sit out the rest of them," Maryann said, lifting one foot and attempting to ease the cramping arch. "My feet are killing me."

"I told you not to save the new slippers for a ball," Deborah chided.

"I shall follow the advice for my other pair, mark my word. I only did not want to get them dirty by wearing them prior to tonight." She extended her foot forward to admire the shimmery gold of the satin in the candlelight of the ballroom. They really were fabulous slippers, cramps and all.

Deborah touched Maryann's elbow, and she looked up to see what had caught her sister's attention. As soon as Maryann saw him, she felt her shoulders relax and the corners of her mouth turn up. "He's here," she said under her breath.

"Indeed he is," Deborah said, as self-satisfied as though Timothy's arrival had been her doing. Deborah made no attempt to hide the fact that Timothy Mayfield was her choice for Maryann.

Lucas had been friends with Timothy since Cambridge, and Deborah had insisted on introducing him to Maryann as soon as she could. The little sister in Maryann wanted to reject her sister's choice as a matter of course—she would never hear the end of it if Deborah chose her husband, whoever he might be—but such a rejection would be silly rivalry, and Maryann was beyond such things.

Timothy was lively, kind, and handsome in a boyish way that put her at ease regarding her own rather plain looks. From their first introduction, she'd felt a warmth in his presence, a sparkle of . . . something that had only grown since. She never felt as though he were keeping up pretenses with her, an aspect he had proven at his last visit when he'd admitted to being in the market for a wife of fortune. Maryann had been peckish that day, her head throbbing and her mood as gray as the skies. She'd been shocked by Timothy's answer to her surly question regarding his intentions, and even mildly put off, but by the end of the visit, she had been grateful for the truth. That he was not seeking her out *only* for money deepened the connection she'd felt to him from the start. Being married to such a man would bring laughter and adventure into her life as well as a reprieve from the shadows that had moved in during the years of her mother's declining health.

Maryann had been the natural choice to be her mother's companion, and it had not been difficult to forgo her own ambitions in order to attend her. When Mama died last fall, Maryann had lost her closest friend. It had been a very long winter, and she would not have come to London except that Deborah had convinced their father that Maryann needed to get out from under the cloud that had darkened the skies for all of them. Timothy, more than anyone else Maryann had met, had opened the drapery and let sunlight back into her life. Now that word of her fortune was drawing impoverished men to her like ducks to bread, she appreciated his friendship more than ever.

She watched as Timothy made the rounds of the room, saying hello to everyone, it seemed. At one point, he looked up and caught her watching him. She ducked her head, embarrassed, before looking coyly away. When she looked back, he was leading Miss Larkin, a debutante with golden hair and sparkling blue eyes, to the dance floor. There was no reason whatsoever for her to expect Timothy to ask her to dance first. And yet, she had imagined that he would cross to her directly and ask her to the floor. She'd all but counted on it, considering this was the first time she'd seen him since his return from Norfolk.

Timothy whispered something to Miss Larkin as he passed her in the steps of the quadrille. Miss Larkin laughed, then covered her mouth with her hand to hide the reaction.

Maryann turned away completely, feeling foolish, and Deborah raised an eyebrow. Had she been watching Maryann watching Timothy?

"I must step outside for a few moments," Maryann said, coming up with a quick excuse for escape. She put her cup on one of the nearby tables. "It is quite warm."

"Quite," Deborah said, but she had not looked away, making Maryann feel like a book waiting to be read. An unwilling book.

It was a comfort to have Deborah in London, acting as her sponsor for the season and keeping Maryann from her inclinations to stay at home. But sometimes Maryann felt as though she was expected to lay her entire life open like a map for her sister to peruse and critique at will. If Deborah's pregnancy last summer had come to term . . . Well, many things would be different, including the attention Deborah could direct solely at Maryann. It was unfair for Maryann to think such things, however. No one had wanted that child more than Deborah had, and if managing Maryann's belated season lessened some of the pain her sister still carried for the loss, then Maryann could not complain.

Still, she needed some air and some distance for a few moments at least. Timothy had not even crossed the room to say hello.

Maryann headed for the veranda doors, nodding at a few acquaintances and pausing to converse a few minutes with Susanna Hansen, before continuing outside. The cool air on her warm skin tingled. She welcomed the sharpness. There were not many people out, which suited her, and she found a quiet section of balcony where she could lean her forearms on the stone railing. She inhaled the night air, highly fragranced with smoke from both household fires and the factories from the east end of town. Father said that industry would soon take over society, but she hoped industry would not bring *this* part of life to an end completely. There would always be a place for fine evenings and pretty gowns, wouldn't there?

She let her eyes drift closed and, against her better judgment, invited a new fantasy to mind now that her original fantasy—that of Timothy crossing to her immediately—had come to naught.

This time, he'd look about the ballroom after his dance with Miss Larkin only to find Maryann missing. Determined to find her now that he'd fulfilled his duty to Miss Larkin—perhaps he'd lost a bet or owed her brother a favor—he'd begin a search for Maryann, eventually finding her on the veranda, looking over the moonlit garden with the gentle breeze stirring the curls that dripped down her back. In the moonlight, she would *almost* look beautiful.

She imagined him standing in the doorway even now, watching her, then crossing to her as silent as a falling petal. He would reach her, but not speak. Instead, he would put out his hand and brush his fingers across the back of her neck, inviting a shiver of such delicious heat that she would be more grateful than ever to have stepped outside.

"Miss Morrington?"

"Hmm," she said, captured within the image of Timothy leaning closer, repeating his words in her ear. She angled her chin so as to put her profile at its most alluring.

"Miss Morrington?"

The voice was too direct to be fantasy. Her eyes popped open, and she spun around to see Mr. Barney Fetich jump back, startled by her reaction. She put a hand to her chest as fire shot up her spine and filled her cheeks. "Goodness," she said, trying to catch her breath and feeling like the most idiotic of women. "You frightened me."

"I am sorry," he said, his cheeks red, too. "I had thought you heard me the first time I said your name. My apologies."

She *had* heard him the first time. Only she'd thought it was Timothy within her daydream. She forced a smile and squared her shoulders, though her cheeks continued to burn. "Yes, well, I am sorry to have been so distracted. Um. How are you this evening, Mr. Fetich?"

"I am well." He spoke as though he were not entirely sure how he was doing. "I had wondered if you were already engaged for the waltz. It shall begin in a few minutes."

She had, of course, hoped to waltz with Timothy, but he had not asked her before taking Miss Larkin to the floor, nor had he found her on the veranda when that set had finished. "I am not already engaged, Mr. Fetich."

His face relaxed into a smile. "Would you, perhaps, consider waltzing with me, then?"

"Certainly."

He put out his arm, and they walked back into the ballroom, making small talk about the party and the weather as they waited for the set to finish. Maryann had no trouble locating Timothy dancing with yet another blonde debutante. She furrowed her eyebrows at that. Granted, she had not been part of the London society for long, but Timothy had tended to be a bit less . . . cliché at other events.

The dance ended, and she lost sight of Timothy as dancers stepped off the floor and new dancers stepped on, her and her partner included. Once in position with Mr. Fetich, Maryann scanned the crowd yet again, her mouth nearly falling open as she watched Timothy escort Genevieve Crawford onto the floor. Genny was the forerunner of the debutantes this season. Diamond of the first water, they called her. A paragon. She was a lovely girl, but her father was a gentleman farmer, and Genny had only been able to come to London through the graces of a family friend. Genny was the oldest of seven children, and there was no doubt she'd been sent to London in hopes of making a match that would work in favor of herself as well as her younger brothers and sisters. Not only was Timothy not in a position to give her such security, but Genny could not give Timothy what he had confessed he needed in a match—money.

The orchestra began, and Maryann forced herself to meet Mr. Fetich's eyes. She would not be so rude as to be distracted by another man, but her chest prickled with questions and irritation.

Not only did Timothy not ask Maryann to dance, he was only within her vicinity long enough to share a simple hello before moving off to another corner of the room to converse with yet another of the leading set of debutantes this season. To cover the pain of her unrealized expectations, Maryann adopted her most inviting smile and made eye contact with every man she could, ensuring that she danced every set of the night, flirting with more ardor than was her usual habit. Through it all, she kept her eyes on Timothy, who moved from blonde to blonde like a bee at a honeysuckle bush.

By the time the ball ended and she was seated in the carriage across from Deborah and Lucas, she was a complete muddle of pain. Her feet were throbbing, and her chest was filled with irritation, frustration, and . . . regret. Had she been so out of sorts that day Timothy had come to see her that she'd put him off? Had he left believing that she was not a woman he could spend his life with, while at the same time, she was believing he might be the very man she'd come to London to find? What of his insistence that he would not court women he could not expect to marry?

"What a lovely event," Lucas said. He reached for Deborah's hand and raised it to his lips, holding her eyes as he kissed the back of her hand.

Maryann looked away from the affection; Deborah and Lucas had been married just over a year, and their lovebird habits were nauseating tonight. She'd have been happy to walk home, pinching slippers and all, but it was dark and London was not safe at night. Still, she longed for some cool air to help with her temper, and a solitary walk might have helped her work through some of her feelings.

"Do you agree, Maryann?"

She looked up at her brother-in-law and forced a smile. "Yes, it was a very nice evening."

He raised an eyebrow. "Very nice?" He turned to Deborah. "I believe she said the same thing about last night's fish."

"Yes," Deborah confirmed, watching Maryann closely. "I do believe she did."

Maryann sighed dramatically and lifted one foot. "My feet are all but numb from these blasted shoes, and I am very tired."

"I am sure both of those things are true," her sister said. "But that is not all, is it?"

Maryann refused to meet her sister's eyes as the carriage bounced and bumped along the cobbles.

"Perhaps you did not notice, my dear," Deborah said, addressing her husband, "but Timothy barely said hello to Maryann tonight." She leaned toward Lucas as if to whisper, though she spoke as loudly as ever. "I believe that has set Maryann's back up a bit."

"Really?" Lucas drawled.

Maryann felt like she were on stage as both of them stared at her. She let out another breath and straightened. "Yes, I had expected he would say more than 'Good evening, Maryann' before running after the next blue-eyed beauty like every other lovesick buck in this town."

The silence that followed was fierce, and she felt the blood rush to her cheeks. Had she just opened her mouth and let out these petty words to bounce off the walls of the carriage like frogs? She cleared her throat and opened her mouth to apologize, but Deborah spoke first.

"'Blue-eyed beauty'?" Deborah repeated, embarrassing Maryann even further because of what those words really said. *I am not blue-eyed nor am I a beauty.*

"Never mind," Maryann said, shaking her head and wishing she'd not made a habit of blurting out things like this. She was behaving much as she had when Timothy had visited her and she'd put him on the spot to define his motivations. Was there something about him that made her forget manners and polite behavior?

"Only, I thought . . ." She stammered. "I thought Timothy was interested in other things."

"He is." Lucas knit his eyebrows together. "I had not noticed it in the ballroom, but you are right. He danced with all the belles, didn't he?"

Maryann growled low in her throat but was not sure if that was because Lucas had confirmed what she'd seen, or because apparently everyone knew who the belles were—and that Maryann was not one of them.

I do not care for such things, she told herself.

Deborah chimed in. "I think what Maryann was most aware of was that he did not dance with *her*. He had all but promised her a dance at this ball."

"He promised me nothing," Maryann defended.

"I think that he did," Deborah said.

"He didn't!" She was too loud, adding one more layer to her embarrassment. She covered her face with her hands and forced herself to take three deep breaths before lowering her hands and speaking again. "He danced with me at the Guthries' ball some weeks ago. *That* was what he'd promised, and it is fulfilled. He owes me nothing, so let us be done with this conversation. As I've said, my feet hurt and I am so tired I clearly cannot control my tongue, therefore I should not use it at all."

"But I think—"

Lucas took Deborah's hand, silencing the rest of her words. "Let us do as Maryann says and speak no more of this tonight, dearest."

Maryann appreciated his help, but she did not thank him

because she was determined not to speak for the rest of the night in hopes of preserving some measure of dignity.

She knew Deborah would pick up the thread again, but Maryann had a reprieve for tonight at least. She closed her eyes and leaned her head against the seat, letting it bounce on the cushion in time with the movement of the carriage. *He can dance with whomever he likes*, she reminded herself. And yet, she had so wanted him to *want* to dance with her.

Chapter Four

Timothy was admiring the carved marble mantelpiece when Miss Morrington entered the drawing room. The detail of the mantel was remarkable, and he told her so after he bowed over her hand and complimented her appearance. She wore a straw bonnet with lavender ribbon that matched the small flowers on her cream-colored dress. Her pelisse was yellow, which made her look like springtime, except for the slight tightness of her smile. If she hadn't wanted to go for a walk, he wished she'd have responded and said as much. Truly, she was one of the harder females of his acquaintance to read, but he hoped to understand her in time. He generally liked a challenge.

"Are you ready then, Miss Morrington?" he asked, raising his eyebrows expectantly.

"Yes, Mr. Mayfield."

He put out his arm, which she took, and they turned from the room together. Once on the street, walking toward the west entrance to Hyde Park, he asked if she was feeling better since their last visit some two weeks earlier.

"I am, thank you," she said. "And how was the visit to your uncle? Does he live in Norfolk? I think that is what you had said."

Timothy could not keep from smiling broadly, as he did each time he thought of his visit to Uncle Elliott's estate and how his life had changed since then. "The visit was nothing short of exceptional," he proclaimed. "Exceedingly so."

"Exceedingly exceptional?" she repeated, looking at him but not smiling, though he thought she probably should since she was obviously teasing him.

"Exactly," Timothy said with a nod.

She faced forward again, and they took a few steps in silence. "And since returning to London? Have you been enjoying yourself?"

He heard the dash of judgment in her tone, and it was his turn to look her direction without a smile. "I always enjoy London," he said. "Is there something wrong?"

"Oh, no, nothing," she said in that tone particular to women who were put out with a man. Unlike many women, however, she was not missish, so she could probably manage him confronting her on it.

They were approaching the park entrance, and he waited until they were within the green before he spoke again. "That, Miss Morrington, is not true. I can see right through your words because of your *tight ears*." He leaned close enough to bump her shoulder playfully. She glanced at him quickly. "So, tell me why you are put out? Is it with me in particular, or some overall complaint with life that has turned your thoughts away from such a lovely day as this?" He waved his hand at the blossoming trees around them. A breeze would now and then send a flutter of petals into the air—it looked like pink snow. They passed two women and nodded in greeting, but didn't stop to converse.

Timothy silently sighed in relief. Some ladies he walked with made a point of talking to everyone they passed. Hours could go by when one walked that way.

Maryann remained silent even after they were "alone" again. Acting on impulse, he reached over and pulled at one of the ribbons of her bonnet, unraveling the bow beneath her chin.

She let go of his arm in order to catch the ribbon before the knot came undone too, then she turned wide eyes to him. She had lovely eyes, golden-brown with flecks of green near the center. "Mr. Mayfield!"

He laughed at the scolding. It was too lovely of a day to be serious.

Other girls would likely cry if he teased them such, but Miss Morrington merely glared at him, though he felt sure he could see the beginnings of a smile. She attempted to retie the bow, but her gloves apparently made the task awkward without a looking glass, so he lifted his own hands and pushed hers away.

"I am sorry. Let me fix it." He poked his tongue between his teeth as he concentrated, making sure each loop was equal to the other. His sister, Donna, had taught him to tie a bow, and he felt sure she would have been proud of her little brother's accomplishment on Miss Morrington's behalf today—though she would have scolded him for untying the bow in the first place. He was close enough to Miss Morrington that he could smell the scent of her perfume—a very nice blend of florals and musk.

When he finished the bow, he met those golden-brown eyes again and realized she'd been watching him. The awareness gave him a shiver. She didn't look away as the moment stretched a bit longer than necessary. And then a bit longer still. He was the one to step back, clearing his throat and fiddling with the cuff of his coat to give him reason to look away from those lovely eyes that had captured him.

Once he'd recovered from the odd . . . connection, he put out his arm again, smiling brightly at her. She was still watching him but took his arm after a few moments. They resumed their walk through the park.

"*Now*, you have reason to be put out with me, Miss Morrington."

"Perhaps I had reason to be put out with you before you attempted to upend my bonnet on the street."

He imagined if that had actually happened and her bonnet had been blown from her head and they'd spent five minutes chasing the thing. That would have been hilarious! But that wasn't the point, and he returned his attention to the discussion at hand. "I suspected as much, but when I asked what was wrong you said 'Nothing.'" He said the last in a falsetto voice and celebrated when she pinched her lips together to keep from smiling in response. "Come now, Miss Morrington, we are friends, are we not? If you are upset with me, I would prefer you tell me."

She sighed, then opened her mouth to speak. Timothy saw a couple approaching from down the way and steered Maryann to the side of the path, bowing politely as the couple passed. Privacy was restored soon enough, and Maryann took a deep breath. "All right, Mr. Mayfield, since you want to know my mind, yes, I *am* a bit put out with you."

He put his free hand on his chest. "I am wounded. Whatever have I done to earn your put-out-ed-ness?"

"You have been back from your uncle's for almost two weeks, and I have seen nothing of you."

"Not true," he defended, raising his hand to stop her. He held up one finger. "First, I saw you at the Harrows' ball, and then at the Sorensons' garden party, Almack's on Wednesday, and then, today, I came to take you on that promised walk." He wiggled his four fingers for emphasis before lowering his hand. She did not seem impressed.

"I was frankly surprised you remembered having promised it at all." She looked past him, at a bird or some such distraction, but the color was high in her cheeks and her intent was pointed. This was not an exaggerated feeling, she truly was upset with him.

"Obviously, I did remember. I believe I deserve credit for following through, not criticism."

"I do commend you for following through on your promise, but you cannot blame me for questioning your attention since you barely spoke to me at the other events you mentioned." She fiddled with the string of her reticule. "Could we walk again, please?"

He obliged, and after a few steps, he spoke again, "I am genuinely irritated by your determination to accuse me of neglect, Miss Morrington. I greeted you at each and every event."

"Yes," she said with a nod, her chin high and confident. "You greeted me and every other person there."

So many young women were soft and sweet all the time, but he liked feeling that Miss Morrington did not hide any portions of her nature from him.

"I should not have greeted you? Or should I have not greeted the others?"

She sighed, and he sensed a weariness in her as she looked at the ground. "There is no need for me to be vague any longer, is there?" She took a breath. "I had felt, before you left town, that you and I had reached a certain understanding of one another, and yet now, upon your return, I can't help but feel as though you are avoiding me." She stopped, and he turned to face her on the path. "Are you avoiding me, Mr. Mayfield? Because if you are, you need not have followed through on this engagement today. I do not need your pity nor your attention if it is not wholly given."

"So," he said slowly, moving through his thoughts as though picking his way in the dark of night. "You are upset with me because I asked you for this walk?"

"I am upset with you because you have all but ignored me at every other engagement."

"I am unsure what you expect, then, Miss Morrington, since we have both agreed that I *did* speak with you at each of those events."

"Did you ask me to dance?"

"Well, no," he said, only now realizing the truth. Dancing was a perfect way to introduce himself to the debutantes he had not let himself get to know before his situation changed. "But in my defense, there are far more ladies than sets, so I did not dance with *most* ladies."

She cocked her head to the side and dropped his arm. "Just say it out. Have you been avoiding me?"

"No," he said with a laugh. The idea was ridiculous. He spread his arms wide. "Am I not here, right now, attempting to walk with you in Hyde Park? If I were avoiding you I certainly would not have done that, now would I?"

"No, I suppose you wouldn't." Her tone held confusion, and perhaps some embarrassment. He felt she deserved to feel the latter, but maybe not the former. They agreed that he'd promised her this walk and that he'd delivered on that promise and that he'd not *ignored* her at the other events. He prayed that would be the end of it.

Only, it wasn't the end of it because now he was reviewing

how he'd interacted with her at those aforementioned events and could see why she had made the conclusion she had. He had not given her any special attention, which apparently, she had expected. Was he responsible for that expectation?

"Right. Might we continue?"

She nodded and took his arm yet again, sheepishness replacing her defensiveness.

They walked in silence while Timothy reviewed the day he'd visited her in her father's drawing room. It was reasonable that his boldness that day—and hers—would create an expectation different from what she had of other men. Men who flattered her and . . . were after her money. Was that the root of her insecurity? Did she see him as just one more man after her fortune and therefore not to be trusted? But he wasn't one of those fortune hunters. Not anymore. She did not need to be wary of him or attempt to interpret his every action or every word. It must be exhausting to have to suspect every relationship with every man who approached her—poor girl. The realization made him glad he had kept his unexpected financial boon to himself so that he might not face the same fate as Miss Morrington when the town learned of it and changed their treatment toward him.

"I am sorry it seems as though I have been avoiding you, Miss Morrington," he finally said. "That was not my intent."

She was quiet for a few steps, seeming to be looking at the trees and flowers that decorated the park. "I am glad to hear it, but I wonder what changed. Your . . . intention at these events has been different than it was before you left."

He imagined her watching him during those balls and dinner parties, expecting him to give her some attention while instead he lavished it on women he had only been cordial with before because he could not risk engaging his heart.

"Don't hear what I've said wrongly," she added. Was that repentance in her tone? "You owe me nothing, Mr. Mayfield. Our connection is chiefly due to your friend and my sister's marriage and—"

"It is not true that our connection is based upon them," he cut in.

"It *is* true, and that is all right," she said. "I value your friendship, but you know my position in this carnival of matchmaking, so I hope you understand why I am so . . . sensitive. Not just to you, of course, but to all men who seek to be a *suitor*. I do not mean to hold you to that place, Mr. Mayfield, and I fear that is the impression I have given this afternoon."

He nodded an understanding of her apology, but his discomfort continued. *She does not consider me a suitor?* That was likely for the best. At least he knew for certain she considered him a friend.

"So then, enough of that. You must tell me of your visit to your uncle," she said. "I have never been to Norfolk."

"It is lovely country," he said, but he felt he could not discuss a new subject without settling her mind first. "Miss Morrington, as we are friends and as I have caused you some discomfort, I think I should confess something to you that will explain the change of my recent . . . pursuits." He swallowed nervously, debating the wisdom of sharing his secret with her, but landing on the portion that would benefit her. And him, really. He would not feel responsible for her confusion once she understood, and he quite liked the idea of being able to say out loud the things that had been turning like a mill in his chest and mind. If anyone would understand the change of his position it would be her.

"Oh?"

"My visit to Norfolk was exceptional for a variety of reasons, but one reason in particular. If I tell you, may I count on your absolute discretion? You and I both know how loud the whispers can be in town, and I do not wish this to become a matter of gossip. But neither do I want you to take responsibility for something that is unconnected to you."

"I can promise you, Mr. Mayfield, that I am no gossip."

He looked at her and drew her to a stop. "You cannot even tell your sister, or Lucas—certainly not Lucas." Lucas had not revealed Maryann's financial situation to Timothy, and so Timothy saw no reason to confess *his* circumstance to Lucas. At least not yet.

She raised her eyebrows. "Of course, I shall keep your secret, Mr. Mayfield. Even from them if you ask me too."

Though he had not known her long, he believed her to be a woman of character. And so, in a big, rolling jumble of words and gestures and expressions, he told her the whole of Uncle Elliott's offer, even easing her to the side of the pathway when two women came upon them so that his explanation might not be interrupted. She listened without taking her eyes from his face. Timothy found himself experiencing the same excitement he'd felt when he'd first learned how his destiny was forever changed. When he finished, he felt the flush in his cheeks.

"Is it not remarkable?" he said, almost breathless.

"It is remarkable," she said. "Um, congratulations."

"Thank you." He pushed out his chest a bit. There was something validating in having someone else agree that this was as much a boon as he thought it was. "After all these years, it is as though a tiny hole in a curtain has been torn wide open. I can now let my heart make the choice without restraint. I can, literally, find the perfect woman without having to factor something as gauche as money into the equation." He was tempted to throw his arms toward heaven in a display of gratitude. Perhaps dance a little jig.

"The perfect woman," Miss Morrington repeated. "And, what are the aspects you are now able to look for since money is no longer your goal?"

Timothy immediately ticked the desired traits off his fingers: blonde, tall, graceful, with blue or green eyes, a bow-shaped mouth, dainty fingers, and rosy cheeks, even in winter. His perfect wife must come from a large family, possess a hearty appetite without giving toward plumpness, and have a tinkling laugh. She should enjoy dogs and riding horses, traveling at a moment's notice, dancing in the rain, fine wine, and society events. She should have a mother who thinks Timothy is wonderful. She should speak French and Italian, have musical prowess, love babies, and possess an affinity for art, especially watercolor.

"I adore a solid watercolor." He grinned, feeling light as a balloon to have put these words out into the world. They felt more real, now that they'd been spoken. And, oh, so very possible.

"*That* is your perfect woman?" she asked.

He nodded. "I might make some exceptions for things like eye color and language proficiency, but, yes, for the most part what I have just described is the woman I have always wanted. And now, I can have her. Upon my return from Norwich, I wrote it all down."

He patted his coat pocket, where he kept the list. Each time he remembered how wonderfully things had changed for him, he would touch his pocket and imagine the woman he was determined to find amid the finest city in the world.

Maryann blinked at him, then looked away for several seconds. She took two deep breaths. When she looked back, he noticed that the warmth of her golden-brown eyes was missing, replaced with an emotion he did not know how to interpret. "Mr. Mayfield, such a woman does not exist."

"Oh, she does," Timothy said with a grin. "I am sure of it. She is my destiny."

"What you have described is a fantasy—a caricature of what a real woman is. And it is extremely shallow."

His joy wavered and fell to the ground between them like a stone. "I am not shallow."

"No, you are not," Miss Morrington said in a way that sounded like an agreement but wasn't. "Which is why hearing such *shallowness* from you is so surprising. You have described what a woman looks like and what a woman knows and does, yet you've said nothing about a woman's character and virtue and flaws."

Timothy harrumphed. "I hate to be the one to tell you this, Miss Morrington, but a man does not go looking for a woman with flaws."

"No, but that is what he will find. Every time."

"With the right woman, even the flaws will seem like virtues."

She shook her head and laughed dryly, not her usual bark. No one enjoyed laughter as much as Timothy did, but not when it was at his expense. He felt himself tightening. "I shared this with you because I thought it would help you understand why my intentions have seemed different of late. I did not want you to feel that there was some failing on your part—"

"Except that there *are* failings on my part." She began ticking off his list with her fingers the same way he had done. "I am not tall, blonde, green-eyed, nor do I have—what was it?—oh, yes, perpetually rosy cheeks or a bow-shaped mouth. I speak French but not Italian, though I can read Latin. I am not particularly musical, I do not come from a large family, and my mother is *dead,* so she cannot think you are wonderful. Apparently, all those things are failings when compared to this *goddess* you are searching for."

"That is not what I said." She was twisting his words, and he hated the heat burning his neck. "I refuse to apologize for seeking out certain qualities in a wife now that I have the chance to do so."

She raised her eyebrows. "Instead of having to settle for one of us who is so far below your standards?"

"You have aspects you are also looking for in a husband, Miss Morrington. Does that make you shallow?"

"If I wanted only beauty and accomplishment, yes, it would, but my hopes include things like an appreciation for my honesty, the ability to look past physical beauty, a temperament that lends itself toward being a good father, and devotion to me and our future family. Those things will take time for me to know about a man, and through that process, I fully expect to learn even more about him, including those imperfections which every man possesses. To say I shall only consider fair-haired men or men raised in the north would make me as shallow as are all the men seeking my attention only because I am wealthy."

Timothy shook his head and looked around as though there might be some mode of escape nearby. But they were standing on the side of a path in the middle of Hyde Park. Plus, he was Miss Morrington's escort back home so he could not storm off, though he was tempted.

"Well, I am very sorry that I burdened you with this information," he finally said. He put his arm out stiffly, barely containing his anger. "I had best return you home as we have both worked up to far more temper than is comfortable."

She narrowed her eyes, and he turned back the way they had come—back when the day had still been lovely and his mood cheery. They walked to her house in silence. It had been so freeing to tell someone of his good news, but she had turned it inside out to the degree that he looked like a fool. And he *was* a fool. Obviously, he and Miss Morrington were not friends the way he had thought they were. Well, at least now they both knew where they stood with one another. She could focus on all those other men vying for her attention and her fortune, and he could see to his own happiness. They would never have made a solid match. It was best they knew it sooner rather than later, but he hated the discord.

When they reached the front walk leading to her father's house Timothy stopped and turned to face her, keeping his expression guarded, which was not his strong suit. He was relieved to see she had lost some of her tension. He hoped that would help his apology find its mark.

"I apologize for upsetting you, Miss Morrington. That was not my intent. I had only . . . I had only meant to try to explain so that your feelings would not be hurt at what seemed like my slighting you. I have never meant to annoy you, but I seem particularly adept at doing so."

"And I am sorry for reacting so strongly, Mr. Mayfield." She spoke calmly, and he was relieved that she was not going to continue the flogging. "It really is none of my business nor my concern. I hope you can find what it is you are looking for and that you realize every happiness." She met his eyes and smiled, though there was sadness behind her expression. Or maybe just discomfort. All of this *was* terribly uncomfortable. "I truly do want your happiness. I am only sorry that I won't be the woman to share it with you."

They said their goodbyes, she went inside, and Timothy turned toward his rooms. He was a few steps away from the house when he stopped in the middle of the sidewalk. *I am only sorry that I won't be the woman to share it with you.*

Gracious. She'd thought . . . She hoped . . . And he'd . . .

Timothy groaned as his eyes closed and his chin dropped to his chest. After a few seconds, he began walking again, but his steps dragged as he replayed the afternoon—what he'd said, what she'd said, and, most importantly, what he now realized she'd *felt*.

When they had spoken in her father's drawing room before he left for Norfolk, he'd told her that he needed to marry for money but that he also wanted to find a woman he could love, which is why he was being attentive to her. Today, he'd essentially told her that since money was no longer his goal, she was no longer a consideration. *Gracious.*

Chapter Five

The day following their walk in Hyde Park, Maryann received flowers from none other than Timothy Mayfield. She'd have thrown them out the window except that they were daisies.

Instead, she fell into a chair in the drawing room, holding the bouquet that had been wrapped in cheap paper, and tried not to cry. It was ridiculous that she should feel so hurt by what he'd confided to her yesterday. But she felt it all the same.

She put her nose into the flowers and inhaled deeply. The fragrance was nothing like roses or lilies or freesias, but daisies reminded her of home and happiness and simple pleasures—all of which seemed far away just now. As children, she and her sister had picked daisies from the woods and made chains and crowns and played "he loves me, he loves me not" while picking off the petals. When Mother had been ill, Maryann and Deborah had taken turns picking bouquets every few days when the wildflowers were in bloom to keep the vase near Mama's bed full. Maryann had wreathed Mama's headstone with a daisy chain made from the very last blooms of the season, having had to search all the woods to find enough. She missed her mother, both the woman who had been vibrant and full of life when Maryann had been young, and the failing woman who had needed Maryann so much in the last years.

Who needed Maryann now? Who noticed her first when she entered a room?

Not Timothy Mayfield now that he did not need her money. *He loves me not.*

She looked at the flowers again, wishing he'd sent roses or something she could dismiss more easily than these. The bouquet was not from a shop, which would have used finer ribbon and paper. Instead, this was a haphazardly gathered bunch, like what she would have picked from the woods at home. He had not picked them himself, had he? From one of the public gardens? She imagined Timothy standing in the middle of a cultured garden and snapping stems as quickly as possible before he was caught. She smiled slightly.

More likely he had bought the flowers from a street vendor who would have the best prices. Did that mean his current allowance was the same as it had always been despite his promised inheritance? He still wore too-small boots and owned just three coats he traded around with his waistcoats—not always in the best combination—for different events. He would be embarrassed to know she'd noticed such things; maybe she would tell him so that he would feel as low as she did.

"You are being petulant," she told herself and stood. A card tumbled out from within the folds of paper. She retrieved the card but rang for a vase before she read it. Only when the bouquet was centered on the table in front of the parlor window did she sit down and open the letter.

Dear Miss Morrington,
I am beyond humiliated at my actions yesterday and
hope you will forgive me for being unkind. I shall always
value our friendship as a great treasure and hope that it
might continue.

Sincerely,
T Mayfield

Maryann curled up in the chair by the window, knees pulled to her chest as she read the words again. *Friendship. Value. Treasure.* She pushed away some of her hurt so she might see his position more clearly than she had yesterday. A great boon had come his way, of course he would take advantage. Any man—or woman—would. Should Maryann wake up beautiful one day, perhaps she would pursue the new prospects that would be opened to her with the same self-interest.

She read the letter again and then tapped it against her chin as she looked out the window to London beyond. A carriage rattled down the cobbled street going one direction, and two women holding parasols crossed before her window going the other way. Life moved forward, and her hurt would not stop or change Timothy's new circumstance. She could respect that he had not hidden anything from her. His honesty was proof that he valued and trusted their *friendship.* However, she faced the prospect of either keeping Timothy at a distance, having now seen a side of him she did not like, or keeping him in her circle for all the things she admired.

She looked at the envelope again, and then at her hand that held it. One of Timothy's requirements had been dainty fingers. All the Morrington children had inherited their father's hands—short fingers, blunt at the tips. Her hands were not masculine, necessarily, but they fit with the rest of her, which was not up to par with Timothy's expectations of feminine perfection. And perhaps not other men's expectations either. She was not willowy and thin. She had square shoulders, though Deborah assured her it gave her a balanced figure that men appreciated. Only penniless men, it seemed.

Her thoughts were interrupted when a young man turned into the walkway of her father's house. She quickly fixed her position in the chair, hoping he had not seen her curled up like a child. She recognized Mr. Fetich the moment before he disappeared from view. It was too early for callers, and yet she had no reason to turn away a man who *was* interested in her company. Timothy's goal, before his uncle's offer of financial independence, had been to find love with the woman he married for money. She could do the same. Never mind that she'd hoped Timothy might have been her match—she felt things for him she did not feel for other men.

When Herrington, the butler at Father's London house, knocked on the door a minute later to see if she would receive before hours, Maryann agreed. Mr. Fetich had arrived merely twenty minutes before calling hours; it was not so poor a breach. "Will you please inform my sister so that she might join us?" she added. Herrington nodded, and Maryann pinched her too-full cheeks to add some color.

Mr. Fetich was shown in, and she welcomed him with a smile. Deborah joined them a few moments later, only somewhat frazzled by the unexpected request of her company, and after exactly a quarter of an hour, Mr. Fetich gave his goodbyes, bowing over Maryann's hand and leaving a rather wet kiss there, which she wiped on her skirt once he'd been escorted out of the room.

"Well," Deborah said, returning to her chair. "At least he has manner enough not to overstay a visit, though why he did not wait until calling hours gives him no credit." She met Maryann's eyes. "You are not overly impressed with him, are you?"

Maryann shrugged. "I suppose not, but he is kind."

"What do you know of his circumstance?"

"I believe it falls to my sponsor to manage such details," she said with a smile.

"Well, I shall be sure not to fall short, then. Lady Dominique will know. We can ask her at tea this afternoon." Deborah's eyes seemed to land on the daisies for the first time. She smiled, stood, and crossed to them, touching one of the petals before turning to look at Maryann.

"Daisies," she said under her breath, and Maryann was sure she was remembering their mother the same way Maryann had. "Did Mr. Fetich present these before I arrived?"

"They arrived *before* Mr. Fetich. From Timothy." The card was tucked in her sash though there was no reason to keep it. It was not a love note to read over and over again so as to relive the thrill of the words. But it *was* the continued offer of friendship, and maybe that was just as valuable.

Deborah's smile widened, and her look become pointed. "What a thoughtful gesture."

"Indeed," Maryann said with her brows lifted. "Because he acted a complete cotton-head yesterday and owed me an apology." She gestured toward the flowers as proof.

Deborah's smile fell, and her hand dropped to her side. "What?"

Maryann had promised not to reveal the change of Timothy's circumstances, so she merely said, "He has changed his interest in me and has chosen to pursue a different sort of girl."

Deborah's voice was heavy. "What?"

"It is fine," Maryann lied, waving her hand casually. "Timothy and I are good friends, Deborah, but not all that compatible when one really considers the intricacies of marriage." She was not nearly blonde enough, for one thing. And quite frankly, he lacked the depth she would put on her list, if she had one. Which she didn't.

Deborah sat across from Maryann, her golden-brown eyes—same as Maryann's—filled with compassion and regret. "What are you talking about? The two of you are perfect for one another. He is so sociable, and you are such a good hostess. You temper his enthusiasm, and he brightens your mood."

"He is not attracted to me," Maryann said, causing Deborah's expression to turn from concern to glowering. "And that is all right. I am not keen on some of his sillier mannerisms anyway. He shall make a wonderful *friend* here in London, and I bear him no ill will."

Deborah glanced at the flowers again, and Maryann felt prompted to explain further. "He did not express himself as well as he should have when we spoke yesterday, but then I responded with unkindness, so perhaps I should be sending him flowers as an apology for my part."

Deborah's eyes snapped back to Maryann. "I'm sure your reaction was perfectly reasonable."

"It was not," Maryann assured her. Deborah would have a fit if she knew how boldly Timothy and Maryann had conversed. "But we are friends again, and the bouquet is lovely. Did you tell him that daisies were so meaningful to me? I have not seen any since leaving home, though the woods would be bright with them now, wouldn't they?"

"I have never mentioned anything about daisies to Timothy," Deborah said flatly. It might be harder for her and Lucas to accept that her relationship with Timothy would only ever be as friends than it was for Maryann to accept it herself. Well, not really, but it helped to tell herself as much.

Something caught Deborah's eye out the window, and she straightened before looking at Maryann. "You've another caller. I don't know him, but I believe you danced with him at Almack's." She lifted the watch pinned to her bodice. "At least it's past eleven; I shall give him credit for that."

Maryann smiled and arranged herself on the chair so that she was ready to receive when the man, Mr. Burkstead, was let into the room. She looked into the man's brown eyes set too closely beneath eyebrows that came together just off center of his nose and kept her sigh to herself. Without any prospects regarding Timothy Mayfield, it may prove to be a rather long day . . . ere, season.

Chapter Six

Two other gentlemen called after Mr. Burkstead, and Mrs. Callifour and her two daughters came as well. Maryann enjoyed that visit best; the eldest Callifour sister was Maryann's age, and they shared a similar, slightly cynical humor they could hide beneath what seemed to everyone else to be polite conversation: "Oh, yes, Mr. Burkstead is a nice gentleman. Those eyes!"

Then there was tea with Lady Dominique, Lucas's mother. Lady Dominique was a powerful woman in London and hosted a weekly tea with her friend, Mrs. Blomquist, where they got to know young ladies they would then recommend to other friends. The two matrons did not specifically cater to the highest social ranks, rather they concentrated their attention on those young women without strong connections in town so that they might have the distinction of helping debutantes find their place. An endorsement from Lady Dominique and Mrs. Blomquist was as much a credential as a voucher to Almack's. Deborah and Maryann attended the weekly "welcome" teas as often as possible to keep the afternoons from feeling like interviews, though that was exactly what they were.

It was through one of those teas that Maryann had met Mrs. Callifour and her daughters. Today was not one of *those* teas, however. Today was sheer gossip, and by the time the macarons were gone, Maryann knew that Mr. Burkstead was the fourth son of a baron and without a living. Additionally, she learned that Mr. Andres would likely have a commission by the end of the summer and wanted to marry before then so he would have someone to kiss him goodbye and someone to come home to.

It was useful information to have, but it was not hard to imagine that at some other tea in some other part of the city—or perhaps over brandy at one of the gentlemen's clubs—Maryann's name was being batted around by others determined to reduce her solely to money and circumstance. A person's character seemed to matter very little. And she was as bad as any of them. Perhaps London brought out the worst in everyone.

There was a dinner party that evening, but it did not go too late and Timothy had not attended. It was a relief to enter her bedchamber and know that nothing was required of her for the next eight hours. Lucy, her maid for ten years, was waiting for her, and Maryann smiled at her gratefully. She sat at her vanity, and Lucy began to take down her hair.

"You seem out of sorts, miss," Lucy mused after a few minutes. "Are you unwell?"

"I am well enough," Maryann said, arranging the pins on her vanity in straight lines, side by side. At least she could enforce order amid her accessories. "Only . . . unimpressed with this city, I suppose. Everyone seems to wear a mask, and I wonder how a woman is to ever know a person." Except Timothy, she realized. He did not wear a mask. He was exactly who he said he was. But he didn't want her, so what did it matter?

"I am sorry, miss," Lucy said with a thoughtful nod.

"Have you enjoyed London, Lucy?" The woman had been far more excited to come to town than Maryann when the decision had been made at Christmastime. Maryann envied her maid's simple joy of things; she did not have markers to reach or motivations to sift through.

"Oh, very much," Lucy said, grinning. "They have assemblies for the serving class three times a week at a variety of different halls throughout the city. The housekeeper arranges schedules so that each of us might attend at least one. I went last night in fact, while you attended your ball, and I enjoyed it very much."

Maryann met Lucy's eyes in the mirror and smiled at the maid's enjoyment. Lucy was seven years older than Maryann, and a bit of a flirt. "I am glad to hear that."

Lucy nodded, still smiling to herself as though remembering the evening.

A few minutes passed as Lucy finished taking down Maryann's hair. Maryann thought about Lucy's social nature among her own class. Then she thought about tea that afternoon. Lady Dominique knew so much about so many people, but not everything or everyone. Mr. Fetich, for example, was someone Lady Dominique knew nothing about.

"Lucy, do you remember that time you learned that the curate was paying inappropriate attention to the maid in the Jaberstone house?"

"It was far more inappropriate than *attention*, miss." Lucy's eyes sparkled. She liked to talk, which was why Maryann was careful not to share too much of her own information, but then again, she did not have much to hide. "I was glad to see that curate leave the village," Lucy continued. "I tell you that for sure. A man of the church must live as such."

Maryann had told her father what Lucy had told her. Father

had then told the vicar, who had investigated, proven Lucy's story true, and sent the curate packing. "I agree. He was of no character to represent the church. It reminds me, however, how very good you are at learning about households, and I wonder if you and I might make an arrangement."

Lucy lifted her eyebrows and removed the last pin. She used her fingers to further separate the locks of hair that had been twisted up all day. It was all Maryann could do not to close her eyes and melt into the sensation. Instead, she picked up the brush and handed it over her shoulder, forcing herself to focus.

"What sort of arrangement?" Lucy asked, running the brush through Maryann's hair.

"If I could work it out with the housekeeper for you to attend *all* the gatherings through the week, could you seek out servants from other households and learn information for me?"

"If those servants are at the events, I suppose I could, but there are a great many servants in this city, and learning specific information from a specific person might be difficult. This is not Dunster."

Excellent point. Maybe her plan would not work, but it was worth a try, was it not? "And if you cannot find information, that is fine. I have ways of learning what I can above stairs, but it could be quite a benefit should you learn a detail or two as well."

Lucy was thoughtful. "What sort of thing are you looking for? Immoral conduct?" Her eyes were a little too bright. Maryann was quick to shake her head. This was not an opportunity to share salacious stories. At least not *only* salacious stories.

"You know of my trepidation regarding the men who have been calling on me these last few weeks, now that my inheritance is known in the city."

Lucy nodded.

"While many of them have circumstances that are publicly known, there are some who are not so forthcoming, and I am hesitant to open my heart to them until I know the reason for their interest. To marry a man who wants only my money seems a fate worse than spinsterhood."

Lucy looked thoughtful as she continued to draw the brush through Maryann's hair. "You want me to learn about the men who call on you?"

"I specifically want to know if the men who come to see me are in need of my fortune. I suspect they all are, but perhaps I am wrong about some of them. I could interact with them differently if I better understood their situation. Could you determine that, do you think?"

"Why not just ask them, as you did Mr. Mayfield?"

Lucy had been in the room for the bold conversation that day and afterwards had deemed Mr. Mayfield exactly the sort of man Maryann should fall in love with. So much for that.

"Most men are nothing like Mr. Mayfield." Her heart ached to say it. "They do not tell me the truth and instead act out a part as well played as Mr. Mayfield's tribute to Hamlet was."

Lucy laughed. "That was great fun."

"Yes, it was," Maryann said dryly. "But Mr. Mayfield has made his intentions clear, and they are not pointed toward me."

Lucy frowned and shook her head.

"I must therefore make the most of my other prospects, and I think your particular skills would be just what I need to do a good job of it. I would pay you for the service, of course."

Lucy's eyes snapped up. "Yourself, miss? It would not go through your father or the staff?"

Interesting, but not too surprising. Lucy would not want any other staff to know she was gathering information. Maryann did not want that either and had a generous enough allowance that she could keep things discreet between them.

"Payment shall come directly from me, and no one will be the wiser. Anonymity is paramount." She thought of Mr. Andres heading off to fill his commission. She admired his patriotism but did not want to marry only to be left alone weeks afterward. Character mattered more than anything to her, and Lucy could help her better determine what a man's character truly was. "To be clear, I want more than financial reports. I want an understanding of who the man is, where he comes from, and what his intentions might be. Perhaps we can agree on . . . six shillings for each man you are able to gather information for."

"Could we instead deal in stockings?"

Maryann pulled her eyebrows together. "Stockings?"

"London is a town of commodities," Lucy said, sounding very modern for an uneducated girl from Somerset. "Silk stockings are worth more in trade than money and difficult for women in service to buy for themselves."

And they cost more than six shillings. Lucy was a frighteningly savvy woman. "If you would like silk stockings, then silk stockings it shall be. One pair for each man about whom you find solid information."

A stealthy smile grew on the maid's face, and she nodded with satisfaction while plaiting Maryann's hair. "I shall do my best by you," Lucy said.

"And we shall keep your actions between the two of us, agreed?"

Lucy tied the end of Maryann's plait and met her eyes in the mirror, looking like a child on Christmas. "Agreed."

Chapter Seven

*M*iss Morrington."

Maryann put on her hostess smile and extended her hand so Timothy could bow over it. It had been a few weeks since their walk in Hyde Park, and they had shared little more than polite greetings since. Tonight, Deborah and Lucas were hosting a dinner party at Father's house, and as an assistant hostess for the event, Maryann could not avoid Timothy as she had at other events.

Maryann hoped that, in time, she would not feel so much embarrassment for her part of the conversation that had caused the breech, nor so much regret for his. She also wished she hadn't missed him so much nor felt the rush of pleasure when she'd watched him enter the front doors of the town house a few minutes before. Trying to determine how to be *friends* was proving to be more difficult than she'd expected.

"Lovely to see you again, Mr. Mayfield."

"The pleasure is all mine, I am sure."

He may have held her eyes an extra moment, and she may have seen some regret there, but then he moved on to greet

Deborah. Maryann did not let herself watch him circulate the drawing room even though her mind seemed to track him of its own accord. He was the last of the thirty guests to arrive, and so she turned her attention to Mr. Fetich, who had been hovering just beyond her elbow for the last quarter of an hour. He'd continued his attention to her these past few weeks, and while she had not necessarily encouraged him, she was not particularly discouraging either.

Lucy's investigation had turned up that he owned a small shipping company out of Portsmouth but he kept the information quiet because the *ton* abhorred tradesmen. Maryann, however, did not. Her father had done well in his own ventures; the *ton* did not mind basking in the glow of his gas lamps, only that he'd had a hand in the industry of the innovation.

It had been a relief to learn that Mr. Fetich wasn't necessarily after her fortune. He did, however, ask after her father a great deal. When would Sir Wayne be in London? Did he ever give lectures about his rise in business? What did he think of the mining operations taking over Manchester?

It was frustrating that Mr. Fetich seemed to want a connection to her father more than he wanted a connection to her—inheritance or no. He was a nice enough man, but there was no spark between them, and she suspected she might have the superior wit. All three of those considerations kept him below the mark she was still hoping to find among the men who sought her out.

The dinner was excellent and the entertainment lovely. Miss Hansen played the harp, which had been delivered by her man that afternoon since Father's house was not equipped with one. Miss Morningside then gave a reading from her favorite Jane

Austen novel. Maryann suspected she did not know that her chosen excerpt was meant to be satirical.

Maryann's eyes moved to the vase Timothy had used the day he acted out the scene from *Hamlet* in this very room. *That* had been superior entertainment. Unable to resist looking in his direction, she was surprised to find him watching her from where he sat beside Lady Dominique. He winked, and the warmth that flooded her body helped her relax for the first time all night. Playing hostess alongside Deborah meant ensuring other people's comfort before her own. Yet he had set her at ease with such a small gesture. She smiled softly and gave him a nod of acknowledgement, before looking back at Miss Morningside and keeping her expression of rapt attentiveness in place though her mind began to wander.

The London Season was in full swing, which meant there were multiple balls a week, dinner parties, teas, shopping, theater, opera, and readings. Maryann had attended all of them. Or at least as many as she could, often three events in a single day, which meant three different dresses with matching gloves and bonnets and a dozen other fripperies. Deborah had told Maryann from the start to be mindful of the other debutantes and see them as allies and lifelong friends rather than competition. It had proven good advice, and Maryann appreciated the friendships she had made with the other women more than any other part of the experience.

With the men she had met in town this last month, Maryann was more circumspect. Her conversations with Timothy had taught her how *not* to converse with anyone else. She held back her boldness and was careful not to appear too . . . attainable. Instead, she fell into the same games many a woman had played before her: carefully crafted questions that helped her learn more than the man would generally tell her, coy smiles, not too much eye contact, a repertoire of small talk. She was careful not to give too much attention too quickly or show too much interest, ever. Keeping such arrows in her quiver kept her from making herself too vulnerable, as she had with Timothy. *Lessons learned*, she would tell herself whenever she found herself missing the comfort she'd felt with him. She glanced at him again, but he was looking at Miss Morningside now. Accepting his rejection would be far easier if she had another prospect upon which to focus her attention.

After the performances, the guests began to depart. Maryann fell into conversation with Mr. Fetich and told him about a letter she'd received from her father earlier that week, in which he'd explained that he would not be joining them in London as he'd originally planned. He would instead continue to oversee his interests in the north and in Wales—which needed more attention than expected—and return to Somerset in September. Maryann had wanted to be sure she did not want Mr. Fetich's continued attention before she informed him of Papa's plans. For whatever reason, she was ready now.

"So, I shan't have the chance to meet him here in London?" Mr. Fetich confirmed, his whole face drooping.

"I'm afraid not," Maryann said, only slightly stung by the dejected look on his face. "But should you wish to correspond with him, I am sure he would welcome it. Shall I ask him?"

Mr. Fetich brightened substantially, and he did not even try to hide the fact that she'd uncovered his true interest. Maryann promised to write to her father on his behalf before the end of the week. Mr. Fetich thanked her before turning and heading straight to Miss Callifour, who was in the process of leaving with her mother and younger sister. He helped Miss Callifour into her cloak before they all left the house together. Interesting.

Maryann returned from showing the Bensons to the door a few minutes later to find Timothy studying the artwork on the wall. Every time she had encountered him in this room he was looking at some piece of art or workmanship—why was that?

Her feet took her in his direction until she was standing just behind his left shoulder. He was wearing his blue, superfine coat tonight, with tails that almost reached the top edge of his boots. The only thing that would have improved his appearance would have been black trousers instead of light gray. Then he could wear his black-and-pink-patterned waistcoat and present a very sharp picture. He did not have a valet to make such arrangements for him, and sometimes it showed.

He looked over his shoulder, and then stepped aside so as to invite her to join in his admiration of the painting. "This is a lovely seascape," he said.

She glanced sidelong, wondering if he were making some sort of jest. He did not break his concentration on the piece, which led her to believe his sincerity. "It is a Joseph Turner, I believe." She was sure she'd heard her father say as much once before.

"Yes." He waved toward the signature, a squiggly thing that resembled the letter W. "I've not seen one in someone's home before."

"You know art as well as that?" she asked.

He shrugged without looking at her. "I *enjoy* art," he said simply and continued to look over the painting for a few more seconds, leaving Maryann at odds with herself. Should she leave him to his study? He had listed "watercoloring" as one of the traits he wanted in his "perfect woman." Was that because he enjoyed painting himself? If so, it took that attribute beyond a mere item on a list and changed it to a hobby he could enjoy with a woman who also appreciated the art form. The pettiness of that one item on his list was now in question.

"Do you paint, Timothy?" She caught the slip of his Christian name as soon as she said it and felt herself flush. It was what Deborah always called him, and how Maryann always thought of him, but calling him by his name was a liberty she had not been granted.

He looked at her with a lifted eyebrow and a half-smile that made her traitorous heart flutter in her chest. "I do not, *Maryann*. Do you?"

She smiled back and ducked her head in hopes of hiding the blush on her too-prominent cheeks. Well, then, this would be something new for their odd relationship. Well enough.

She looked back at the painting. "Not well, I'm afraid. My mother hired a painting teacher for me once, but he gave up after four lessons. I believe his exact words were 'There are many who would benefit from my tutelage, but your daughter does not seem to be one of them.'"

Maryann had not cared that he'd insulted her, she'd only been glad to no longer have to try her hand at something she had no interest in. She preferred such things as household management, schedules, and account books—all of which she had taken over during the years of her mother's illness. Artistic endeavors had never held much appeal. Timothy, on the other hand, seemed to flourish in the creative aspects of life—theater, art appreciation. They were so different.

"I think I would have enjoyed lessons," Timothy said. "But we never had the option of such things when I was young, and painting is not something they teach once a boy starts school. It is a girl's talent, everyone says." He knocked her shoulder slightly with his own and gave her a grin. "But apparently not every girl's."

"Apparently," she said, smiling fully so he would know she was not offended. Friends could tease one another, and she truly wanted to be friends. "And in Joseph Turner's case, I suppose talent is not restricted to only my sex."

"True," Timothy said with a nod. "I *would* like to try my hand at it one day."

"I hope that you will," Maryann encouraged. They lapsed into silence, which made her panic slightly, not wanting to lose this accord. "I like to think I was awarded an extra dose of wit and wisdom in place of the artistic portion of talent I do not possess."

Timothy laughed. "I would put money on it. Do you enjoy *looking* at art, Miss Morrington?"

"Mostly I think I appreciate how a piece accentuates a room rather than the individual aspects of one piece over another. I do like seascapes, however. They remind me of home." She missed the sea more and more with every passing week.

"I have never seen the sea," he said.

She looked at him. "Truly?" If he had not seen it, then he had not smelled the brine or watched the waves crash against the shore in hypnotic rhythm.

Timothy shook his head. "Raised in western Norfolk, schooled in Cambridge, lived in London ever since. Funny that I haven't realized until this moment that I've never been." He shrugged. "Perhaps I am lucky. One cannot miss what one does not know."

It would be a small thing to invite him to visit them in Dunster after the season had ended so that he might witness the majestic sea she'd grown up with. Lucas would likely come if

Timothy did. But Timothy had his perfect woman to find, and Maryann had a match to make as well. They fell into an awkward silence for several seconds.

"It was a very nice dinner party," Timothy finally said.

"It was," she said, relieved that he'd continued the conversation. "You enjoyed yourself?"

"Certainly." There was something too polite in his tone.

"Hmm," she said. "I sense a certain tightness around your ears."

She braced herself, fearing he would retreat from her attempt to recapture their earlier teasing. Instead, he smiled widely, showing his fine teeth, and looked at her in that particular way of his that made her feel as though she were the only thing he were seeing. It made her shoulders tingle.

"Ah, I can't fool you, can I, Maryann?" He sighed. "I must admit that I am especially tired tonight." He looked toward the door. "I have been waiting for Lucas to return so that I might make my official goodbyes."

"Your color does look rather gray," she said, looking at him more closely. When he was smiling, the smudged rings below his eyes hadn't been so noticeable. "Are you all right?"

"Just tired," he said.

"Of what?"

He laughed, then shook his head. "Of people less diverting than you, to be sure."

She did not know how to respond to the compliment, but suddenly felt his hand at her elbow.

"Would you mind if we sit while I wait for Lucas?"

"Not at all."

He moved his hand to the small of her back and guided her toward the chairs grouped around a low table. She had to swallow at the physical sensation of his touch. *No, no, no*, she chastised herself. *You will not respond to him this way.* Not him. She'd been waiting weeks to feel some sense of this energy from the other men she'd met—and she hadn't. But Timothy was the man who didn't want her. Didn't need her.

Thankfully, they both sat in chairs, so she did not need to feel the warmth of him beside her on a settee. "You look very well tonight, Maryann," he commented.

She told herself he would say as much to any woman, but she still liked that he'd said it to her. "Thank you." This was her first time wearing her new pink silk overdress with daisies embroidered around the hem, and she'd received many compliments. His compliment, however, somehow meant the very most. Which was aggravating.

They went quiet again, and in the space between them, she felt as if there were an invisible line keeping them from being fully comfortable with one another. The moment whispered in her ear that this could be her chance to build upon the friendship he had offered with his flowers and his note of apology. She had sent him a note of forgiveness and thanks weeks ago. Wouldn't she like the assurance that their friendship was intact? Then, perhaps their next encounter would not be as uncomfortable as this one.

She cleared her throat. "At the risk of making this conversation even more awkward, how is your perfect-wife-campaign going?"

He eyed her, clearly suspicious.

She waved her hand through the air between them. "I ask as a *friend*, and I promise not to harass you. I am genuinely interested. The last time we met you were so excited about your change of circumstances, as I've come to realize anyone would be."

"Well, as a *friend*, I suppose I can tell you that it is not going as well as I had hoped. In fact, your words about the impossibility of my 'list' have been haunting me."

She was tempted to make a flippant comment about having been right, but his mood was too serious.

Timothy continued. "I have met dozens of women who matched the aspects I desire, yet none of them are . . . right."

What misery it was not to tell him that they weren't right because they were mere women, not the goddess Diana. She restrained herself, however, and settled for stating the obvious. "This is very upsetting for you."

He nodded, leaning forward and putting his elbows on his knees so that he was looking at the rug. After a few seconds, he looked up. "I have this one chance, and I am so frightened I will get it wrong." He sighed, loudly but not dramatically, as he sat back in his chair. "I suppose you shall now tell me that you knew this would happen."

His expectation of her superiority erased any residue she had been feeling of it and unlocked her own honesty. "No, I will not say such a thing. Everyone is looking for something. Perhaps you were more honest than I was prepared for, but I do not think I am much different. I have tried to get to know any number of men, for example, and not found one of them who meets my expectations, which I was certain were far more reasonable." She shrugged, wishing she was exaggerating more than she was. All she really wanted was a man not *solely* in want of her fortune and who made her feel the way Timothy did. She may as well have had a list of a thousand qualifications.

He let out another heavy sigh. "It is a very difficult prospect— looking for the person who will be your perfect match. I suppose that is why so many people settle for less than what they want."

"And yet many of them end up happy together."

He did not smile as she thought he might. "Do they?" he said quietly. "I have been watching married couples as well, and I wonder if many of them do not simply accept their lot and make the best of it. I do not want that for myself, or for my children."

"Your children?"

"My parents were . . . not well matched. My father died a few months before I was born so I only knew my mother, but she spoke poorly of him and pulled away from everyone, even us—my brother, sister, and myself." He looked up, the pain in his eyes showing through. "If you do not love the person you marry, does that affect the love you can feel for your children, do you think? I want so much more than what my parents had, yet sometimes I wonder if I have been chasing fantasy all along. I was so sure that this . . . change would solve what was missing, but now I wonder if it's only made things worse."

Maryann swallowed, taken off guard by his confession. Timothy was always so cheerful and full of energy that she'd never guessed he had a painful history.

"My parents married after having met only three times," she said. "They came to love one another very much and loved their children equally well. Hearing how deeply you have thought about this topic makes me feel that perhaps I have taken for granted the security that came from knowing my parents were so mindful of each other." A tenderness rose up within her as it always did when she thought of her mother. "When my mother became ill, my father would not leave our home, even though his business suffered and it was painful to watch her decline. He read to her every day for almost five years, even when we doubted she knew any of us."

"*That,*" Timothy pronounced with a soft smile that said he

knew she was sharing something sacred with him. "*That* is what I want. It is what my brother found in his wife, Sybil—they were excellent partners and parents."

"Were?" Maryann asked.

"Sybil died four years ago, but the bond she and Peter shared has continued to bless their daughters. Sybil was Peter's perfect match, and he knew it early on. I want to find the same."

"I admire that a great deal," Maryann said, treading softly.

"So you see why I cannot leave the smallest aspect to chance. It feels too much of a risk. I must know from the start that the woman I take as my wife is the woman who can create *that* future with me."

"You want to fall in love before you marry, then?"

He shook his head. "Love without commitment can be fickle. I am not such a romantic to believe that love will conquer all things. Rather, I believe there is a woman out there who can be the perfect match of my own attributes. I believe I will recognize her, and then love will come after."

"Recognize her?" Maryann repeated. "What do you mean?"

"Yes, recognize her." He leaned forward, his energy increasing. "It cannot be an accident that I am drawn to art." He waved toward the walls. "That must mean that the woman who shall make me happy will love art just as I do. Perhaps she may even help me to unlock a talent within myself I have not yet discovered."

Ah, he was looking for a soul mate: one person in existence who was his other half. She had to resist debating him about the realistic nature of such a belief. "And blonde?"

He picked at something unseen on the knee of his trousers, avoiding her eye. "I have always found blondes to be particularly attractive and imagined a houseful of blonde children."

"You are also blond. Perhaps you are looking for a female version of yourself, then."

"Precisely." He flashed that adorable smile, and she bit back a laugh. His earnestness felt misguided, and yet he was so sincere. Had he not said a moment ago that he was not such a romantic as to expect love to strike him like lightning? The irony was that he expected *more* than lightning. He expected a soul's recognition.

"I would not say my parents were the same person of each sex," Maryann said, trying to disagree diplomatically. "Rather, they were good people evenly situated and committed to each other and their family. That commitment encouraged both of them to do their part toward building a happy marriage. They worked toward what they wanted and challenged one another through their differences."

"Hmm," Timothy said. "I cannot see how differences can be helpful in forging a trustworthy future."

She did laugh then, which startled him. She sobered quickly so as not to shut down the conversation. "I *just* told you that it worked for my parents."

"And I just told *you* that it did not work for mine." He shook his head. "It feels to be the wiser choice to keep looking for that woman who is perfectly suited for me. I am certain she is out there, and I am certain I will know her when I see her."

"And yet we began this conversation because you were feeling discouraged in your pursuit so far."

He frowned as he considered that, but then shrugged. "I think mostly I am simply tired. I go from one event to another, day in and day out—often not getting home until early morning only to be making morning calls a handful of hours later."

Though her feelings were still complicated when it came to Timothy, it made her sad to think that his uncle's boon was becoming a burden. They had already established that she was not in the running for the role of his "perfect woman" so, maybe, if he met every woman who seemed to fit the list he would realize he should be looking for different things.

"Have you met Natalia Rushford?"

He pulled his eyebrows together, then shook his head.

"She is from Wales and new to England, though her mother is connected to the Connellys. I met her at Lady Dominique's tea a few days ago. Lovely girl. Granted, she has brown eyes, not green, but she is blonde and an exceptional flautist. She probably likes babies, though I did not ask directly."

He eyed her with suspicion. "I have not met her, no."

"Well, I will be seeing her tomorrow, I think. Deborah and I were going to make a visit, and I shall find out the next few events she might attend. If you are both there, I shall help make an introduction."

"Why would you do that?"

"Because I am your friend," she said as though that were her only motivation. "And because I meant what I said when I told you that I wished for your happiness."

She saw a flash of pity in his eyes, a reminder of when she had pointed out how she had not measured up to his list. "I have come to realize many ways in which you and I would never suit, Timothy." She laughed—lightly—though it stung. "But we are still friends, are we not? And thanks to Lady Dominique, I am in a position to meet any number of women when they come to England. Deborah and I have become a part of her committee, so to speak."

Timothy laughed, though dryly as though he did not entirely trust her offer. "Yes, Lady Dominique likes to be the first to vet newcomers."

"Precisely. If you have, in fact, made the rounds and come up empty-handed, perhaps I could help you be among the first to meet those who join the season later. Deborah assures me that girls continue to arrive through the end of May."

"You would do that for me?"

"Certainly."

He leaned forward suddenly, quick enough that she startled and her loud, bracing laugh escaped. She quickly covered her mouth but kept her eyes on Timothy as he stared at her face. "I am checking you for tight ears."

She lowered her hand and narrowed her eyes at his joke. "Well, you shan't find them because I am telling the truth."

Lucas suddenly flopped into the chair next to Timothy, wine nearly sloshing out of the glass in his hand. "My apologies," he said, then yawned and rubbed his head with his free hand, making a mess of his hair.

A quick look about the room showed it had emptied, which explained his casualness. "One would not expect that getting people to leave would take an entire hour." He downed the rest of his drink, then set it to the side on a small table already sporting three other wine glasses. He looked between Timothy and Maryann. "What are we discussing? Have I missed out on my share?"

"You have no share," Timothy said, casting a quick but pleading look at Maryann. She had promised discretion regarding his situation, and she was a woman of her word, though she had longed to discuss the issue up one side and down the other with Deborah a dozen times over the last weeks. She gave him a nod in response and turned her attention to Lucas.

"I was only asking Timothy why he was so tired."

Lucas looked at his friend, pulling back as though that was

necessary to get a full view. "He does look rather haggard, doesn't he?"

"I have been attending too many parties," Timothy said.

Lucas laughed. "*Too* many? I never thought you could get *enough* parties."

"Well, it seems I can."

Maryann wished she had someone looking for her with as much determination as Timothy was looking for his perfect woman. Regardless of whether she believed in soul mates, what would it be like to have a man choose you above all others?

She hurried to speak before her thoughts swallowed her resolve. "We were just discussing how he might better choose his events so he might not wear himself out so."

Lucas looked at Maryann with raised eyebrows. "Were you now?"

Lucas and Deborah had had a difficult time coming to terms with Timothy's distance this last month. Maryann had told them that she and Timothy did not suit, but it seemed they were unable to completely let go of their hopes. Maybe this would help convince them. She looked at Lucas coolly. "Is that so surprising? Are Timothy and I not friends?"

Lucas shrugged, but Timothy caught her eyes, half of his mouth pulled up in a smile. It was as good as a written contract, the way he held her eyes with his lovely blue ones. Yes, they were friends. Yes, she would help him. But she had additional reasons. She had enjoyed this one conversation during this one evening more than any other she'd had in the last month. She was never so happy as when she was with him.

"And, as a friend," she continued, "I was about to tell him that the next time he wears this blue coat, he should pair it with his black breeches and the black-and-pink-patterned waistcoat."

"You'll make him into a dandy!" Lucas exclaimed at the same time that Timothy took hold of his lapels and looked down at his clothes in surprise.

She gave Lucas an irritated look. "Not in the slightest. Timothy owns some very nice pieces of clothing. Pairing them differently will not only show them in greater variety but improve his overall fashionability. Some women quite like a man of fashion."

"I believe I have just been insulted," Timothy said, still clutching the edges of his jacket. "I am capable of dressing myself."

Maryann waved toward Lucas. "Deborah chooses his evening dress."

Lucas sat up straight, sputtering. "Well, now."

"Does she?" Timothy asked his friend, eyebrows lifted.

Lucas looked between them, completely caught. "Well." He pulled at his waistcoat—a lovely thing of silver and apricot that looked very nice with his charcoal coat. "My valet is a bit old-fashioned, and, well, women do have a knack for color and such." He sat up even straighter. "And men have better things to do than put this with that and that with this!"

"Oh, yes, such important things to do," Maryann said with a nod and a smile because they all knew Lucas spent most of his time at the club drinking and smoking and talking about horses.

She looked at Timothy. "Wear the combination I recommend and see if I am not right."

He smiled at her, his eyes bright, and nodded. "I shall."

Chapter Eight

Timothy finished a jig that left him dabbing his forehead with his handkerchief as he waited for the next dance to begin. Almack's was stifling tonight. He thought he might sit out the next set after having such a lively time of the first, but he hated to see young ladies without partners and he liked to dance. They needed more waltzes, that's what. No one worked up a sweat during a waltz. Opening some windows would help as well, but the day had been particularly humid, which was likely why the night held no relief.

"Mr. Mayfield?"

Timothy turned to his right, a ready smile on his lips, which grew wider when he saw that the interruption came from none other than Maryann Morrington. Beside her was a young woman he'd never met before, and slightly ahead of them both was an older woman he belatedly recognized as Countess Cowper, one of the patronesses always willing to facilitate introductions. Timothy bowed over the older woman's hand, deftly pocketing his handkerchief at the same time, hoping none of them would notice. "Lady Cowper," he said as he rose. "What a lovely gown."

"Thank you, Mr. Mayfield," she said with a smile. She'd always liked him, but then most people did. "I would like to introduce you to Miss Natalia Rushford. Miss Morrington thought you would like to meet her."

Timothy flashed Maryann a quick smile of thanks, and then centered his attention on the lovely young woman beside her. A very *young* young woman. Timothy suspected she was not yet sixteen.

"It is a pleasure to meet you, Miss Rushford. Miss Morrington was telling me about you just yesterday." He took her hand and bowed over it, then thanked Lady Cowper for the introduction before she moved on to her other duties of the evening.

"A pleasure to meet you as well, Mr. Mayfield," Miss Rushford said. Her voice was so soft he had to lean in to hear her. "Miss Morrington says you are delightful."

He turned raised eyebrows to Maryann. "Did she also tell you that I am a very fine dancer?"

Maryann very rudely—but expectedly—rolled her eyes. Only Timothy could see it, however. Timothy smiled at Miss Rushford. "Would you like to partner me this set? I would be much obliged."

"Oh," she said, surprised, her whole face brightening. "That would be lovely."

He put out his arm, winking at Maryann as they left her on the edge of the floor. It was a relief to be back on good terms with Maryann. The weeks when they had been out of favor had been uncomfortable, but he had not known what else to do to bridge the gap. To not only have their friendship back on solid ground, but to also have introductions to the new arrivals in the city was something he appreciated very much.

Miss Rushford was not a confident dancer, but she knew

the steps well enough. He complimented her on her dress and hair so that by the end of the dance, her face was bright and her manner engaged. In turn, she complimented his attire, which was the second compliment of the evening on the ensemble Maryann had challenged him to wear. Perhaps he did need help dressing himself.

After the set concluded, Timothy returned Miss Rushford to Maryann, who had reappeared at the sidelines as though she were the girl's mother. No sooner had they stopped when Mr. Hawthorne asked Miss Rushford for the next, which she gladly accepted. Timothy stood by Maryann's side, watching the new couple take their places on the floor.

"Well?" Maryann asked quietly through her society smile, not to be confused with her teasing smile or her reprimanding smile or even her "I can barely stand you" smile. "What do you think of Miss Rushford?"

"She is lovely," Timothy said politely.

"What do you *really* think?"

He laughed. "That is what I really think."

She slapped him on the arm, playful but harder than was polite. "You need not protect me. What about her is not quite right? You are not swooning over her."

"First of all, I do not imagine I am the swooning type," he said. "Secondly, she *is* lovely, and I stand by that summation. Thirdly, she is . . . very young. How old is she?"

"Sixteen."

"Gracious," he said, shaking his head. "There are two types of sixteen-year-old girls, Maryann. Those who look sixteen, and those who look twelve. Miss Rushford is of the latter group, but neither type interests me all that much."

"You did not have an age requirement on your list."

"Well, I shall add it as soon as I return to my rooms, then." He nodded sharply, the decision made. It felt unseemly to imagine anything of a romantic sort with such a young girl. "But she is lovely, and I hope she finds London to her liking and that she is given the chance to grow up before she becomes a man's wife."

"Your attention will do her well even if she is not to your tastes."

Like the dog in Aesop's fable, men liked better what another man had, though it embarrassed him that Maryann knew this truth as well. The attention he showed to Miss Rushford would draw the eyes of other men, and thus she would be assisted on her way. Which is one reason why he made a point of dancing with as many women as possible, even though his interest was very specifically focused. The *ton* liked Timothy—his lack of consequence and cousin Harry notwithstanding. They trusted his judgment and character. Timothy did not take such trust lightly and did all he could to be a good steward of such.

"I hope that it does help her," Timothy said humbly. The set began, and he realized they were both standing there, unpartnered. "Um, would you care to dance, Maryann?"

She did not look at him and instead gazed about the room. "You do not need to ask me to dance, Timothy."

"I know I do not *need* to, but I am asking if you would like to dance with me."

She gave him a dull look. "No, actually, I would not because I know you are asking me simply because you and I are standing beside one another without partners and you are being polite."

"Well, I *am* a gentleman," he said, lifting his chin slightly. "It is my creed to be polite."

She huffed through a smile and shook her head. "I am going to have some punch." She turned, and he followed, staying beside her as they made their way toward the refreshments. It was too late to join the set now, and he appreciated the reprieve; the room was not getting *more* comfortable.

"It was very kind of you to facilitate the introduction to Miss Rushford," Timothy said. "You have kept your word to me."

"Are you saying this so that I do not facilitate future introductions?"

"Not at all," Timothy said, slightly offended at her accusation. "I am intrigued by the idea of your inside information on new girls to London and appreciate your offer to introduce me."

She looked over her shoulder and nodded once. "You are welcome."

They reached the refreshments, and she reached for a glass. He took hold of her wrist and pulled it back before selecting a glass and handing it to her. She smiled sardonically at him but thanked him all the same.

"You are most welcome, Miss Morrington," he said formally before taking a glass of his own. They took their first sips at the same time and turned to one another with equally unimpressed looks, which made them both pinch their lips together and look away to keep from laughing.

Maryann moved toward one of the tables for used glasses and added hers to the other mostly full ones already in place. Timothy followed suit.

"The lemonade is never anything to crow about, but something was amuck with that punch," Timothy said, trying to get the bitter taste out of his mouth. What he wouldn't give for a swallow of wine or brandy, or even water, for heaven's sake.

"Anise," Maryann said, then coughed slightly and put a gloved hand to her mouth. "It is far too heavy on anise."

"Yes, that is it exactly." He shuddered dramatically. "I may never recover."

She pinched her lips together again, but her eyes were dancing. "Do not make me laugh."

"I shan't if I can help it." He added an even more dramatic shudder to emphasis his teasing.

She chuckled as she turned to him. "What?"

They were friends. Good friends. The kind of friends who could tease one another as he and his schoolmates did all the time. Her eyes were dancing and her smile was in place—all felt safe and well between them. "Your laugh is very much like the bray of a donkey. I should not want to unleash that on such an unsuspecting crowd as this one."

He expected her to cover her mouth to keep from laughing again, but instead her expression fell and a hot pink flush filled her cheeks. She blinked, then turned quickly and made her way through the crowd away from him.

Blast. He'd hurt her feelings. Why had he not realized that this particular teasing would be over the line? He followed her but quickly lost sight of her in the crowd of colorful gowns and bouncing headdresses.

"Mr. Mayfield?"

He scanned the figures ahead of him once more before looking to his side at Miss Larkin. He'd sought her out first thing upon his return from Norfolk but had not remained attentive since. She talked of nothing but her hair and figure. It was one thing for him to admire her qualities, quite another for her to admire herself. It had taken only two dances and one partnering at dinner for him to know they would never suit. He had lessened his attention after that, and other men had quickly filled the space he'd left behind.

"Miss Larkin, so good to see you."

"I thought it was you," she said, bouncing on the balls of her feet. "Would you like to meet my cousin—Constance Larkin? She is just come to London."

"Oh, of course," Timothy said. He scanned the room once more but could not see Maryann. He felt he had little choice but to meet cousin Constance, who was a middle-aged version of Miss Larkin. He would plan an appropriate apology for Maryann in the meantime.

"We matched our frocks tonight," Miss Larkin said, leaning into her cousin to show that, indeed, they both wore light-yellow gowns. "I think they look very nice with our hair, though mine is lighter than Constance's. What do you think of our slippers? Which do you like best?" She lifted her skirts—too high— and turned her foot this way and that so he might admire her footwear. To his further dismay, her cousin did the same—two women holding their feet out to him at Almack's.

Timothy searched the crowd for Maryann again, but she was no longer in view. Surely, as friends, she would forgive him. Wouldn't she?

For now, there was nothing to do but compliment footwear. Yes, London was losing its charm more and more with every passing week, and he was apparently losing control of his manners in the process.

Chapter Nine

The second bouquet of daisies arrived the next morning. Again, they were not florist quality, but the imperfections made them better. She inhaled their fragrance as she had with the first bouquet and ached for home. What she would not give to be back in Dunster, picking her own daisies, wearing her hair long down her back and walking barefoot in the wet sand along the shoreline. Tears pricked her eyes with a fierce longing. She blinked them away and focused on Timothy's flowers of apology. Maryann had not yet overcome the feelings he had sparked the night before: Small. Angry. Hurt. Rejected.

She'd known Timothy did not like her laugh, she'd seen him bristle enough times over it, but to compare it to the bray of a donkey . . . Her cheeks flushed all over again to remember it.

Why can I not be the woman he wants? The thought brought tears to her eyes, making her feel even more pathetic and ushering in an even more pathetic thought: *Why must I continue to* want *to be the woman he wants?*

She rang for a vase for the flowers, then opened the card tucked inside the cheap green paper.

Dear Maryann,

I cannot apologize enough for my cruel words last night. I was caught up in the wit and banter which has always been so good between us and let myself tread too heavily on sensitive topics. I could see in your face how much I hurt you with my words, and I have been ill over it, knowing that you must feel even worse. There is scarcely a woman in the world I admire more than I admire you, and I cherish our friendship as dear as any I am so fortunate to possess. I hope I have not lost your regard, for that would be the worst suffering I can imagine. Please forgive me for being such a buffoon.

Your friend,
Timothy

She did not doubt his sincerity. It was not in his nature to be cruel on purpose, but he was proving rather adept at hurting her despite his intentions. Was it even more hurtful because she could not be angry at him for something he'd done in ignorance? If he'd meant to hurt her, she could count that against him, but he'd thought he was teasing her the same way she had pointed out a better combination of coat and waistcoat for him the night before.

One of the items on his list of a perfect woman had been "a tinkling laugh." Was that on the list specifically because of how he felt toward *her* laugh? It was such a specific, personal element. And one she had no control over. She had tried to change her laugh when she was younger, but when something took her by surprise, she could not hold down the burst of joy in response. Her family had helped her accept and even appreciate her laugh.

And Timothy hated it. Thought it sounded like a donkey. How many others were equally appalled by her laugh?

I will never laugh in his presence again, she decided.

The footman returned with the vase, and she took a moment to arrange the ragged bouquet of flowers before putting it on the table in front of the window. It brightened the room, and she told herself that it was impossible to stay angry with such charming things as daisies in the room. But it wasn't impossible to feel tired. And frustrated and . . . sad.

Morning visits would start soon and new gentlemen would present themselves to her and she would feel nothing for them. And then she would send Lucy to learn of their circumstances. And she would discover that a match with them would never work. Mostly because they wanted her money. But also because she was in love with someone else. There was the rub, painful and raw and wholly acknowledged.

Just as she believed that Timothy would never find the woman he described on his list, Maryann feared she would never find a man to drive Timothy out of her heart. *He has ruined me for any other man.* Then she took a breath, held it, straightened her spine, and let it out. Enough pity. She had survived the decline and death of her mother, she had managed two months in a town where no one saw her as anything more than a bag of money, and she would survive the fact that Timothy Mayfield did not love her.

She threw the note in the fire, not because she wasn't glad to receive the apology or because she doubted the sincerity. She burned this one because she could not read the words again. They hurt too much.

Chapter Ten

$\mathcal{M}$aryann was surprised, and not entirely pleased, to be seated next to Timothy at dinner three days later. She did not feel ready to see him. Thirty-five other guests should have made the chance of being seated beside any man her own age nearly impossible. She caught Deborah's eyes across the table as she found her chair, and her sister winked. Maryann narrowed her eyes and cocked her head to the side, which was as much displeasure she dared display in company. Deborah just smiled as Maryann sat in the chair held out by the footman.

It did not seem to matter that Maryann had told Deborah that Timothy had offended her again, hence the second bouquet, or the continued reminders that she had no interest in Timothy nor did Timothy have any interest in her. Because Maryann would not tell Deborah the reason for the apology daisies, Deborah was determined to see them as a sign of Timothy's affection and had apparently convinced the hostess to seat them beside one another. What luck.

Maryann let the footman push her chair under the table and made small talk with the older man on her left for a few minutes until his attention was captured by the woman on his other side who could have used at least two more inches on the neckline of her dress. Really, had she no self-respect at all?

"So, you are left to me," Timothy said quietly as she looked ahead and filled her spoon with soup.

She took the bite before she answered but did not look at him. "It seems so, yes."

"Am I to suppose you do not accept the apology I sent with the flowers? It *was* sincere, Maryann, I assure you. I did not mean to hurt your feelings. I fell into teasing the way I would tease a male friend, but it was not right. I am grateful Deborah was able to arrange an opportunity to explain myself."

Fantastic. Timothy had gone to Deborah for help, and Deborah had clearly interpreted his request as something different from apologizing for his idiocy. Very well, they would put it behind them—but she *would* be heard, even if she had to speak quietly enough to not be overhead by anyone else.

"I have been embarrassed by my laugh all of my life, Timothy, and I tried for years to change it, but it seems, like my plump cheeks and short fingers, it cannot be changed. I have come to believe that the people who care for me do not mind it. I have *never*, however, had anyone compare it to the braying of a donkey." Saying it out loud caused her cheeks to catch fire all over again.

"I am so sorry," he whispered. "Truly."

She nodded and took another bite. She had already vowed never to laugh in his presence again and wanted to be done with this conversation.

Silence fell heavy between them, and Timothy was caught into conversation with the woman on his other side. Equal numbers usually ensured everyone had a partner to talk to, but it was not a perfect system and Maryann wondered who else on this circular table was being left out of conversation.

The soup course was removed after what seemed to be far too long, and the fish was served. She'd managed half of her plate before Timothy returned his attention to her.

"How have you been the last few days, Timothy?" She kept her tone cheerier than she felt in hopes he would follow her lead.

"I have been well, save for regret over having acted like an imbecile to someone whom I care for."

Someone whom I care for. She could not let those words go to her head. "We are finished with that topic," she said. "What have you *done*? Any walks in the parks with a belle of the season? Trips to Tattersalls with the other bucks?"

He obliged her and talked about riding with his cousin Harry through Hyde Park and attending a card party where he spent through his five pounds before even the first hour had passed.

"I can see how men get themselves in distress through cards," he said. "Had I deeper pockets, it would be easy to chase my limit with five more pounds, and then another five in hopes of winning back the lot. I shall always credit my thin pockets for my having avoided such a fate. Harry goes to the gambling hells nearly every night. I don't know how he still has a coat on his back."

Maryann had heard a bit about his cousin Harry, who was extreme in many ways. She'd only met him once, at a card party where he'd already had too much to drink and made embarrassing overtures toward a married woman who did not welcome his attention. She would choose Timothy over his cousin any day of the week, not that it mattered, as she would not choose him and he would certainly not choose her.

"My brother taught me to play loo with pennies," she said to keep the conversation going. "I could not believe how much money he made from me over the course of two days. When my father learned of it, he made James return every cent plus a shilling so he would not take advantage of my youth again."

Timothy laughed, and she smiled at the slow return of their easy friendship. She wanted this, she reminded herself. Even with the difficulty of being so close to Timothy, she preferred his friendship to his absence.

"What do you think of my ensemble tonight?" he asked, leaning against the back of his chair so she could see the emerald-colored waistcoat he wore with his charcoal coat and black breeches. "I have been trying to be more . . . creative with my dress since your counsel."

"The tones work well together, but when wearing different-colored coat and pants, it is best to have a multicolored waistcoat to blend them."

Timothy's face fell. "Oh, I had thought I had done well."

"You *did* do well," she said, patting his forearm as though he were a small boy on the brink of a pout. "Next time, wear your black breeches so your coat and pants are the same color; *two* solids makes for a striking look. I saw that you wore the combination I recommended to Almack's on Wednesday." She felt it brave of her to bring that night back into conversation.

"I received *seven* compliments," Timothy said in awe. "I could not believe it." He let his face fall along with his shoulders in an exaggerated expression of disappointment. "I had so wanted to prove your recommendation wrong."

She'd have laughed if she hadn't forbidden herself to do so in his company. Instead, she smiled widely. "I shall not let it go to my head, I promise."

She glanced toward their feet beneath the table. "Might I share one more observation about your dress?"

"I am not sure my ego can handle it." He took a deep breath and let it out slowly while placing his hands on his knees as though bracing himself. Then he nodded. "All right, I am ready."

"Why do you wear those boots when they are too small?"

He lost his stiff posture and looked at her in surprise, the widening of his eyes making the blue of them seem even bluer. "How can you tell they are too small?"

"You take careful steps, and by the end of an evening, you wince slightly even when standing. You only own one pair of black ones." She regretted saying as much when color flushed his face. "I am sorry; I have embarrassed you." Would he think she was taking retribution?

Timothy shook his head. "No apology necessary. I am just disappointed to know it is so obvious."

"Probably not to anyone else." She hurried to cover the comments with other, less embarrassing, ones. "You must be completely miserable at the end of a night."

"I am," he admitted. "But they are such nice boots. I, uh, have little funds to spend on such things. I got a very good price on these."

"A cobbler could stretch them for not very dear a price."

"The bootmaker said that to stretch them would distort the shape."

"Perhaps a bit," Maryann said with a nod. "And I can see how a craftsman would find that beyond consideration, but I do not believe anyone else would notice. My father often gives his shoes to my brother, whose feet are a full size and a half larger than my father's. He's had many pair stretched by the local cobbler in Dunster. You should try it and spare your feet. Fashion is not worth that dear a price."

"I shall look into it," he said, but she could tell he was still embarrassed as he finished his fish.

"Now I give you equal opportunity to give me some advice." She put her hands in her lap demurely. "What is something I can improve upon?" She could only hope he would not bring up her laugh again.

He looked at her, eyebrows pulled together so that two lines ran vertically between them. "I have no advice for you, Maryann."

"Of course, you do," she said. "For instance, I was not sure I liked this color when I got the dress back from the seamstress earlier in the week." The green was not quite the same shade as Timothy's emerald waistcoat, but darker than she was used to. Deborah insisted that since Maryann was of "advanced years" for a debutante the richer hue was acceptable.

"It brings out the green in your eyes," Timothy said after a few seconds.

She was not prepared for a compliment, and it filled her up like wine to an empty glass. "There is green in my eyes?"

Timothy nodded, smiling at the surprise she had apparently not hidden very well. "Toward the center, there are little sparks of green that are enhanced tonight because of the dress. You should wear this color more often."

The compliment burrowed in too deeply for her to pluck it out before it became a part of her. She had green in her eyes. Timothy was the first to have ever told her. "Thank you."

He shrugged shyly. "You're welcome."

Their plates were empty but not yet removed. At this rate, the meal would last another hour and a half at least.

"But," he said, turning to her, "I do not think that light yellow does you many favors. You have that one frock that you wear for morning visits—the one with lace at the collar." He waggled his fingers at his neck.

"I know the one," she said, feeling a bit defensive but determined not to show it. She liked that dress, though perhaps more for fit than color.

"The lace is very good quality, you should retain it, but the dress itself draws out your coloring somehow," Timothy said. "I do not know how to explain it, but I saw you wear it once and determined I did not like it. I think you look better in darker colors. Although that pink dress with the flowers at the hem is very nice on you."

"This is very helpful," she said, surprised he knew her dresses so well. She refused to follow where that feeling wanted to lead her.

"Well, we are friends," he said with a shrug. "Friends help friends."

"Yes, they do."

They lapsed into another silence as they waited for the next course. Why was it taking so long? She sensed Timothy was thinking the same thing as his knee began to bounce beneath the table.

"Do not bounce your knee," she said, though she smiled because this sort of boyish quirk was so endearing.

"It keeps me from giving in to my nerves that are telling me to jump up and run around this table fifteen times."

She smiled at the image. "It shakes the table."

"It does not."

"Look at your neighbor's glass."

The wine in question was shivering within the glass. He stopped his bouncing and the wine stopped moving too.

"Drat, you're right. *Again*."

She grinned. "It has been known to happen."

Timothy looked at the footmen standing at the sides of the room, their hands behind their backs despite the fact that every guest was finished. He leaned toward Maryann and spoke quietly. "The hosts are going to regret this when they realize how much more wine everyone will be drinking if there is no food."

Maryann looked around and smiled in acknowledgment of the detail. Then she reached for her own glass and took a swallow. He grinned and did the same, draining his glass and then lifting it slightly so a footman would refill it for him. Maybe if enough guests refilled their wine, the course schedule would improve. Maryann filed that away for when she was in charge of a dinner party on her own.

A full glass of wine later, the plates were removed and the entrée—pork tenderloin—was set before them.

"Have you walked with any young ladies recently?" she asked, keeping her voice casual. She was feeling fuzzy from all the wine. "You seem to like the more active entertainments—dancing, walking."

"Ah, you know me so well, Maryann," he said. He dabbed at his mouth with his serviette before returning it to his lap. "I do prefer to be moving. I am very poor at sitting still for an extended period of time."

"What about church?" she asked.

He chuckled. "I confess this to you only because we are such good *friends*." He leaned in conspiratorially, and she tried not to inhale the heady scent of his aftershave. "When I finish services, I walk in the opposite direction of my rooms, and when I know I am away from anyone who might recognize me, I run as fast as I can for as long as I can in order to make up for all that sitting."

She imagined him running at full speed in his Sunday suit,

arms pumping at his sides, and chuckled under her breath. "Where on earth do you find a place to run without being recognized?"

"I walk east from the church a few blocks," he said, a sparkle in his eye. "And pull my hat down low, just in case. I feel for the people who think I am mad, but, well, without the remedy I could not attend church at all so I believe it is a worthwhile trade. What do you think of it?"

"I think you are mad."

He laughed, and she wished she could join him.

They finished their pork, and once again the plates were not cleared. The wine in Maryann's glass began to shiver, and she moved her hand from her lap to Timothy's leg, pressing down to stop the nervous movement. His whole body stilled and he turned sharply to look at her in surprise. She quickly withdrew her hand.

"I only meant to stop the shaking," she said, nodding toward her wine glass, now still.

He blinked and looked forward again. She looked forward too, not knowing what to make of his reaction. "I am sorry," she said when the silence between them continued. She caught Deborah looking between them, a slight air of confusion about her. Maryann shook her head slightly, wishing she could yell "Stop looking at us!" No one else had noticed, had they?

After the plates were cleared, Maryann said quietly, "I am sorry." The silence was becoming excruciating. "I didn't mean to make you . . . uncomfortable."

"I know."

The pudding course was placed before them.

Timothy cleared his throat as he picked up his spoon. "You must promise never do to that again."

"I promise." Was it that extreme a thing for her to have done? She felt wholly chagrined.

"To *any* man, *ever*."

"All right, I will never put my hand on a man's knee again." She paused before giving in to the need to defend herself. "But I was only trying to be helpful."

His expression was as serious as she had ever seen it. "We shan't talk about it again, then." He turned back to his pudding, took a bite, and then glanced at her, though his smile seemed a bit forced. "If you're not going to eat yours, I'll take it. It's very good."

Maryann narrowed her eyes at him. "You can't have my pudding."

"If I finish first, I might." He began eating quicker, and she hurried to match the pace. It was childish and bad manners to do such a thing at a formal dinner. But not as bad as her putting a hand on his knee? Men were so confusing.

Chapter Eleven

Maryann did not see Timothy for a nearly a week. When she saw him at the Thompsons' garden party, she remembered his reaction to her hand on his knee and swallowed her embarrassment. Upon reflection, she'd realized how out of line she'd been. She hadn't meant it to be intimate, of course, but to apologize further would make everything worse.

So, she'd focused on other things and followed through on the introduction to Susanna Grimmley, whom she'd met at Lady Dominque's welcome tea earlier that week. Timothy was kind and charming to Miss Grimmley and asked her to take a turn with him around the lake. A pond, really, but Maryann supposed it was the closest thing to a lake one would find in the city. He was friendly and relaxed and Maryann felt comfortable putting the dinner party incident behind them.

Deborah had not been feeling well, and since Lucas was not the sort of man to attend social events without his wife dragging him there, Maryann had come alone, meeting up with the Callifours, who were happy to absorb her into their group. Maryann spent the next two hours moving in and out of conversations beside the elder Miss Callifour. After a few months in London, Maryann knew which women to be on her guard with and which she could be relaxed with, who to trust and who not to. Maryann's connection to Deborah and Lady Dominque had put her in solid placement within the *ton*, though her inheritance certainly helped.

"Mr. Fetich has been very attentive," Maryann commented after the man, who had been visiting with them some quarter of an hour, jumped up to fetch Miss Callifour a fresh glass of lemonade.

Miss Callifour smiled after her admirer. Then she turned a concerned look toward Maryann. "Does it bother you?"

"Not in the least. You both deserve someone who sparks your interest, and I daresay there were no sparks between myself and Mr. Fetich. I wish you both the very best."

Her father had commented in his most recent letter to her that Mr. Fetich was a very enterprising young man. Clearly, Mr. Fetich hadn't wasted any time writing to him.

Miss Callifour leaned in to whisper about a walk they had taken beside the Serpentine just that morning, and a stolen kiss when no one else was in view. "Are you so very shocked?" The look in her wide brown eyes betrayed that *she* was shocked, even if Maryann was not.

"I am glad to hear that his interest is so ardent. I would caution you not be too amiable to his attention until things are secure, of course."

"Of course," Miss Callifour said, but her eyes were dancing.

Though Maryann did not envy her for Mr. Fetich's sake, she would not mind a stolen kiss or two of her own. As the season moved on and engagements were announced all around her, the pressure was becoming uncomfortable for those like Miss

Callifour and Maryann who were not as young and pretty as some of the others.

Miss Callifour thanked Maryann for her blessing, then excused herself for a turn about the "lake" when Mr. Fetich returned with a full glass of lemonade. Maryann smiled at the couple and dipped her head in approval. He nodded back, which she took as his thanks that she was not standing in his way.

Without the company of Miss Callifour, Maryann prepared to leave, glad not to have an evening engagement. She'd had some event or another every evening for the last ten days, and the sociality was beginning to wear on her. Sometimes she worried that her false society smile had made her forget what a true smile felt like anymore. It would be wonderful to sit in her bedchamber and simply read a book. Alone. Wearing her nightdress and the pink shawl her mother had knitted for her many years ago.

She made her way to the drive, where she ordered the carriage and then visited with some other guests while she waited. She was standing alone when someone tapped her right shoulder. She looked that direction at the same time Timothy stepped forward on her left side.

"You are such a child," she said after turning to her left, but she could not hold back a smile—a real one. No one made her smile like he did.

"Lucky for me, you like childish games," Timothy said, then winked. He knew that she did *not* like such things, but it was such a part of him that she could not protest. "Did you enjoy yourself this afternoon, Maryann?"

"I did," she said. "You?"

"Certainly," he said. "Anywhere with women, wine, and fine food is a good time to me, though I am enjoying them much more now that I'm not trying to attend every event."

"I'm glad to hear you are being more attentive to your schedule," she said. "And what did you think of Miss Grimmley?"

"She was . . . lovely."

"Lovely?" Maryann repeated. It was the same account he'd given of Miss Rushford a few weeks earlier. "What is wrong with her?"

"Nothing is wrong with her."

They argued for a full minute until Timothy finally admitted that Miss Grimmley had very odd thumbs. "They are short and flat, and, well, they look like badminton paddles, honestly." He waggled his own finely-formed thumbs.

"For heaven's sake," Maryann grumbled, shaking her head. "You are impossible."

"I am not impossible," he said with faux wounded pride. "I am just . . . particular. I introduced her to Mr. Anders, who has those excessively big ears, so he shall likely be more patient with her affliction than I am. And I am not dismissing her because she is not a wonderful woman, only she is not the woman for me. There is no shame in that."

"There cannot be any shame in being rejected by Mr. Timothy Mayfield because women rejected by Mr. Timothy Mayfield is becoming a bigger and bigger group. Goodness, nearly all of us are within its confines these days."

He looked at her with raised eyebrows

She had not meant to be quite so transparent, but she also did not step away from the truth. "Am I not one of them?" Before he could answer with something that would likely make them both uncomfortable, she continued. "I thought you were being more flexible regarding your list."

"I am," he said with his chin held high as he rocked back on his heels. "I took Miss Justin on a walk yesterday, and she is a *brunette*." He smiled at his heroic gesture, though it quickly fell back to its ordinary level. "But I have realized that I am in no hurry to marry. I am only twenty-seven years old."

"Lucas is also twenty-seven, and he has been married a full year and a half *and* he was engaged for two years before that due to my mother's illness that stood in the way of a wedding."

Timothy grinned at her. "Ralph Bington was thirty-*two* when he finally married."

"And will be dead before his children marry."

"Oh, you are a saucy one." Timothy reached over and pulled at the ribbon of her bonnet, undoing the bow with a single tug.

She had four pins in place, so the bonnet did not shift in the slightest, but she gasped and glared at him. She tried to retie the bow with gloved hands, but, as he had that day in Hyde Park, he pushed her hands away and retied it himself. She looked above his head to keep from staring at his face so close to her own and willed her heart to keep a steady pace. If she wanted to, she could lean forward and steal a kiss of her own.

Oh, Maryann. Really.

"So, I have been thinking," Timothy said as he gave the loops a final tug.

She glared at him once more before looking down the drive for the carriage, feeling oddly uncomfortable now that she'd thought of kissing him. If he knew, he would laugh.

"You have gone out of your way to introduce me to some prime candidates for making a match, but I have done nothing for you in return."

"I mean this as kindly as I possibly can," she said, smiling sweetly at him. "But what could you possibly do for me?"

He narrowed his eyes at her playfully, then ran his hand through his overgrown hair. "I can introduce you to potential husbands, just as you are introducing me to potential wives. It seems only fair."

"Except that I don't need your help," Maryann said. "I have plenty of men to choose from." Men visited her every day, with bright smiles and tight ears as they complimented her dresses and her hair and the lovely room her father had built and the extraordinary gas lamps in the drawing room. Each man was as insincere as the next, but she was not lacking in numbers.

"You have *fortune hunters* to choose from," Timothy said. "Men looking to line their pockets and pay off debts."

"Hmm," she said thoughtfully, tapping her chin with one of her non-dainty fingers. What did Timothy think of *her* thumbs? "It seems you were one of those men not too long ago."

"But I was honest about it," he reminded her, putting a hand to his chest to emphasize his magnanimity. "I know men who do not necessarily move in our circles but who would be a good match."

"If they don't want money, they'll want beauty and youth, and I am equally low on both."

"Do not be unkind to yourself, Maryann. You have plenty of both those aspects."

She blinked at him. Was he saying that he thought she was pretty? She did not dare believe it because she was reminded every day that she was not. She looked away before he could see the surprise in her face. "I thank you for the offer, but, again, I do not need your help."

"Why not?"

"Because I do not need it," she snapped.

"So, if I were to introduce a man to you who fit the parameters you were looking for, you would snub him?"

"I am not mean-spirited," she said, feeling rather cornered by the discussion.

Lucy had become proficient at vetting potential suitors through their household staff; Maryann had purchased eleven pairs of silk stockings these last weeks in payment. Mr. Martin owned an estate in Surry—with a heavy mortgage attached. Lord Bromley had land of his own—and five younger sisters in need of being launched into society. His estate had not been profitable for almost a decade due to severe flooding and inadequate repair. His wife would be expected to sponsor each of his sisters, which would take the next ten years of her life. No, thank you. One by one, each name that crossed her salver ended with a financial need for which she was seen as remedy and nothing by way of romantic connection. Each man who joined the ranks of the others made her miss home even more.

"Let me help you," Timothy said, smiling at her in that way that froze the argument on her lips. "I shall only offer introduction to those men of the finest character, those whom I know would benefit from a fine woman like you."

She finally nodded, but her mind was repeating "a fine woman like you" over and over in her head. He felt her a fine woman—but not fine enough for him.

"I shall agree if you will get a haircut."

He ran a hand through his hair, causing it to stick up so badly that she used her fingers to comb it back into place. She worried after the first pass that it was another intimate, and therefore inappropriate, gesture, but he did not react so it seemed she was safe. She wished she were not wearing gloves so she could feel his hair moving through her fingers. It seemed very soft.

"We are still in public, Mr. Mayfield, do mind your manners."

He laughed as Lucas's carriage finally rolled up. Timothy put out his arm to escort her the ten steps down the drive.

"Thank you for your concern for my future," she said when they reached the carriage door held open by the driver. Timothy bent his head and kissed her gloved hand before handing her inside. She told him goodbye, he shut the door, and she collapsed against the cushion. She would introduce women to him, and he would introduce men to her. What a carousel, one that she knew with greater clarity every day would end in heartache. For her at least.

Chapter Twelve

Maryann paced back and forth in the drawing room while Deborah sat in a chair near the fire. "I am tired of attending events alone, Deborah. If you cannot go, then I should be able to stay home as well." She looked pale, but not *that* pale.

"Lucas and I cancelling is a hardship on the hosts already, but at least the numbers are kept even. You'll better understand this when you plan your own parties and someone else is inconsiderate of the details you spend hours toiling over."

"Then make Lucas go and I shall stay home this time." Her desire to return to Somerset grew stronger each time she thought of it, and attending events alone did nothing to lessen her discomfort. She was so tired of the marriage games of London.

"Again, it comes down to the numbers," Deborah explained patiently. "Equal men and women. Lucas and I, as a married couple, are easily extracted. You, as a single woman, are not. It is a very fragile balance, and it will reflect poorly on all of us if you do not go."

Maryann sat in the chair beside her sister with a scowl on her face. Between her headache and too many callers, she had not gotten any rest that morning. To hear that she would have to attend the Hornbergers' dinner party alone was the proverbial straw on the back of her diminishing sociability. She was in no mood to be good company and make small talk and drink punch. She wanted a good strong brandy, truth be told. Father had occasionally allowed it when she had one of her headaches, but Deborah would not. Maryann was still a debutante and debs did not drink brandy. Even medicinally.

"Is it really so bad?" Deborah asked kindly, her head cocked to the side in a gesture that reminded Maryann of their mother. "You have met so many people that surely you shall be familiar with the other guests. Won't the Callifours be there? I know Lady Dominique is attending."

Maryann sighed and scolded herself for acting like a child. "It is not *so* bad," she admitted. "But when we attend together, I know you are looking out for me and I can go to you with any difficulties. You have extracted me from more than one awkward conversation." Once, a young man had been droning on about his cattle for nearly half an hour before Deborah was able to draw Maryann from the conversation; she later gave Maryann some tips on how to remove herself in the future. "The whole point of having a sponsor is so that I do not have to attend events alone. Plus, I have a headache." She pointed to her head as though Deborah could see the slight throbbing that had been keeping Maryann company all day.

Deborah frowned and crossed her hands in her lap. "I am sorry, Maryann. You have done well this season; I have been so proud of you. However, tonight is not an event you can easily miss. There are only twenty guests, eighteen without Lucas and myself."

"Can I at least have some brandy for my poor head?"

"Maryann, dear."

Maryann waved away the inevitable refusal because Deborah did sound sincerely apologetic. "It is all right. I know I am being petulant. But this is the fifth event in the last two weeks I have attended alone, and I am beginning to feel strange arriving by myself. As a debutante, I am *expected* to have a chaperone." Saying it out loud made her sound even more childish. "But, enough of that. I should be more concerned for your health than I have been. Perhaps it is time to send for a physician." It was not the first time that Maryann had suggested such a course. After caring for Mother for so long, she was not one to drag her feet when men of medicine needed to be involved.

"The physician is coming tomorrow," Deborah said, as though admitting a secret. She removed the light shawl she was wearing and began to fold it in her lap.

"That is good, then," Maryann said. "With a little luck, and perhaps the right treatment, you can be joining me again by Saturday night."

Deborah shifted her in her seat and kept her eyes on the shawl. "If I am right about the reason for my discomfort, I do not expect I will be feeling much better for a while. Perhaps we should discuss another arrangement for your chaperone. Lady Dominique might—"

Maryann slipped from her chair and knelt down in front of her sister. She put her hands on the arms of Deborah's chair, trapping her in her seat. "You're pregnant!"

Deborah blinked back tears but nodded. "I believe so, but I am so nervous. After last time, I don't know that I could bear another loss."

Deborah had married in February of last year, after waiting

almost two years after Lucas's proposal due to their mother's illness. *Two years*. It was Maryann who had convinced her family to move forward with the wedding when it became obvious that Mother would not improve.

That June, Deborah had announced she was expecting. Mother had not been aware of anything, but Deborah had told her as though Mother understood every word. "I know you are happy for me," Deborah had whispered that day as she held their mother's crumpled hands in both of hers.

In July, Deborah lost the baby.

In August, Mother was unable to swallow properly, which led to issues with her lungs.

In September, all of them were sitting around her bed as Mother took her last breath.

The hardship of those months was more than Maryann could articulate even now, but the pain was even sharper for Deborah, who had lost her child and her mother in a few months' time.

Maryann raised on her knees enough to wrap her arms around her sister's shoulders. "Everything will be all right this time," she said even though she had no way of knowing such. She pulled back, remembering something she'd heard the women discussing at a tea a few weeks ago. "That you feel ill is a good sign, I think. You were not ill last time, right?"

Deborah shook her head. "I have heard that, too, but it does not displace my fear." She put her hands over her stomach though there was no physical change yet.

"Well, it *should* displace your fear and give you hope," Maryann said with confidence. "And you are to forget I whined at you about anything at all and know that I am well enough on my own for as long as needs be. I shall be an aunt!"

She hoped that the child would be a girl and Deborah would name her after Mother—Katharine Landsing had a nice ring to it.

"You are already an aunt three times over to James's children," Deborah reminded her.

"And they are lovely." Maryann smiled, remembering that Timothy used that word to describe the women who did not meet his requirements. "But this will be *your* child, my sister's child, and I shall be the most doting aunt you can possibly imagine."

"You shall have to be, as Lucas has no brothers or sisters and James's wife is not one to dote on her own children, let alone someone else's."

Maryann barked a laugh, then covered her mouth quickly with her hand. Deborah laughed as well but stopped when Maryann cut hers short.

"My apologies," Maryann said after removing her hand.

"Apologies for what? I believe laughing at someone's joke is a compliment. Why did you stop yourself?"

Maryann stood, shaking out her skirts and attempting to turn the subject. "I am so happy for you and Lucas both. This is the most wonderful thing I have heard in a long time."

"Thank you," Deborah said. "But why did you cover your laugh?"

Maryann shifted her weight to her other foot. "Does Lady Dominique know? Have you told anyone else?"

Deborah would not be put off. "Tell me why you covered your laugh, Maryann. You have not done that for years." She waited a few moments, then added another stick to her fire of demand. "I am a woman existing on the brink of emotion and reason, tell me or I shall burst into tears."

It might have been a joke, but it very well may not have been.

"Timothy compared my laugh to the braying of a donkey, and since then, I have tried to be more circumspect."

Deborah's eyes flashed wide, and her hands went to the arms of her chair as though she would push herself up and march across town to throttle the man. Maryann crossed to her quickly and put a hand on her shoulder just in case that truly was her intention.

"It is all right. I have known my whole life that my laugh is hideous."

"It is not hideous."

Maryann cocked her head. "Deborah, I don't need to be placated."

"Good, because I am not the placating type. Your laugh is loud and full and reflects the joy you feel. I shall beat that boy about the ears for saying otherwise."

"He thought he was only teasing me. He did not understand how deep my own regret of it has been."

"But he hurt you and that is unacceptable to me after he already rejected you. I shall have Lucas give him a piece of—"

"You will not tell Lucas to do anything. In fact, it would be best if you told him nothing," Maryann said, realizing she had underestimated Deborah's emotional state. "I have forgiven Timothy, and as things are so strange between us, I will not risk resurrecting the topic by having you or Lucas breathe a word of it. He apologized, and I forgave it."

Deborah's cheeks were pink and her jaw was set, but at least she was not trying to stand any more. "He should not have said such a thing."

"But he did, and it is true and all is well."

"All is not well if you are not laughing. You must laugh, Maryann, I need you to laugh. And I will not allow you to change any single thing about yourself to please anyone, least of all a man."

Maryann returned to her chair. "Ah, but it is not just a man, it is Timothy."

That brought Deborah up short, and her stare was a little too hard. For the second time today, Maryann had said too much, and yet she did not fully regret this one. Deborah had shared her secret, why should Maryann not admit hers?

"You do care for him, then? Things have been, as you said, strange between the two of you, and Lucas and I have wondered what to think."

For a moment, Maryann considered telling Deborah the depth of her feelings, the ache in her chest when she was with Timothy and how much she wanted his company when he was gone. She imagined telling her what it felt like to see another woman on his arm. To unburden herself felt like the most irresistible temptation . . . except that she knew it would not change his heart, or hers, or ease Deborah's mind, which was Maryann's first priority now.

"He is Timothy, Deborah, and a very good friend." Maryann hid her discomfort behind a smile.

Deborah opened her mouth to respond, but Maryann spoke before she had the chance. "I had best ready myself for tonight, and you are not to worry yourself at all. In fact, I think your happy news has even relieved my headache." She crossed to her sister and gave her another hug. "You rest and eat toast and drink peppermint tea, and I shall dance and socialize enough for the both of us."

Chapter Thirteen

*M*iss Morrington?"

Maryann turned from the conversation she'd been having with a few other ladies, lemonade glass in hand—much better than that horrid punch from a few weeks ago—and smiled at Timothy. She had not seen him arrive and excused herself from the conversation so she could devote her full attention to him. It was only when she noticed the man standing beside Timothy that she realized what was happening. He'd found her a suitor. Her heart froze a beat in her chest.

"Good evening, Mr. Mayfield," she managed.

Just then, Lady Jersey bustled up to them. She was flustered as she looked between the three of them, and her ostrich feathers shivered over her head as though in a breeze. "Miss Morrington, I would like to introduce you to Mr. Timothy Mayfield of Norfolk."

Timothy cleared his throat to draw the frazzled woman's attention to him, and then nodded toward the other man.

"Oh, yes, my apologies," Lady Jersey said quickly. "Miss Morrington, I would like to introduce you to Colonel Berkins.

Now if you'll excuse me." She hurried off, and Maryann was glad to have very good ears and the ability to be attentive, otherwise she'd have missed the man's name completely.

Colonel Berkins stepped forward and bowed without fanfare over her gloved hand. He was only a few inches taller than she was and wore evening clothes instead of his military uniform. "It is a pleasure to meet you, Miss Morrington. Mr. Mayfield sings your praises."

"Does he?" Maryann asked, raising her eyebrows. "What does he praise the most—my laugh, perhaps, or my simpering manner?" Deborah's news had added some spice to Maryann's mood these last few days.

She'd meant to throw Timothy off his expectations, but he only grinned wider, his blue eyes sparkling like the sea. "Simpering you are not, Miss Morrington, but wit you have in spades." He put a hand on Colonel Berkins back. "Colonel Berkins is new to London and not the usual fare." He wagged his eyebrows at Maryann though she was the only one to see it. "I thought to introduce him to the best woman this town has to offer."

"Well, if he likes his women plain and old, very good," Maryann countered with a slight curtsy. Because why not be who she was?

Colonel Berkins laughed at that, a deep sound that drew her attention. "It seems Mayfield was correct in believing you and I would get on, Miss Morrington. I am no great beauty myself nor have I been young for some time."

Indeed, he had some gray above his ears, and though she would not say he was plain, neither was he handsome. But had he just confirmed that she was no beauty either? She should be offended, yet she was the one who had brought it up. She smiled and nodded slightly, accepting what was.

"Mayfield said you had a beautiful smile, and that seems to be true as well."

Maryann looked at Timothy. Had he truly told this man she had a beautiful smile? *Did* she have a beautiful smile? Father often said that her smile lit the sun just as Mother's did, but no one had sincerely commented on her smile here in London. She wondered if she had forgotten it was an attribute simply because no one had pointed it out. Until Timothy had said as much to his new friend.

"I thank you both for the compliment, then," she said, looking back at Colonel Berkins and wondering if perhaps he would be her rescue from the feelings she could not unfeel regarding Timothy. How she longed for that relief.

"Well, I am off to find a partner for the next set," Timothy said before he bowed, turned, and left her alone with Colonel Berkins.

"Um, well, how long have you been in London?" Colonel Berkins asked.

"Nearly four months now. Since February," Maryann said.

"And you are not married yet?"

Ouch. "Those of us short on looks and long in the tooth tend to stay on the shelf a bit longer."

"Good grief, I may be in London for years." He made a face, but then smiled again and shrugged. His self-comfort was engaging. The set currently taking the floor came to an end, and the couples applauded for the orchestra.

"Would you care to dance?" Colonel Berkins said.

She heard a tremor of hesitation in the offer. "Do *you* want to dance, Colonel, or are you offering because you find yourself at Almack's and that is what is expected?"

He laughed again, and the sound moved through her. "You have caught me, Miss Morrington. I do not love to dance, but I am willing if you would like to. It is a good way to interact, and, as I understand it, there is not much more to do here but to drink poor punch. Mayfield warned me away from it quite directly. Said he has never been the same since a particularly bad batch."

"Perhaps you have not known Mr. Mayfield long enough to know that he has a flair for the dramatic. As I have already vetted tonight's concoction, I can assure you that it will not do you any harm. There were some empty chairs near the window on the far side of the room last I looked—perhaps we could take the set to get to know one another rather than force you to dance."

"Oh, you are the holiest of angels," he proclaimed and put out his arm. She smiled, took it, and hoped that Timothy was watching.

One set's worth of conversation turned to two. On the third, Mr. Ramsey, one of Maryann's newer admirers, found them and asked her to dance. She excused herself from Colonel Berkins's company, but as she made the steps and turns of the dance with Mr. Ramsey, she kept thinking about Colonel Berkins. About how he had sat with her so long. About how he had kept her from thinking of Timothy. Still was, in fact, except that when she thought about how he kept her from thinking about Timothy she actually *was* thinking about Timothy.

When the dance finished, she was surprised to find Colonel Berkins moving toward them.

"Might I have the next?" Colonel Berkins asked.

"Certainly," Maryann said.

The men traded her off, and she reentered the floor with Colonel Berkins.

"I would not make you dance if you wish not to, Colonel Berkins."

"It was unfair for me to keep you from the floor for two whole sets, and I feel sure that other men have noticed the same so I shall not miss my chance to occupy your attention one set longer, then I shall not impose any more."

"You are not imposing if your attention is welcome."

He smiled widely, and she returned it, remembering how Timothy had told this man she had a beautiful smile.

They took their places and moved through the dance. Though he may not have liked dancing, he was confident of the steps. She wondered if he knew about her fortune.

Colonel Berkins was true to his word and did not take any more of her time that evening, save for sitting beside her during the cold supper. She was glad for the chance to speak with him again and by the end of the night could honestly say that he had been the brightest part of the evening. Brighter even than Timothy.

The next morning, the colonel called and they had a lovely visit, with Deborah acting as chaperone. When he left, Maryann caught Deborah watching her.

"You like this one," Deborah said bluntly.

"I do," Maryann said, picking up her needlework. She was working on a new cover for the piano stool back at Orchard House. She'd wanted daisies, but white silk did not always wear well, so she'd chosen pink instead. She hoped to have it finished by the time she returned to the estate in another month.

"And he is a friend of Timothy's?"

"I do not think Timothy knows him well—I daresay I have spoken with him more than Timothy has—but they share a mutual friend, though I don't remember who."

"What is Colonel Berkins's situation?" Deborah asked, also picking up her embroidery. She was planning a set of handkerchiefs for Father for Christmas.

"He has recently finished a commission in the King's army, where he spent a great deal of time in Spain, mostly. He's returned to a bit of acreage left to him by an uncle in Shropshire and is in negotiations with a mining company in regard to its use in that industry. He has come to London for a wife."

Deborah's head snapped up. "He told you that?"

"Well, I asked him, so it is only polite that he answer me." She could not hold back her grin as she pushed her needle through the fabric.

"*You* asked him if he had come to London for a wife?"

Maryann lifted her eyes. "Yes. I tire of the games, Deborah, and feel that I have lost most of them. Why not change them up and be honest and direct?"

"Because it is ill-mannered," she said tightly. "And it reflects poorly on your character and your family."

Maryann had not thought of it in quite that way, but she was not fully dissuaded. "I have only spoken so boldly with him, no one else, and I did so because I thought to put him off in order to get back at Timothy when I started. But then it turned on me and ended up being a very nice evening."

"Get back at Timothy? What do you mean by that? You mean for the horrible thing he said about your laugh?"

That seemed ages ago. "For thinking I needed his help in finding a husband."

Deborah set down her stitching. "But you are trying to help him find a match, are you not? What is wrong with him doing the same for you? You've been in London four months. I think it fair of him to help after being such a disappointment himself."

How could Maryann truly explain the complexity of her relationship with Timothy? She tried to find an answer, then gave up. It barely made sense to her and would certainly make no sense to anyone else. She kept sewing and tried to keep the topic easy, though it was anything but. She did not like to upset Deborah in her delicate condition, but her sister's heightened emotions made that difficult sometimes.

"It does not matter," Maryann said. "Suffice it to say that I like Colonel Berkins very much. Time will tell if my opinion stays as rosy, but for now he is the most interesting prospect I have met so far."

"Oh," Deborah said, finally returning to her work.

Maryann had expected more and glanced up from her silk to see Deborah wipe quickly at her eyes.

"Deborah," Maryann said, setting her work in her lap. "Whatever is the matter?"

"Nothing." Her sister sniffled and wiped at her eyes again. "Pregnancy does such things." She sewed a few more stitches, but likely could not see well enough through her tears. Maryann waited her out, and finally Deborah looked up, her chin trembling. "I had so hoped you and Timothy would find an accord, and I have held out hope all these months that what I see between you two would blossom. Even after you told me of the horrible things he'd said about your laugh. I talked to Lucas and he said that it might yet come together." She lifted her shoulders. "I felt better, but if Timothy is introducing you to his friends, then, well . . ." She wiped at her eyes again, and Maryann set her work aside fully so she could cross to the settee and put her arm around her sister's shoulder.

Deborah sniffled. "Timothy is Lucas's closest friend, and his only friend who does not annoy me, well, until recently. Were the two of you to marry it would keep you and me connected. After losing Mother, and with James being married to that ninny, I see my family slipping away from me and . . ." She sniffed. Took a breath. "And so I had hoped that the right match would keep you closer. It seems silly now, especially after Timothy's cruelty to you, but, well, there it is."

Maryann remained quiet until she trusted herself to speak evenly. "My dear sister," she said, then kissed her sister's forehead—had she ever done that in the whole of her life? "I do not need Timothy to keep me connected to you. Please do not worry yourself over that in the slightest. I am not going to disappear into my husband's life, no matter who he is, and I cannot imagine my future without you in it."

"If Colonel Berkins is from Shropshire, he will want to take you there with him and I shall have this baby without you and . . ." She began to cry again.

"And I am a woman of fortune," Maryann reminded her. "And I shall not enter into any marriage contract that limits my ability to travel wherever and whenever I choose. You will not lose me."

"I could not bear it," Deborah whimpered.

"And you shall not. I should like your blessing to try to find my happiness with Colonel Berkins—or another man if necessary, however." She would be wise not to put all her eggs in the Berkins basket. After all, she had only known the man for the space of one evening and one morning visit. "Can you grant me faith that I will not let anyone or anything separate me from you?"

"Of course, I want you to be happy," Deborah said and sat up straight. "I am sorry. I am so undone."

"For good reason." Maryann returned to her chair where she picked up her stitching. "Now, tell me how you are feeling and what plans you have made." Deborah had not been out of the house in well over a week.

Deborah cried happy tears when she explained that Lucas had agreed to name the child after Mother if it were a girl, but then sad tears when she confessed that Lucas's mother wanted them to move in with her until the baby was born. Deborah could not abide having the baby anywhere but in Orchard House, and Lucas had not yet taken up the campaign with his mother.

The next callers arrived, and Deborah excused herself while Maryann entertained Miss Callifour and her sister for half an hour. She sewed for another quarter of an hour alone before telling Herrington that she was finished with her visits for the day.

She rang for Lucy even though she felt guilty about the errand she was going to ask of the girl.

When Lucy arrived in the drawing room, Maryann asked her to close the door and then waved her to share the settee with her away from any prying ears or eyes.

"What is it, miss?" Lucy asked, her eyes sparkling with delight at the subterfuge. They always talked in Maryann's bedroom, but this newest task was not one that Maryann felt could wait—Lucy would be going out tonight.

Maryann kept her hands in her lap. "Last night, you asked if I had met anyone you should follow up on and I told you that I hadn't, but that was not true."

Lucy's pale eyebrows shot up. "Miss?"

"I had not thought I needed to have him investigated as he is so forthcoming and open." She met the maid's eyes, promising herself that should she and Colonel Berkins marry she would never tell him of this. Unless by then she knew he would find it funny. That was something to ponder on later, as well as whatever Lucy might learn in the meantime. "I am reminded today, however, of how complex a thing love and marriage can be." She paused for a breath. "Could you find everything you can on Colonel Charles Berkins as quickly as possible? He hails from Shropshire and says he has a piece of land there he is looking to mine. He's been in the King's army until recently and spent time in Spain but is now renting a modest home in Kensington. Will you make sure he is everything he has said he is?"

"Of course," Lucy said, patting Maryann's hand. "I'll ask one of the other girls to help with your hair tonight."

"You are not getting any complaint from the other staff, are you?"

"Oh, no," Lucy said, smiling and shaking her head. "I gave the housekeeper a pair of fine silk stockings, and she has given me all the margin I could ever want. No one dares question her."

Chapter Fourteen

*M*aryann stood at the window, fiddling with the strings of her reticule as she watched the phaeton come to a stop in front of the house. She had never gone on an open-carriage ride with a gentleman, and though she was excited, she was oddly nervous. There was something silly about riding around town in his carriage where people could see them. As though they were trying to advertise their interest in one another; it had only been a few days since the colonel's morning visit.

It also seemed to her as though carriage rides were reserved for the young. *And* she worried that he had suggested it so he might impress her with his fancy carriage. Not that he shouldn't want to impress her, she wanted to impress *him*, but she didn't want him to think that she was interested in material things. Because she wasn't.

Being a woman at times came with too large a capacity to think all the thoughts at once.

"Relax," Deborah said from where she sat, still working on Father's handkerchiefs.

"I'm trying," Maryann said. She was a grown woman, so why was she feeling like such an inexperienced girl?

Perhaps what really had her unsettled was Lucy's report that had come from a chambermaid hired with the house he'd let for the rest of the season. Apparently, Colonel Berkins was everything he said he was. It was the first report Lucy had ever given that had not revealed some ulterior plan. Maryann was glad for it, but it meant there was no reason not to invest herself in his attention. Was she ready to do so? Was Colonel Berkins the man she'd been waiting for? Her perfect man, even though she did not believe in such things?

She backed away a step from the window, watching as he hopped down from the high seat of his carriage and came around the front of the horses. He had no tiger—not for a two-person carriage—so he waited for a footman to secure the horses before he came up the walkway, straightening his coat as he did so. His confident stride seemed to tell the world that he was in accord with himself and therefore they may as well be in accord with him too. Timothy held himself in a similar way. Was that why she admired it in Colonel Berkins? Did she like the colonel for his own sake, or because he reminded her of Timothy?

So many thoughts!

She heard the knock at the door and placed herself in the center of the room so she could smile when he came in. And he did come in. And she did smile as he crossed the room and bowed over her hand. He wore buff-colored trousers, a black coat, and a simple cravat. "You look lovely, Miss Morrington."

"Thank you, Colonel Berkins."

They said their goodbyes to Deborah, and then went out into the lovely afternoon of blue skies and just the right amount of breeze to keep the air moving but not plaster her skirts to her legs.

Maryann startled when Colonel Berkins put his hands on either side of her waist and lifted her completely off the ground so her foot might reach the step, but she went along with it—what else could she do? He winked once she'd found her balance on the seat, and she narrowed her eyes playfully in response, making him laugh. He crossed round to his side and climbed up to his seat. It was a relief to feel her anxiety settling. She was with a man she liked, who was everything he said he was, and they were in a carriage on a fine afternoon. What was there to be so worked up about?

"Timothy says you hail from Somerset," Colonel Berkins said once the phaeton had found its pace. Though the carriage was known for speed, he did not seem intent to show off that aspect, which she appreciated. "I imagine that contrasts with London a great deal."

"Yes, it is very different here," she said, adjusting her position. The seat had a back, but no side so she found herself leaning toward Colonel Berkins in order to keep her balance. She felt so far off the ground.

"I have been to Somerset once, many years ago with a military friend. A little town called Broomfield, do you know it?"

"I do," she said, looking at him in surprise. "My sister has a friend who lives in Taunton. We stayed the summer once when my parents were traveling to Wales."

They continued to talk of Somerset and the sea; she'd grown up beside it, and he'd come to love it during his time in the army and the years he'd lived in Spain.

"Lovely country," he said, nostalgically. "And the people are beautiful and openhearted. Only there is still so much rebuilding to be done there. It was a relief to return to England. The structure of it all—laws and roads and decency."

"You will not miss Spain, then?"

"Oh, I miss the land every day, but I hope to keep the best parts of it here with me." He put a hand to his chest.

"Where will you live after your time in London, then? If your land will go to mining, will you need to be there to supervise the work?" It hurt her heart to imagine the rich countryside being destroyed. But mining was the future, everyone said so, even her father, and it was a primary topic in Parliament to make sure too much land did not fall victim.

"I am unsure, which I realize is an unpopular answer. A man is expected to be certain of all things."

She liked that he could be honest with her, and then she had to take hold of his arm as they rounded a corner into Hyde Park. It was a crush of carriages, and they likely could have walked faster than the carriage was moving. Despite the silliness she'd felt earlier, she found it rather exciting to be in the place where so many people went to be seen. She would be seen with Colonel Berkins, who was growing handsomer each time she saw him and who was the only man able to replace a certain *other* man in her thoughts. She was officially glad she'd accepted the invitation.

"You are among friends here, Colonel Berkins," she said once their pace and position were constant. "And if anyone can appreciate your uncertainty it is I. I am meant to make a match here in a city I've never been in before and then to live at the whim of my husband. At least you know what your choices are." Sometimes when she thought of not living in Orchard House again, she could barely breathe. Especially lately as the blush had faded from London.

He laughed. "I hadn't thought of that, Miss Morrington. Perhaps you and I are not so different, then. I suppose I have choices to make, but I still feel at the whim of things."

"So, what are your choices of where you might live?" Maryann asked. "What have you considered?"

They spent the rest of the ride nodding to acquaintances—hers, mostly, since he was so new back to England, let alone London—and talking of his possibilities while the horses kept a steady pace.

Colonel Berkins explained that he had a house on the far end of his land, away from the mining operations, but it was small and currently occupied by a steward he was hesitant to turn out—the man had five children. Or he'd considered keeping a house in London where much of the business side of the industry would take place.

"I could set up residence nearly anywhere, so long as my wife was patient with my necessary absences, which I fear shall be the case regardless of where I decide to settle. I shall simply have to find ways to make it up to her, I suppose."

He bumped her with his shoulder, just as Timothy often did. This comradery with promise was something she could learn to like very much. "Perhaps you could even live in Somerset," she said in as casual a tone as she could manage even though she feared her meaning was entirely transparent.

"I don't see why that shouldn't be a consideration," he said. "In fact, as I shall be traveling and managing business no matter where we live, I don't know why I would be the one to make the decision at all. I imagine if a man marries a sensible woman, he ought to consider her wishes as important as his own, don't you think?"

Oh, Deborah, if you could only hear this! "What a very modern and reasonable man you are, Colonel."

"I should hope so," he said. "The world is changing, and I don't know why people resist changing with it. Far easier to adapt to new ways and ideas, says I."

Chapter Fifteen

*M*aryann would have been sad to see the ride come to an end if not for the fact that the constant bouncing had dislodged one of the hatpins holding her bonnet in place and it was now stabbing her in the back of the head. Every bump since leaving the park further convinced her that the pin had drawn blood.

It was a relief when Colonel Berkins finally came to a stop in front of her house. She was prepared for him to lift her from the carriage this time, and she put her hands on his shoulders, letting them linger once her feet were on the ground. He was not quite as tall as Timothy, but tall enough that she had to look up into his face. He kept his hands on her waist a few moments and then surprised her by kissing her quickly on the cheek.

"Colonel Berkins!" she said in sincere surprise when he straightened and released her. She did not hold back her smile, though, nor regret the way the kiss shivered through her most pleasantly.

"Forgive me," he said. "I could not help myself after such a thoroughly enjoyable afternoon."

"Well, I can't argue that," she said, then leaned in and dropped her voice. "But the next time you choose to show your thanks, perhaps select a location that does not afford my family a front row seat."

She looked past him to Deborah, framed in the front window, and gave her a finger wave. Deborah raised her eyebrows and stepped away.

Colonel Berkins looked over his shoulder in time to see the retreat, then looked at Maryann and cringed. "Forgive me, Miss Morrington. Your sister will think me a cad. I did make sure the street was clear."

"More likely she will think me a wanton woman for not slapping you." But she smiled as she said it because the kiss felt as genuine as he professed it to be.

They shared their farewells on the small porch, and then she closed the door behind her. She was surprised Deborah was not waiting in the entry with her arms folded and her toe tapping.

Then Maryann entered the drawing room.

Deborah sat on the settee facing the door, with Lucas beside her and Timothy standing at the mantel. What was he doing here? All of them looked at her with such equally expectant expressions that she laughed. She did not miss Timothy's slight tightening of his jaw when she did so. So be it. She had laughed out loud three different times with Colonel Berkins, and he had laughed along with her.

"Don't the three of you look like a trio of broody hens."

"What on earth are you thinking, letting him kiss you like that?" Deborah said. "And on the street!"

Maryann undid the ribbons of her bonnet, eager to pluck the offending pin from her scalp. "First, he did not ask permission. He just kissed me so I had no opportunity to ask him not to." She pulled out the two long, sharp pins holding the bonnet in place as well as the pointed culprit—the six-inch pearled pin. "Second, there was no one on the street." She removed the bonnet and wished she could take out all the hairpins keeping her bun in place, but of course she couldn't let her hair down with Timothy and Lucas in the room. "And third, it was a lovely gesture."

"It was *not* a lovely gesture," Deborah said. "It was a liberty, and beyond his right."

"Well, if you count a kiss on the cheek as a *liberty* then it is about time someone took one."

Lucas groaned. Maryann looked at Timothy for support. He would find that funny, wouldn't he? But his expression was blank, and his stare was hard.

"Goodness, what is wrong with the three of you?"

"He put his *hands* on you," Timothy said.

"When he lifted me from the carriage? Yes, he did. I would like very much to see you in skirts and petticoats get yourself down from a perch such as that." She gestured toward the window as though the high-seated carriage was still outside for reference.

"He should have provided you a ladder," Lucas explained oh so helpfully.

Maryann put her hands on her hips and glowered at both men in turn. "As if navigating a ladder is any easier in skirts and petticoats."

"Maryann," Deborah said in a tone that quivered on the edge of calm. "That display on the street was very brazen and will make you the center of gossip."

"Only if the three of you wag your tongues. No one else was about."

"If you are willing to allow him such . . . familiarity on the street, then you will likely allow more of the same in public, and that *will* be the ruin of your reputation," Lucas said.

Deborah nodded. "There are girls who never recover from such things."

Timothy added his opinion to the fray. "And no true gentleman would treat a young woman as Colonel Berkins just treated you because he would understand all of those things."

Maryann narrowed her eyes at him. "And who are you to chastise me on this, Timothy Mayfield? You are not my father nor my brother."

That extinguished some of the flame in his eyes but did not douse it completely. "I am your friend—and a member of the same circles you are moving in. I don't want to see you hurt."

"Oh, you don't?" She opened her mouth to tell him that no one could hurt her the way he had, but luckily, she did not let her tongue run away with the words. Instead, she closed her mouth and lowered her hands from her hips. Someone had to diffuse this and it may as well be her because she was certainly the most uncomfortable.

"I had a lovely ride with Colonel Berkins, and I suspect that, as he is newly back to England, he is less familiar with the constraints of polite society. His kiss was only a reflection of how much we enjoyed one another's company, and I would ask the three of you to give me more credit. I would never stand for anything such as *that* in a public setting. But I will not apologize for enjoying the attention of a good man after so many months of having nothing of the sort."

She deliberately did not look at Timothy just then. "I am very tired and pray you will excuse me. Good afternoon."

She turned to leave, then remembered her bonnet and came back to the room to retrieve it and her pins.

"I'm sorry, Maryann," Timothy said quietly as she passed by him. "You are right. I have no position in which to reprimand you."

She looked at him and felt her insides soften. She hoped such sensations would soon fade as Colonel Berkins took priority. She let out a breath. "Of course, I forgive you, Timothy." She looked toward her sister and brother-in-law. "I am sorry for upsetting all of you. I will be more circumspect if you will not treat me like a child."

"That will be easier to do when you do not act—" Lucas said, but stopped when Deborah put her hand on his knee. Apparently, it was all right when a married woman did so to her husband.

"We trust you," Deborah said in that motherly voice again. "And we apologize for our reaction. Perhaps we can all retain whatever wisdom has come from this exchange and then carry on as though it did not happen."

She looked pointedly at her husband, who nodded, though his expression was still tight. Timothy nodded as well, but Maryann no longer wanted to look him in the eye.

"Thank you," Maryann said. "If you'll excuse me."

She left the room, knowing that as soon as the door closed behind her they would be discussing her actions. Was it *so* inappropriate?

She reached her bedchamber and tossed her bonnet onto a chair and her pins onto her vanity before falling face first on the bed. It was not fair that their reactions should ruin such an enjoyable afternoon. None of them knew how difficult it was for her to watch Timothy with every other woman but herself.

And why had Timothy reacted so strongly? She ascribed the heat in her chest partly to embarrassment for him having seen the display, but mostly to anger that he thought he had any place to reprimand her for it. She knew he had stolen his share of kisses from the debutantes in town. How would he feel if she had told him what was whispered about *him*? And how it made her want to cover her ears each time she heard it.

But then . . . he hadn't only been worried for her reputation. He'd been angry. Even jealous?

She sat up on the bed and shook her head. What would he have to be jealous of? He must simply be feeling protective. She knew he'd often told people he regarded her as a younger sister. She'd rolled her eyes when she first heard that, and she rolled them again now remembering it.

There was a knock at the door, and Lucy poked her head in. "It is time to get ready for the opera," she said.

Was it? Maryann sighed and stood up. "Yes, I suppose it is."

Lucy held a royal-blue velvet gown over both arms. Maryann wondered how she'd managed to knock and then open the door. The gown was new from the seamstress that morning and freshly pressed. It was the perfect distraction for Maryann's mood. At the final fitting last week, it had none of the beading on the bodice or piping along the seams. She especially loved the white fur trim at the neckline; it would be like wearing a cloud.

Deborah felt sure she could manage attending tonight. Maryann was glad for that. She hoped the shared excitement of the event would help them overcome the disagreeable afternoon.

Lucy laid the dress reverently across the bench, and Maryann ran her finger down the fabric as soft as kitten fur. "It is magnificent," she said in a church whisper. Too bad Timothy would not be attending with them. She shook the thought out of her head. Too bad *Colonel Berkins* would not be attending with them. *His* was the opinion that needed to matter to her now.

Chapter Sixteen

Timothy blinked in the muted light of the pub, scanning the occupants until he found the two he was looking for. He did not move toward them right away, taking a few moments to gauge the mood. He'd spent time with Uncle Elliott and he'd spent time with his cousin Harry—they had met at school— but he'd never spent time with them together.

The stiffness of Uncle Elliott's posture contrasted with the establishment, which was just a step above grimy. Harry probably chose the place specifically to make their uncle uncomfortable. Timothy let out a breath and steeled himself to play well his part of peacemaker. He'd received the invitation to join them just an hour ago, but it had said the meeting was casual, so he'd been able to still his concern that there was some emergency involved.

"Good morning, gentlemen," Timothy said cheerfully when he approached the table.

Harry, who had been lounging against the bench opposite their uncle, grinned up at him and scooted over so Timothy could join him. He wore a shirt but no cravat beneath a black coat more suited for evening than a late breakfast. Timothy wondered if perhaps Harry had not yet returned to his rooms since the night before.

He looked at their uncle, keeping his society smile in place. "Hello, Uncle."

"Good morning, Timothy. I am glad you could join us."

"Of course," Timothy said with a nod. "I would never miss an opportunity for your company, Uncle."

Harry snorted and turned so he could lean against the corner of the booth, one leg propped on the knee of the other. Uncle Elliott and Timothy looked at him in tandem, then back at one another as though making a silent agreement to ignore him if he were going to be petulant.

Timothy pushed his smile a shade brighter to compensate. "What brings you to London, Uncle?"

"Business mostly," Uncle Elliott said. "But I thought to visit with my nephews while I was here and see how the two of you are faring."

"I am very well—"

"I am exhausted," Harry said, cutting off Timothy. Harry yawned loudly, his mouth stretching wide and releasing a less-than-polite odor that made Timothy hold his breath and wish he had not sat so close. "Other than that, I fare just fine, no thanks to you." He narrowed his eyes at their uncle, and Timothy shifted.

During prior conversations, Harry had called their uncle a "Grande Dame," "Hopeless Windbag," and "Old Codger." Timothy had laughed off the titles and changed the subject. He did not agree with Harry's assessments, of course, but he didn't want to raise contention. Harry hadn't needed their uncle's support as he had inherited his father's estate in west Norfolk a few years back. He had no reason to be so ungracious as far as Timothy could see.

"Well, I suppose I have my answer as to what terms you and I are on, then," Uncle said, his eyes flashing as he lifted a mug of ale and took a hearty drink. He turned his attention to Timothy. "Harry did not take well to my presentation last month, left in a bit of a tiffle."

Harry straightened from his languid posture and leaned forward across the table. The cords in his neck stood out, and the angles of his jaw were sharp in the muted light. "I've no space for your management, old man."

"Harry!" Timothy said, staring at his cousin. "Watch yourself."

Harry turned his red-rimmed eyes on Timothy. "I will not take direction from you any better than him." He spat the last word, and Timothy was taken aback by the anger infused in every syllable. Before Timothy could manage a response, Harry put his hands against Timothy's shoulder and pushed, nearly sending Timothy to the floor with the force. "Let me out," he said as Timothy stumbled from the bench.

"For Heaven's sake," Uncle Elliott said with disgust as Harry stood up.

Timothy stood several feet away, surprised by this side of his cousin, though he'd heard about Harry's temper. He imagined how Harry would relay this story to a friend, "And then I called him an old man, pushed myself from the table, and left him to his beer." His friends would roll with the telling and Harry would grin.

Harry pointed at their uncle, staring down his finger. "You will see me ruined—and where will all your conniving manipulation put you then?" He cursed, then turned and stormed out of the pub, a dozen eyes following him.

Timothy did not sit back down until the door had closed behind his wayward cousin. Even he could not smile through the tension left in his wake.

"I marvel," Uncle's voice was even as Timothy returned to his seat, "that your cousin has not pulled your reputation down with his in this city. How have you managed such a thing, Timothy?"

"I move in different circles."

"Not that different," Uncle said, shaking his head. "You must put a great deal of effort into showing the contrast. The two of you look more like brothers than you and Peter do; I'm sure people have noticed."

It was true that Peter favored their mother's coloring while Timothy and Harry had the fairer features of the Mayfield line. Harry had sharper lines and a few more inches in height, however.

"I made a concerted effort to befriend men of character in school," Timothy said. "Those friends took me home on holidays, and I was polite to their parents and brothers and friends so that I would be welcomed back. I am good with names and remembering details, which allows me to strike up conversation years after my first meeting someone. I have tried hard to earn people's respect and good graces." He shrugged as though that were a simple thing to do, rather than a goal he had spent a decade working toward.

"And you avoid the gaming hells, brothels, and other unsavory society that your cousin immerses himself in."

Timothy did not approve of Harry's behaviors, or his treatment of their uncle, but he also did not like to stand in judgment. "I do not think Harry feels the need for society's approval the way I do." Harry's father had been of a good family, with a successful estate for Harry to rise to. Harry had come into that inheritance some five years ago and lived well from the proceeds. To succeed in London, a man needed two of three things: manners, money, or connection. Timothy lacked money, but had managed to keep his connections and his manners sharp. Harry lacked manners, but had strength within the other two.

Uncle Elliott grunted, which Timothy chose to interpret as agreement.

"He seems rather put out with you, Uncle."

Uncle Elliott chuckled just as the barmaid brought out three plates filled with sausages, eggs, and beans. Timothy leaned back to allow the woman to slide the plates onto the table in front of them.

"Where's the third?" she said, holding the last plate with a dirty towel.

"He remembered an appointment," Uncle Elliott said, then looked across the table. "Do you think you can put away his portion?"

Timothy nodded quickly, his stomach growling, and soon had two plates before him while trying to keep his excitement in check. For the most part, Timothy subsisted on whatever fare was offered through the visits, parties, and balls of the *ton* during the season so as to avoid the expense of purchased meals. They did not serve sausages at soirees, and he had not had such a meal as this in weeks, let alone two plates' worth. The pub might be dirty and dark, but the food was first-rate.

"As I was saying," Uncle Elliott said a few minutes later when Timothy's eating had slowed enough to allow conversation. "Your cousin did not take well to my marriage campaign."

"Marriage campaign?" Timothy repeated after he swallowed.

"That is what Peter called my . . . gifts. A friend has taken it as a title—marriage campaigns—as though I am some knight of valor." He shrugged, but also smiled.

Timothy nodded and wondered at this *friend*. It seemed his uncle was deliberately not giving details.

"Harry has deemed it a meddlesome manipulation."

"Really?" Timothy said, genuinely surprised. "He is not being forced to accept."

"Precisely," Uncle Elliott said with a touch of exasperation in his tone. "How I wish your cousins would see this campaign as you do, Timothy. It is supposed to be a help, not a hindrance."

Did that mean all of his cousins had reacted as Harry had? "How can it be a *hindrance*?" That made no sense to Timothy.

Uncle Elliott did not answer right away. Someone lit a pipe, adding the sweet fragrance of tobacco to the other smells of baking bread and sizzling sausages. "I have refused to pay off Harry's debts." He followed the confession with a bite of sausage.

Timothy lifted his eyebrows. "Debts?" Harry lived in one of the more expensive boardinghouses in the city and had just purchased a new curricle. "But his father's inheritance, surely—"

Uncle Elliott shook his head. "The motivation behind my campaign was to encourage each of you to live respectable lives. Harry, it seems, is not interested in doing so."

"But he expects you to pay off his debts?" Timothy still found that shocking. He was so careful with his expenses and had never asked for additional funds, already feeling unworthy of his uncle's generosity. Harry had income. Land. A spark of anger rose in Timothy's chest, and he shook his head.

"Just one last time," Uncle Elliott said. "Which is what he said the time before. Suffice it to say, I have refused."

Timothy considered that. "Did you not worry that, upon

presenting the . . . campaign, he will simply marry to secure the funds to pay off the debts?"

"Indeed, that is a worry," Uncle said with a pucker between his gray eyebrows. "And I also worry he will attempt another mortgage on his estate or sell off more of the land he cannot afford to sell or end up beaten senseless in the gutter." He shook his head. "At least the marriage campaign requires he measure up to *something*—I have to approve his choice just as I have to approve yours."

That did not seem to be an exact prevention, and Timothy felt sorry for whichever woman might end up in Harry's net. Timothy had been gifted a London house and acres of land upon a respectable marriage—what had Uncle given Harry?

"Enough of that," Uncle said, flourishing his fork as though to punctuate his sentence. "How are things for you, Timothy? I assume *you* are not angry with me for the campaign."

Timothy laughed. "Between the campaign and a double breakfast, I am anything but angry with you, Uncle. You have my absolute devotion."

Uncle Elliott speared another bite of sausage and asked after Timothy's own endeavors of wife hunting.

Timothy did not want to give his uncle reason to worry on his account, so he kept the details vague. "I am determined to make the right choice, now that I have the choice to make," he concluded. "If not this season, then the next. I have to remind myself that I am not in any great hurry." And yet he was tired of this lifestyle.

"I am glad to hear it, but what of this young woman you wrote of in your last letter who is introducing you to new debutantes? That is quite an advantage."

"She is a good friend," Timothy said simply. "Her sister is

married to my friend from school, Lucas Landsing. That is how Maryann and I met."

"But you have no accord with Maryann herself?"

Not . . . exactly. "We have accord," Timothy said carefully, thinking of how seeing her at an event would make him smile and how he appreciated her honesty with him. "But we are ill-suited as a couple."

"Why is that?"

In that instant, Timothy could not remember why they were ill-suited, only that it was a determination they had both made. Then he remembered that she was not blonde or possessed with a tinkling laugh or musical ability. It embarrassed him to think of his list, which was feeling more and more like folly, and yet he could not answer his uncle's question. Without the list to serve as his guide, why wasn't he seeking further accord with Maryann? Oh, yes. Colonel Berkins. He remembered Colonel Berkins's hands on her waist and his kiss on her cheek yesterday afternoon, and his stomach tightened.

"She has a connection with another man." Timothy's mouth twisted when he said the words.

"And you do not want to interfere," Uncle Elliott concluded.

Timothy nodded and took his last bite of sausage—it was very good sausage.

"And if she did not have this connection with another man, would you be interested in furthering your *accord*?"

Timothy chewed thoughtfully as he considered the question. He was comfortable in Maryann's company, enjoyed their banter, and found her engaging. While he'd once thought her not particularly beautiful, with her round face and rather bland coloring, he'd taken note of her shape these last few weeks—particularly when Colonel Berkins's hands had emphasized her waist a few days earlier. And her eyes were quite spectacular, to say nothing of the way her smile transformed not only her face but the very air around her. It surprised him that he had not noticed such things the very first time he'd met her. Yet, it felt silly to think he could be *attracted* to Maryann. She was Lucas's sister-in-law and . . . not blonde or willowy or demure.

He swallowed his bite and shook his head. "In all honesty, I do not know, Uncle," he admitted. "She fairly ties me in knots sometimes with the things she says and the way she confronts me. Last week she told me to get a haircut, a few weeks before that she advised me on which waistcoat to pair with which coat, and she's told me more than once that she thinks I am a silly man."

"And yet you look forward to seeing her, don't you?"

Timothy looked up in surprise and met his uncle's eyes. "I do," he said. "Which is rather irritating because I do not feel she cares a fig about whether I show up at an event or not."

"Really? She does not return your feelings?"

Feelings? Did Timothy have *feelings* for Maryann? She had once had *feelings* for him, but he'd denounced them in a way that still made him cringe. "She has feelings for this other man," he said to both give an answer and avoid one. "She reminded me recently that I am not her father or her brother and that I should mind my own business."

"Did she now?" Uncle Elliott said with a laugh. He took a bite, following it with a drink of his ale. "Women are extraordinarily complex creatures."

"Indeed they are."

"But," Uncle Elliott continued, "the right one can light a man from within in ways he will never find otherwise."

Timothy raised his eyebrows. "You speak with a certain level of authority, Uncle. Dare I suspect you have found a light from within?"

"Not necessarily," Uncle Elliott said. "She remains simply a complex creature for now, but perhaps time will reveal more than that."

Timothy grinned and put down his fork. "I am happy to hear such possibilities. Tell me all about her."

Uncle Elliott shook his head. "I've nothing more to say, but, on the subject of women and lights and whatnot, has Peter told you his news?"

"Peter?" Timothy had not seen his brother since before the season and could not remember whose turn it was to correspond. "What news?"

Uncle Elliott grinned. "I shouldn't want to be a gossip, but I expect you'll be hearing an announcement soon."

Chapter Seventeen

$\mathscr{I}$ am sorry that your sister was unable to join us, Miss Morrington," Mrs. Blomquist said from the other side of the table. Maryann didn't mind Deborah's absence so much now that she knew the reason.

"As am I," Maryann said easily. "I hope she will be restored to her usual self soon, however." She shared a conspiratorial look with Lady Dominique, the only other person aware of what truly ailed Deborah. Lady Dominque gave a smile and a nod. As Lucas was her only son, she had a great deal of investment in this growing child.

"Was she not at the opera Monday night?" Mrs. Blomquist frowned, clearly displeased that Deborah had apparently been well enough for something as trifling as the opera but not in fine enough fettle for tea today.

"She did attend the opera," Maryann said in a sympathetic tone. "But I am afraid she likely should not have. She was quite ill through the finale, and it laid her flat for all of yesterday."

Deborah had even been sick during the carriage ride home, having had to use Lucas's cloak to contain the mess. And then, of course, she'd cried for being such a burden. Maryann had helped Deborah calm down upon arriving at home and assured her that Lucas did not regret having married her and that she was not the most ridiculous woman ever created. Deborah had slept most of Tuesday, and had only tea with dinner that night.

"I'm afraid it is my fault she did not attend today as I insisted she stay at home to rest and work on the seating chart for Lady Dominique's ball." She shared another smile with Deborah's mother-in-law. "I am afraid I was quite fierce with my orders. I can only hope she will still be speaking to me when I return."

Mrs. Blomquist brightened at the thought of sisterly rivalry on her behalf. "Well, of course she must rest, then. Please give her my sympathy and wishes for good health to be restored soon."

"I most certainly will."

"And your ball?" Mrs. Blomquist asked Lady Dominique. "The plans are formulating well?"

"Yes," the dame said, inclining her head. "This is the first year I have had someone to help me, and Deborah has proven to be quite capable."

Away from Lady Dominque's presence, Deborah was scared to death that she was going to ruin the annual ball that had been twelve years running. Lucas and Maryann took turns reassuring her that she was an adept hostess and all would be well.

"Who have you invited to tea this week, Martha?" Lady Dominique asked, drawing the hostess's attention.

"The Middletons will be coming again. I find them so very intriguing."

And rich, Maryann noted. Old money was Mrs. Blomquist's most respected virtue, and the Middletons were as old money as old money could be.

"And then there is a lovely girl just down from Nottingham

this last week. Nineteen years old and being sponsored by her aunt, Mrs. Wallace. She had her coming out in her own village."

Mrs. Blomquist frowned at that. It was her opinion that all young women should have their coming out balls in London. She did not understand that not everyone could afford the expense of renting a hall and hosting two hundred people. To say nothing of how nice it was to come out among people you had known all your life. Maryann had never regretted having come out in Somerset, though it had been years ago. She wisely kept her thoughts to herself in this respect.

"No mother to attend her?" Lady Dominique asked.

"There is a mother, but five or seven or twelve other children as well. Mrs. Shaw will join the party a fortnight from now but cannot stay away from home for long due to her responsibilities there."

Lady Dominique took in all the information, catching the details in the steel trap of her mind. The woman was as brilliant as any man. Alas, her skills were relegated to parlors and assembly halls while men far less capable than her strutted about in Parliament.

Mrs. Blomquist continued. "Her father is only a physician, but he is also the grandson of the former Earl of Wooston, so his connections are good. Apparently, all the children are lovely and well-mannered; the boys are sent to Harrow and then Cambridge, though only one son is of age at the moment. The girls are educated in Brighton at a highly reputable school there."

"Why is she coming to London so late in her season, then?" Lady Dominique asked.

"She is the eldest, and her parents maintain that a girl ought to be closer to twenty before she finds a husband. Something of her father believing that too young a wife leads to too young a mother which brings with it . . . ahem . . . complications." She shook her head. "I don't feel the same, of course. I think youth is preferable for marriage and children. A woman adapts better to her role when she is young."

"Still, she will come to London *very* late in the season," Lady Dominique commented. Maryann did not nod, but she agreed. It was the end of May and Parliament would only sit another six weeks, unless they filed for an extension as they often did. Several engagements had already taken place between couples who had made their match in town and attendance to the *ton* events was getting thinner by the week.

Mrs. Blomquist nodded. "Apparently, the aunt suggested she come for the last portion so that Miss Shaw might have a better feel for London when she attends the whole of the season next year. Not necessarily a poor choice, but I must tell you that I have seen this girl, and I would not be the least bit surprised if she didn't make a match before *this* season ends. She is as lovely as a lily."

Maryann lowered her gaze to the tablecloth to hide the scowl she was unable to prevent. It was no wonder that men only cared about a woman's looks because it seemed that was all women cared about as well. Not all men were like that, however. Colonel Berkins, for instance, seemed to be looking for more than just a pretty face.

Maryann took a breath and then raised her head, composed once more. "What of her temperament and character?" she asked, which was not really her place. She was here to keep the tea from feeling like an interview, not take the lead of the conversation.

"I'm sure her temperament and character are as lovely as she is," Mrs. Blomquist said, smiling indulgently at Maryann. She turned back to Lady Dominique. "And she is very musical; she plays both the pianoforte and flute. *And* she paints. Let me show you what she sent with her acceptance of our invitation." She lifted the bell she kept to the right of her place at the table and gave it a jingle. A footman appeared before the bell had been returned to the tabletop. "Please fetch me the miniature on my dressing table, beside my hairbrush."

The man nodded and disappeared.

Mrs. Blomquist turned to look at Maryann. "I understand you have been helping introduce some of these new girls at different events." She took a sip of her tea.

"It is the least I can do after everyone has been so welcoming to me." She'd intended to only make introductions to Timothy, but once she knew his level of interest—or disinterest—in a girl, she had begun introducing them to some of the other men of town. Time would tell if any of her introductions played out, but she hoped some of them would. The desperation to make a good match was increasing as the season marched forward, and she wished everyone relief.

"Isn't that lovely," Mrs. Blomquist said, cocking her head to the side and smiling as though the compliment had been chiefly pointed in her direction. "So very kind of you."

The footman returned and handed a small card to the hostess. She sighed, placing a hand to her chest as she looked it over. "In all my years, no one has ever responded with such a gift as this. I find it very thoughtful indeed." Mrs. Blomquist passed the card to Lady Dominique, who put on her spectacles.

"Oh, this *is* very well done," Lady Dominique said. "Such detail on a tiny canvas."

"I know." Mrs. Blomquist nodded, her jowls jiggling slightly. Maryann feared her own plump cheeks would one day sag like Mrs. Blomquist's. What a horror that would be. "It is real talent that can produce such a work as that and then send it along as a gift to the hostess as though the artist can produce a dozen more when needed."

Lady Dominique passed the card to Maryann, who took it with every intention of having an opinion different than the matrons. Was it not rather cheeky to send a piece of your own creation as a gift? Instead, however, Maryann was shocked by the detail of the tiny seascape. She held it closer to her eyes and then further away. The trees stood out above white cliffs and the blue-green waves of the southern sea. The setting was similar to Maryann's beloved Somerset, despite the artist being from Nottingham. She felt she could see which direction the wind was blowing. And all on a two-inch square of paper.

"Is this watercolor?" The image was so crisp, not like other watercolors that had looser lines.

"I believe it *is*," Mrs. Blomquist said. "A very good one."

"Indeed," Maryann said, staring at the card a few more seconds before passing it back to Mrs. Blomquist. This girl from Nottingham was musical, from a large family, nineteen years old, and a talented watercolorist. And what was it Mrs. Blomquist had said—that she was as lovely as a lily? Lilies were light-colored, fair. Was this girl a blonde?

Maryann was about to ask for these details when she heard footfalls in the hall leading to the garden room where they were seated. Three of the walls were glass overlooking Mrs. Blomquist's lovely gardens.

The butler filled the doorway and announced, "Mrs. Wallace and her niece, Miss Rachel Shaw."

He stepped aside to reveal Mrs. Wallace, a woman in her middling years, her brown hair streaked with silver. Beside her stood a young woman, nearly Maryann's height but with porcelain skin, golden-blonde hair that hung in curls over her slender shoulders, and eyes the color of the jade pendant she wore at her graceful throat. Her long-tapered fingers held a folder that likely contained some pianoforte music; Mrs. Blomquist was always keen to have the new girls perform so that she could be the first to praise their skill around the city.

There were still some details Maryann needed to confirm, such as foreign language proficiency, a hearty appetite—Miss Shaw certainly wasn't plump—and whether or not this young woman liked babies. But assuming those pieces were in place, Maryann feared that she was looking at Timothy Mayfield's perfect woman.

Gracious.

Chapter Eighteen

Maryann hadn't seen Colonel Berkins arrive at the Carstons' dinner party Saturday—and then suddenly he was standing beside her. She started, then laughed at her own reaction, but forgot to cover her mouth. Several heads turned her direction, and she felt her cheeks flush. Colonel Berkins, however, did not seem bothered by her "donkey bray."

He leaned into her and placed his hand at the small of her back. "Ignore them," he whispered before he straightened and spoke in normal tones to the women Maryann had been conversing with. "Good evening, ladies, I hope I did not interrupt."

"Of course not," Miss Callifour said with a smile, then lifted one eyebrow in Maryann's direction when Colonel Berkins wasn't looking. Miss Callifour was the only friend to whom Maryann had confided her feelings. Over the last few days, Maryann and the colonel had gone out walking twice, attended a play, and corresponded with letters nearly every day.

Maryann returned her friend's smile and was glad her cheeks were already hot so no one would notice how they burned now. Colonel Berkins had not removed his hand from her back, but she was standing near enough to the corner that no one could know but her. She was fairly on fire with the invigoration of his touch, but it had only been a week ago that she had assured her family, and Timothy, that she would not allow public liberties. If anyone noticed this display . . .

She saw Miss Shaw enter the drawing room, her green eyes wide as she looked over the crowd of strangers.

"Excuse me," Maryann said to the group, giving Colonel Berkins a smile all his own as she slipped away from the circle. She crossed to Miss Shaw and put out her hands in greeting. Miss Shaw visibly relaxed at seeing a familiar face, and upon reaching her, Maryann took both of her hands, leaning in for a faux kiss on the cheek—a greeting Lady Dominique would have approved of. "I am so glad you came," Maryann said as she pulled back. She looked past Miss Shaw to welcome her aunt, Mrs. Wallace.

"You are very kind to have gained us an invitation," Mrs. Wallace said.

"That honor belongs to Lady Dominique," Maryann said. She turned and put herself between the two women, looping her arms through theirs. "It is far better to meet the members of the *ton* in pieces. A small party like this is the perfect venue to start."

Small was a bit of an understatement, there were already at least fifty guests and the hostess, Mrs. Carston, expected another dozen more before dinner. One of those dozen would be Timothy, running late as usual. Each time Maryann thought of the impending introduction between him and Miss Shaw, she winced inside. But it had to be done. It should be done.

I will be happy for them both. And maybe they would not suit. *What if they did not?*
What if they did?
She glanced toward where she'd abandoned Colonel Berkins.

She hadn't explained why she'd left him so suddenly and gave him an apologetic smile. He raised his glass to her, which she took as forgiveness. Easy as that. Thank goodness. She was feeling enough anxiety as it was and would hate to be out of sorts with the man she was coming to like very much.

She began introductions with the hostess, Mrs. Carston, and her daughter, Mrs. Hiller. After a few minutes, she excused them and steered Miss Shaw and her aunt to the next group, which included Mr. and Mrs. Snow, important people to know and good friends of Lucas and Deborah. The Snows had brought Maryann tonight as Deborah was indisposed again. The two Mrs. Websters—sisters-in-laws, both without husbands in attendance tonight—were also in that group and hailed from Nottingham, which was a nice comfort for Miss Shaw.

Maryann was half way around the room with her charges when she caught sight of Timothy talking to Colonel Berkins. Timothy's golden hair gleamed beneath the light of the gas chandelier, not that she cared, and he'd worn his evening blacks with the red waistcoat—two solids, as she'd advised. Part of her was glad that she'd been right about how nice the combination would look, the other part hated that he looked more handsome than ever. Dinner would be served soon, which meant she needed to hurry this introduction so that Timothy and Miss Shaw would have the chance to converse following the meal.

I am doing the right thing for everyone, she reminded herself, hating that she even had to debate this within her head. It should be easy now that she had Colonel Berkins's attention. She tried to remember the sensation of his hand at her back to spur her confidence.

She waited for the aunt to become engaged with Mrs. Blomquist, who had crossed to them, then politely extracted Miss

Shaw. "There is one other introduction I would like to make before dinner is called," she said, leaning toward her new friend.

They reached Timothy, but his back was to them as he spoke with Colonel Berkins.

Colonel Berkins cued him, and Timothy turned, with bright eyes and a smile that moved through Maryann like a breeze on a summer's day.

"Good evening, Mr. Mayfield," Maryann said. "I would like to introduce you to my new friend, Miss Rachel Shaw. She is recently to London from Nottingham and shares your love of art."

She looked at Miss Shaw as she explained the last and saw how the girl's smile turned from polite to quite natural. Maryann then looked at Timothy, who was staring as though every other guest had faded from his view. She swallowed a lump of regret.

"Miss Shaw," Timothy said, bowing over her hand. "What a pleasure to make your acquaintance."

He straightened but did not release her hand as he continued to gaze at her. Maryann remembered how Timothy had told her that he felt sure he would recognize the woman who was perfect for him.

"I am sure the pleasure is all mine, sir."

He laughed, and Maryann's stomach tightened.

"You enjoy art?" Timothy said. "May I show you a particularly lovely piece in the hallway?" He nodded toward the double doors left open to increase the size of the room. "I would love your thoughts before we are called into dinner."

Miss Shaw agreed and slipped her delicate hand around Timothy's elbow. Her manners were excellent, and her carriage straight and proper. They looked like a work of art themselves as they walked toward the hallway.

Maryann felt Colonel Berkins come up beside her.

"What on earth just happened?" he asked in a low voice.

Maryann took a breath to ensure her tone would be level when she spoke, but even so, her words were barely a whisper. "Destiny, I think."

Maryann was seated between two older men at dinner and kept them entertained as was her responsibility. Colonel Berkins was seated across the table and to her right, close enough that she had been able to exchange a few smiles with him throughout the meal. Timothy had somehow managed to sit next to Miss Shaw. But then, if she was his foreordained destiny, why was Maryann surprised? The couple was not in Maryann's view, but she was so attuned to Timothy's voice and his laugh that she could tell he was quite engaged. Miss Shaw's tinkling laugh seemed to bubble up from her bow-shaped lips and float in the air above the two of them. Miss Shaw was everything Maryann was not. She was Timothy's list personified.

I am happy for them, she told herself and asked for a refill of her wine.

Miss Shaw had performed at the tea, so Maryann was prepared for the level of her skill in the drawing room after dinner. Miss Shaw performed Mozart on the pianoforte, then sang an Italian piece a cappella. The applause that followed was not a polite smattering that manners required, but a true show of gratitude from those lucky enough to have been in attendance for such a display of talent. Timothy *stood* to applaud her singing, and Maryann looked away, only to catch Colonel Berkins watching her with a concerned expression.

She shook her head, but then he nodded toward the open

doors that led to the garden. Another couple had left before Miss Shaw's performance and no one had raised an eyebrow, so it must not be out of the ordinary for the evening. The room was stifling, and she told herself she would go only to get some air, not so that she would have distance from whatever was developing between Timothy and Miss Shaw.

Timothy was calling for an encore as she slipped past Colonel Berkins, who then followed at her heels. Once in the garden, she wished she could leave her heavy mood as easily as she had left the room. She had given up on securing Timothy's affection long ago, and Timothy had introduced her to Colonel Berkins, who was wonderful. So why was she not happy?

Maryann took Colonel Berkins's arm, and they began a slow walk through Lady Merrimew's rose garden. She could hear at least one other hushed and giggly conversation somewhere to her right, which made her feel better about being here. It could not be so scandalous if she and the colonel were not the only ones who had extended the party into the gardens. There were even torches lit every so often beside the path.

"Are you all right, Miss Morrington?" Colonel Berkins asked once they had moved a fair distance from the drawing room and away from the giggling voices.

"I am. Forgive me for giving you cause to worry. I think the season is simply wearing me down."

"If I might be so bold, I think it is not the season that affects you this evening."

She looked at him, and he cocked his head to the side. "Mayfield told me he is a friend of your family, but I feel that perhaps there is a bit more between the two of you than that."

She felt her face flush in embarrassment. She could say any manner of things to explain away the reaction, but she didn't.

Because if this man was *her* destiny the same way Miss Shaw was likely Timothy's, what was the purpose of secrets between them?

"There *was* a time I felt affection for him, but that is not the case any longer." So much for being honest. Apparently, she'd chosen to share only what she *wished* she felt.

"But he is still the cause of your current mood."

She was tired of keeping so much to herself, and so she took a breath and told him about the list. "I suppose it vexes me that he is right, that the perfect woman for him was out there all the time."

"They have only first met, Maryann." He turned to face her, a hopeful expression on his face. "May I call you Maryann? I notice that Mayfield does."

"Of course."

He lifted her hand and kissed her white satin glove. "That makes me very happy, Maryann. I hope you shall call me Charles."

"It will take some getting used to, Colonel Charles," she teased.

His smile lifted his cheeks and brightened his eyes. He had dark hair, and she could see where a beard would be if he did not shave. She wondered if he shaved himself, as Timothy did, or if he had a valet do the job for him, like Lucas. "I hope that you will have all the time you need to grow accustomed, then," he said.

He had not released her hand. "As I was saying, they have only just met. Perhaps the accord will not last, and he will realize his folly of the list after all."

"Or perhaps it is love at first sight."

"And that would upset you?"

Maryann let out a breath, embarrassed by her convoluted feelings. She didn't have the words so she shook her head and looked away instead.

"I have lived a full life before meeting you, Maryann. I too have held affections and hopes with others. I can certainly take in stride your affection for a man as charming and handsome as Timothy Mayfield."

To hear *him* call Timothy charming and handsome embarrassed her all over again. She had said far more than the colonel deserved to be burdened with. And yet he was so understanding. That is what she should be focusing her attention on—the kind man before her who had not pouted when she admitted having affection for Timothy and who did not have a list of shallow attributes against which he compared her and found her lacking.

She met his eyes and held his gaze. "Thank you for your understanding," she said softly. "I am fortunate to have such a thing and do not take it lightly."

He took a step closer and trailed a thumb across her jaw. His touch sent shimmering sparks down her back. "I have not had a chance to tell you how lovely you look tonight, Maryann. The pink of your gown brings out your eyes and the bloom of your cheeks."

"It does not take much to bring out my cheeks. They are those of a chipmunk."

He laughed and then kissed her lightly on each of those chipmunk cheeks, warming her to her toes. "I love them," he whispered, and he slid his hand around her waist, gently encouraging her closer.

She offered no resistance, allowing herself to be drawn closer until only a few inches separated their lips and she could feel her heartbeat in her ears.

"I admire many things about you, Maryann, and I hope that eventually memories of our time together will chase all thoughts of Timothy Mayfield from your mind."

This was exactly what she needed, complete distraction. She swallowed the unavoidable anxiety she felt so that all that remained was the longing. "How do you imagine to do that, Colonel Ber— uh—Charles?"

He answered her with a kiss that did, in fact, chase Timothy from her thoughts. Nothing could be more seductive than his acceptance. When he made to pull back from the chaste kiss he had initiated, she placed her hand at the nape of his neck and pulled him closer for a kiss that would chase away even more shadows.

Finally.

Chapter Nineteen

$\mathcal{T}$imothy waited a polite distance outside the doors of St. George Church, trying not to bounce on the balls of his feet as he waited for Miss Shaw and her aunt to exit through the doorway. When they finally did, he positioned himself so he might catch Miss Shaw's eye. Unfortunately, she kept her eyes demurely downcast while her aunt spoke to this person and then that one, and, oh, she mustn't leave out that one. Timothy was near ready to run in circles before the two women finally made their way down the last of the steps. He moved to the right and, instead of trying to catch Miss Shaw's eye, focused on the aunt. She smiled when she saw him.

He took the smile as an invitation and stepped up, then bowed. "Good morning, Mrs. Wallace," he said, then turned to the vision of loveliness at her side. "Miss Shaw." The blush on her cheeks was enthralling, and he looked forward to getting to know her better.

"Good morning, Mr. Mayfield," Mrs. Wallace said. "Did you enjoy services?"

"I always do," Timothy said, looking back at her.

She lifted her eyebrows in surprise.

"I usually attend St. James," he said, "but I rarely miss a Sunday service."

"Really," Mrs. Wallace said, not quite believing him. "Single young men are a rarity in church these days."

"Rare, but not extinct." Timothy had always found church to be a soothing place. Even if it did mean he had to run home after all that sitting.

"One might wonder why you came to a different church today," Mrs. Wallace said.

He grinned wider. "I hope one wouldn't have to wonder too long." He glanced at Miss Shaw again. "I was hoping I might walk Miss Shaw home."

Mrs. Wallace shook her head at his cheekiness, but her smile remained, which led him to believe that he had read her correctly last night and again today. She was not a severe sponsor, nor had she already set her mind against a man without obvious means and distinction. Should his interest toward Miss Shaw continue, he knew questions about him would circulate their way through the *ton* and back to her, but for now she was allowing his attention, and he took that as a very good sign. He would tell both women the truth of his circumstances once he had approval from the one and affection from the other.

Mrs. Wallace looked at Miss Shaw. "If that is acceptable to you, Rachel, I shall walk with Mrs. Peters a short way ahead."

"Yes, Aunt." She briefly met Timothy's eye and smiled shyly. It thrilled him to his toes.

Mrs. Peters was found in the milling crowd, a thousand greetings were exchanged between Mrs. Wallace and every other patron, it seemed, and then finally, Miss Shaw slipped her delicate hand onto his elbow and they began down George Street.

Timothy measured his steps to provide adequate distance between themselves and Mrs. Wallace so that he and Miss Shaw could talk privately.

"It is very kind of your aunt to allow me this privilege," Timothy said.

"Yes, it is," Miss Shaw said.

"She lives here in London, does she not?" He could swear someone had told him that London was Mrs. Wallace's primary residence, as opposed to those gentry who came to the city for the season, then returned to their country estates.

"Yes. My uncle, Mr. Wallace, was a banker here."

"Have you stayed with her in London before?"

"When I was a child," Miss Shaw said. "Twice."

"And did you enjoy London on those visits?"

"I did. It is very different from my home."

"In what way?"

She mentioned the open spaces of her country home and the minimal entertainments it offered, but did not expound overly much. She seemed quite nervous, but Timothy suspected she'd likely never conversed with a man one-on-one like this. He would need to be patient as she experienced so many new things. He forced himself to remain silent, waiting for her to ask a question, though it meant digging his toes into his shoes and biting his tongue.

After a lengthy silence, she finally spoke. "Do you retire to the country after the season each year, Mr. Mayfield?"

Thank goodness. "I do not," Timothy said, shaking his head. "I stay here throughout the year." He chose not to delve into the reasons behind his decision, and she did not ask. Another silence fell, and he said, "I love the energy of this city. There is always so much to do and see."

"Is it not quiet come autumn?"

Timothy laughed and told her all the ways that London was never quiet. Perhaps not as bursting at the seams as when the season was on, but the bustle never really gave way. He hadn't realized how much he'd gone on until he saw Mrs. Wallace say goodbye to Mrs. Peters in front of a lovely gray town house. Mrs. Peters continued on further down the street.

Timothy and Miss Shaw reached the town house a few paces later. He was disappointed that he hadn't managed to learn everything there was to know about Miss Shaw during the walk. Now that he'd found her, he was eager to verify that she was indeed his perfect woman. What a relief it would be to no longer be on the hunt. He vaguely remembered feeling much the same way after meeting with Maryann that day in her drawing room, before going on to Norwich. He'd thought Maryann would put an end to his searching, then things had changed so drastically.

"Would you like to stay for tea, Mr. Mayfield?" Mrs. Wallace asked.

Timothy straightened and smiled widely. Oh, but the day just got better and better. "It would be my greatest pleasure."

Mrs. Wallace laughed and shook her head as though delighted by his enthusiasm. Timothy glanced at Miss Shaw, and she smiled, which added another layer of sparkle to those lovely jade-green eyes.

Mrs. Wallace led the way into the house, speaking over her shoulder. "Rachel will have to show you her portfolio. She is a most exceptional artist."

If it had been possible for Timothy to smile even wider, he would have. As it was, he could not think of a more enjoyable way to spend a Sunday afternoon.

Chapter Twenty

Timothy had just exited a snuff shop with his friends Thursday afternoon, when he recognized a familiar figure a few shops ahead. He excused himself from the group and hurried forward, moving between other pedestrians on the street until he came up behind who he thought was Maryann. She turned to look at her companion—the elder Miss Callifour— and he was able confirm her identity. She wore the same lavender bonnet she'd had on during their walk through Hyde Park several weeks ago.

He moved forward so he was walking right behind her, matching her step for step so closely it would take very little for either of them to trip the other. Maryann's back stiffened and her gait increased when she sensed the unexpected presence, but she didn't look back. He sped up as well. Miss Callifour looked at him first, then smiled and looked ahead. Aha, he had support.

When Maryann finally turned her head to see who was invading her space, he dodged in the opposite direction and fell in step on her left side. She shifted from looking behind herself to side to side until she saw him, then she narrowed her golden-brown eyes.

"I should have guessed," Maryann said, shaking her head and attempting to hold back a smile as the three of them walked together. "If ever there is a childish antic ensuing, one could put a solid wager on the fact that Timothy Mayfield will be involved somehow."

Timothy grabbed his lapels and lifted his chin so he might strut with all the confidence of a rooster.

Miss Callifour laughed, and Maryann lifted her hand to her mouth as though to join her, except that she didn't make a sound. Timothy realized he hadn't heard Maryann laugh for some time.

"How are you this afternoon, Mr. Mayfield?" Miss Callifour asked him.

He leaned slightly forward so he could address the woman on Maryann's other side. "Happy, healthy, and well-fed," he said with a grin. "What more could a man want—other than the company of beautiful women like yourselves."

She laughed again. Maryann rolled her eyes.

"And what brings you *beautiful* ladies to Oxford Street this fine day?"

Timothy was in this part of the city a great deal, not only because his rooms were off of St. James, but because all the best gentlemanly shops and clubs were located in this district—not that he could afford many of them. If not for his many friends who shared their connections, he'd be in the soup.

"I am purchasing some perfume for my mother," Miss Callifour said. "And Miss Morrington wanted to stop in at Hatchers."

Timothy looked at Maryann. "On Piccadilly? You're making quite the circuit this morning."

"It is not so far," Maryann defended.

"*And* we are meeting Mr. Fetich at Gunters in between," Miss Callifour added, though there was a bit of embarrassment in her tone.

"Ah, I see," Timothy said, noting the way her cheeks pinked at the mention of the wily tradesman. Mr. Fetich was not forthcoming regarding his enterprises, but Timothy had heard it whispered and admired the man his ability to exist in both worlds. There was a time when Mr. Fetich had been rather attentive to Maryann; Timothy had not liked him so much then. Now that his interest was so squarely set upon Miss Callifour, however, Timothy had no complaint. "Might I offer my escort as far as the ices, then?" he said.

He met Maryann's eye and winked. Miss Callifour's mother was a rather strict woman, allowing for very few steps away from the middle of the road of propriety for either of her daughters. Meeting up with a young man in the middle of the day would be frowned upon. Having ices with a female friend, however, was an acceptable outing.

The trio made small talk as they continued to the confectioner's shop. Mr. Fetich was standing outside and straightened when they appeared. Miss Callifour increased her pace to meet him, leaving Maryann and Timothy a few steps behind.

"They wish to be alone?" Timothy whispered to Maryann.

She nodded but said nothing further, though she was fiddling with the strings of her reticule.

"But then you would need an escort?" Timothy further surmised.

She hesitated, but then nodded. "Our plan is to enjoy the ices and then the three of us will go on to Hatchers. While I am in the store, they can have some time at Green Park, using my dawdling over books as their excuse."

Timothy clicked his heels together and stood up straight. "Well, fancy my being the rescue, then."

They reached the couple, and greetings were exchanged, and then Timothy took the lead on arranging the particulars: Mr. Fetich and Miss Callifour would sit at a table for three and enjoy their ices with Maryann's reticule occupying what should be her place. In case anyone questioned the couple being alone, they could explain that Maryann had been distracted—only for a moment—by a friend and would return shortly. What young lady would leave her reticule if she were to be gone for a longer period of time?

Maryann's coin purse went into Timothy's pocket as easily as her hand rested at his elbow so that he might escort her to Hatchers, and then perhaps to Green Park to lengthen the escapade. For Timothy and Maryann to be seen together was entirely different than Miss Callifour and Mr. Fetich. Everyone knew Timothy was a great friend of Lucas Landsing, Maryann's brother-in-law. As a friend of the family, he had greater margin.

"That was kind of you," Maryann said as they left the couple and made their way to Bond Street that would take them to Piccadilly.

"Kind?" Timothy said, raising his eyebrows. "It was nothing of the sort. It was complete selfishness because now I have you all to myself." He patted her fingers with his free hand.

She snorted, which he almost remarked upon, until he remembered having called her out on her laugh and how disastrous *that* had been. "You doubt my sincerity?" he said instead.

"Most of the time, yes," she said, smirking at him.

He placed a hand on his chest. "I am wounded, Maryann." It did prick him slightly that she would think he was being false, but since he wasn't being false, he did not dwell upon it.

"I *am* glad to have you to myself," he assured her. "It seems we've had little time together of late."

"Indeed," she said in a way that told him there was far more behind that word than met the eye. "And how is Miss Shaw?"

Timothy smiled again at the reminder of the blonde beauty so recently taking center stage of his dreams. "All that I could hope for," he said. He told Maryann that he had managed to see Miss Shaw every day since Maryann's introduction. He had to speak loudly to be heard over the clattering of wheels over cobbles, shopkeepers' calls, and the usual bustle of the shopping district.

Sunday tea had been lovely, if a bit formal, but it was only their second meeting, and her aunt had been there the entire time. Timothy had talked with Mrs. Wallace more than he had talked to Miss Shaw, but then Mrs. Wallace was an excellent conversationalist. He must have impressed her because Mrs. Wallace made no complaint to Timothy occupying most of Miss Shaw's attention at a dinner party Monday night, and had even sent a footman to attend them on a walk yesterday.

"So you have found your paragon," Maryann said after Timothy had finished his account.

"Perhaps I have." His own hesitation to proclaim her the fulfillment of his list surprised him, but Maryann tended to draw things out of him that he would not discuss otherwise.

"Perhaps?" She looked at him. "I thought you believed you would recognize your perfect woman when you met her."

"But having never met her before, I can't be certain that my reaction wasn't recognition, now can I?"

Maryann shook her head. "You are not convinced, then?"

"Not as yet," he said in a philosophical tone. Then he shrugged. "But I am encouraged, and I have not yet found one reason why she wouldn't be the woman I have always wanted." The formality he felt between them was what stood in his way of proclaiming himself, even to a good friend like Maryann. He had only known Miss Shaw a few days, however. For all of Maryann's accusations that he was shallow and had fantastical expectations, he took his search for a wife quite seriously. He would be certain of his choice before he made it, and with every passing week, he was more determined than ever to be wise.

"Well, I suppose you haven't even known her a week yet," Maryann said.

He turned to her in surprise. "That is just what I was thinking. What a relief for you and I to be of the same mind of something."

"It is rather shocking, isn't it?" Maryann teased back. He liked it when she played along with him.

"And how is your colonel?" It was good manners for him to ask even though his belly tightened at the memory of Colonel Berkins lifting her down from the carriage that day.

"The colonel is all that I could hope for," she said, echoing his sentiments toward Miss Shaw.

"I am glad to hear that," Timothy said, even though it wasn't entirely the truth. "I am surprised I do not see him about the city more than I do."

The man did not seem overly social nor interested in making connections despite the fact that it ought to be his primary intention after so many years out of the country. He should be building a foundation in England, and London during Parliament was the best time to make the acquaintances that would set his future.

"He has a great deal to do, Timothy," she said with an air of reprimand. "His land and inheritance demand a large measure of thought and preparation. I think it is a bit overwhelming, really. After all his years in the military, he is left to manage something completely different than anything he has done before."

That is reasonable, Timothy decided, and he was reminded how little he knew about the responsibilities to be his once he married. He'd met with Uncle Elliott's solicitor here in London in order to go over the details of his inheritance, but the meeting had left Timothy with a continued sense of his insufficiency. He managed nothing beside his allowance and his wardrobe—a far cry from what lay ahead.

They reached Hatchets and spent a full half an hour browsing the shelves. Timothy found a book about central Northampton, where the land Uncle Elliott would give him upon marriage was located, and one on the economy of land management. He felt better already just having the information in his hands. Maryann found three novels for Deborah, who was still not feeling well, and a notebook since Deborah was obsessing over Lady Dominque's party and rewriting every list she made a hundred times—or so Maryann explained. Timothy asked the clerk to bind their purchases in two parcels, which he then carried.

"Shall we take a turn around Green Park?" Timothy asked, reluctant to end their time together.

Maryann eyed him. "Haven't you other things to do today? Footraces with your friends, perhaps, or betting on horses?"

"I do enjoy a good footrace," he said, grinning. "But why are you so determined to believe that spending time with you does not cast all other activities into a paler light?" He deftly steered her toward the park on the other side of Piccadilly Road.

She said nothing.

"Unless you are the one who has better things to do and are looking to make it seem like my fault." What if she'd had some plan to meet Colonel Berkins? The idea caused him to clench his teeth.

"That is not what I meant," she said, shaking her head.

They paused on the curb. Timothy waited for a small break in the flow of passing carriages and then pulled her into a run across Piccadilly Road, loving her slight shriek of surprise. Fortunately, she didn't resist him or they'd have been in trouble.

"Timothy," she exclaimed when they reached the other side of the road. She looked back across the street, her hand on her chest, then turned her flashing eyes to him, her cheeks flushed. "I could have tripped over my skirts and fallen to my death!"

"You think I would let such a thing happen?" He adjusted the parcels under one arm and put out the other. She glowered at him as she put her hand in the crook of his elbow. "Aren't there times, Maryann, when you just want to . . . run? Give all you have to a thing, even if only for a moment and despite what people might think?"

She was quiet for a moment. "Are you speaking literally or metaphorically?"

They entered the path that crisscrossed the green, and he let her set the pace. "Both," Timothy said. "The same energy that we are forced to keep inside physically is represented in manners and procedure, don't you think?"

"I suppose," she said, but she sounded uncertain.

"Take Miss Callifour and Mr. Fetich, for instance. Anyone

can tell they are besotted with one another. She ought to be married as soon as possible—no offense."

"None taken," she replied dryly. But she did not slap him or pull her hand away, so he chose to believe she wasn't offended by his subtle hint at Miss Callifour's advanced age.

"And he is a man of fine character and ambition." He did not know how much Maryann knew about Mr. Fetich's situation and did not want to be a gossip, so he kept the details to himself. "Yet propriety keeps them from spending individual time together, which keeps them from knowing how well suited they are, which leads to guessing and hoping when all they need is some time to focus on one another so that they might know for themselves the rightness of their choice." He paused to take a breath after stringing so many thoughts together.

"So you are saying that they should have the chance to *run* with each other."

He smiled at her. "Precisely. And how good of us to have given them that option, don't you think?"

She shook her head. "I go back to my original commentary on this topic—that it was very kind of you to help provide the opportunity."

"And selfish," he reminded her, then reached up and pulled the ribbon of her bonnet. To his surprise, the bow did not unravel. He dropped his arm to the side and looked at her with wide eyes.

"I double-knotted the bow while you arranged their table at Gunters," she said, obviously pleased with her forethought.

Timothy shook his head. "Gracious, a man has got to get up early to get the best of you, Maryann Morrington."

She chuckled, but it was not a full laugh. She looked around the clear path around them, then met his eye again and gave him a wicked grin. "I shall race you to that tree." She had scarce finished the last word before she pushed him hard in the chest, causing him to stumble backward and bumble the packages in the process. By the time he'd caught his balance, she had her skirts lifted—only high enough that she would not trip—and was running toward an oak tree several yards away far faster than he'd thought possible. He growled in his throat but smiled as he put his head down and raced forward to beat her.

Chapter Twenty-One

*C*olonel Berkins was a patron of Gentleman Jackson's boxing establishment, and the day following Timothy's footraces with Maryann—which he won—Timothy called in a favor with a friend and found himself at the location at the same time as Colonel Berkins. That Maryann was truly interested in this man piqued Timothy's interests. They fenced one another; Colonel Berkins was far better than Timothy but sparred fairly. Afterward, Timothy invited the colonel to Whites. He didn't actually have a membership, but Lucas did, and he had worked something with the desk so that Timothy could come now and again.

Timothy and Berkins enjoyed brandy and pipes and talked of Spain and mining and Parliament. By the end of the afternoon, Timothy was without complaint with the man, other than how he had put his hands on Maryann's waist and kissed her on the cheek that day. That Maryann had not been offended by the behavior made it difficult for Timothy to hold it too much against him, however. What was it Maryann had said—that no other man had given her such attention? Remembering that comment gave

Timothy an uncomfortable feeling in his stomach. She would not welcome additional *attention* of that sort, would she?

On the evening she'd introduced him to Miss Shaw, Maryann and the colonel had disappeared into the garden for a time. He had no reason to suspect anything more than a walk through the roses, but her cheeks had been rather pink upon their return, and Timothy had been thinking about it in more detail since yesterday afternoon. As Maryann's self-appointed older brother here in London, it was his duty to make sure the colonel was properly vetted.

They spoke of the colonel's phaeton; he was already considering selling it and getting a landau instead. "The phaeton is a bit too sporty for an old man like me, I think."

They talked about their future plans, Timothy remaining vague about his prospects since he did not want his fortunate change of circumstances to begin making the rounds. They spoke of races and hunting and every other topic Timothy could think to introduce until he was left with only one. "And what do you think of Miss Morrington?"

Colonel Berkins's smile grew, and Timothy felt his fall. He quickly put it back in place. *I am happy for them both,* he told himself.

"I think a great deal of Maryann," Colonel Berkins said with a confirming nod. "I must thank you for the introduction. She is enchanting."

He called her *Maryann*? And said she was *enchanting*? Timothy forced himself to focus. "I am a great friend of her sister's husband. We were in school together."

"Yes," Colonel Berkins said with another nod. "You said as much when you introduced us at Almack's. She speaks very highly of Mr. and Mrs. Landsing. They have been a great support to her in London and help make up for the loss of her mother, I think."

Maryann had discussed her mother's death with this man? Timothy had liked to think that he was the only man who knew the wound she still harbored regarding that loss.

Colonel Berkins continued. "I *would* like your opinion on a matter, Mr. Mayfield, if you don't mind."

"Of course."

"Maryann and I were speaking of where we would reside after marriage."

Timothy had taken a drink just then and began to cough. He had to lean forward to try to catch his breath. Colonel Berkins slapped him on the back a few times to help the coughing pass.

Once recovered, Timothy stared at the man. "You spoke about *marriage*? You have known her little more than a fortnight!"

Colonel Berkins pulled back from the intensity of Timothy's accusation. "Not a marriage between the two of us. Our *individual* marriages—good grief, man. Are you all right?"

Timothy sat back and cleared his throat, but he was unable to relax enough to strike a casual pose. "My apologies. Do continue."

Colonel Berkins eyed him warily. "She expressed her desire to live in Somerset, if possible, but understands that the man she marries will ultimately make the decision. Since I have not yet established a permanent residence, I wondered what you knew of her family, if that might be something they would accommodate, or would they see me as a layabout not to have a place in hand?"

Timothy mentally repeated what Colonel Berkins had said word for word to make sure he did not react poorly. "You are preparing to make her an offer?"

"Not yet," Colonel Berkins said. "But I am thirty-six, and

I've not hidden from anyone, certainly not Maryann, that I am in London to find a wife and establish my family here in England after so many years abroad."

"You told her this!"

Colonel Berkins's voice was wary but sharp in response. "Yes, and she admitted that was her reason to come to London as well. There is no shame in discussing it if both parties are comfortable with the topic."

"No shame," Timothy repeated and downed his drink before putting the glass on the side table. "It is very bold. I do not think her family will appreciate such forwardness."

He looked chagrined. "Well, then I shall pull back my intention. I apologize for bringing it up. I meant no offense."

They sat in awkward silence long enough for Timothy to chastise himself for handling the man's honesty so poorly. "You must forgive me, Colonel Berkins. I regard Maryann as a . . . younger sister, and I worry for her. Sometimes *her* boldness gets the better of me, but it is unkind of me to react as such to you." He cleared his throat, hoping he was going about this the right way. Why was this so difficult? "In answer to your original question, I do not think her family would object to your situation nor to her wish to reside in Somerset. She loves it there; it is where she has lived all her life and where her mother is buried."

"Thank you, Mayfield, that is a relief to hear. I believe I shall be dividing my time between London and wherever I set up my family. I should like my wife to be comfortable and happy, and I sense that Maryann is an independent woman who will be amenable to a nontraditional arrangement. It is a relief to know that Maryann's family would support such a circumstance if things between she and I should continue as they are. I do enjoy her company and her wit a great deal."

So do I, Timothy thought to himself. "I think that you not being after her fortune will also lend her family's support toward whatever arrangement works best for Maryann. They want her happiness beyond all else."

Colonel Berkins stared at Timothy and set down his glass, though it still had a swallow left. His eyes did not dance and his smile did not grow, rather he looked worried by this news. "Did you just say she has a fortune?"

Chapter Twenty-Two

Saturday night was another ball, and more Colonel Berkins, and more coy glances that led to a whispered invitation to meet him in the library—a room not open to the guests. It was easy to find her way there at the appointed time, even easier to fully enjoy more kisses. More distraction.

She returned to the ballroom ahead of the colonel, and Timothy gave her an odd look from across the room, making her fear that her cheeks might still be a bit flushed. She raised her eyebrows in silent challenge. He narrowed his eyes and looked away. Colonel Berkins entered through the doors at the other side of the room. She met his eye too, flushed again, and then moved around the room in the other direction so no one would be suspicious. Well, no one but Timothy, but Maryann did not care if he disapproved.

She was enjoying herself in London again and finding it easier to be satisfied with herself now that she had the attention of a man whose company she enjoyed. She'd begun to wonder if Colonel Berkins would make an offer. As far as she could tell, he hadn't expressed interest in any other woman, and they had had rather bold conversations about what each of them wanted from marriage. Though she had little regret for kissing the man, she was wise enough to know that she ought not to be too willing until things were set between them.

Colonel Berkins left at eleven, kissing her hand in farewell, and Maryann stayed to talk with the Misses Callifours and a few other friends, including Timothy and Miss Shaw, whose aunt seemed to know everyone in London. It had been a nice evening: easy, entertaining, and comfortable.

Maryann could imagine herself as a married woman—Mrs. Berkins, even—and regularly enjoying the associations in town. Not worried about what other people thought of her. Not wondering at the intention behind a man's attention to her. As a married woman, all that would be behind her, and she longed for it almost as much as she longed for the sea.

Maryann tried not to be too attentive to Timothy and Miss Shaw. They stood side by side, but not touching. At one point, he whispered something in her ear, and Maryann's blood ran hot with an envy she was embarrassed to identify even in her own mind. Miss Shaw had smiled and then looked at him with such adoration Maryann had to look away. The girl was everything he wanted. She wished Colonel Berkins had been able to stay longer so she did not feel like the fifth place setting at a table meant for four.

Mrs. Wallace finally announced her farewell, and Timothy walked the two women out. Maryann did not let herself watch them go.

With it down to just the three of them, Maryann sensed that Miss Callifour and Mr. Fetich wanted some time for private conversation so she excused herself to say goodbye to the hosts and thank them for the night.

"It seems you have had quite the evening," Timothy said from behind her, causing her to startle. She'd assumed he had left for the night but was not displeased to see him. That was part of her problem: she was never displeased to see Timothy.

He fell naturally into step next to her.

She remembered his chastising look earlier in the evening and smiled rather smugly. "In fact, I did. London has become a much more enjoyable place this last week."

Timothy put a hand on her arm and lowered his voice while slowing their step. "Might I have a word before you leave?"

"I've no tolerance for a reprimand, Timothy." They had had such a nice time in Piccadilly, and she wanted *that* to be their new relationship.

"It is not a reprimand," Timothy said. "Rather, it is an apology and a confession."

Maryann lifted her eyebrows, and then moved to the side of the room with him. She looked at him expectantly, and he stared at his boots, taking a moment to gather his thoughts. He lifted his eyes to hers, did not smile, and spoke quickly. "Colonel Berkins knows of your inheritance." He took a breath and then his words continued to tumble out, his tone contrite. "I was only trying to get to know him better and I let it slip, and I am so sorry, Maryann. I know this has been such a burden for you this season, and I was not a good steward of the information. I hope you will forgive me, yet again. I'm so sorry."

Maryann took a moment to make sure she understood the words and the intention behind them before she responded. "I assumed from the start the colonel knew of my inheritance, Timothy. Everyone else in town does."

Timothy blinked. "Oh."

"But you believe he did not know until you told him? How did the topic come up?"

"He was asking about what your family would think if he chose to reside in Somerset, as he expects to travel a great deal for business, and I said something to the effect that they would be relieved enough that he wasn't after your fortune that they would not think ill of him for not having a permanent place of his own." His shoulders fell beneath his blue coat. "I feel terrible, Maryann."

She liked that Colonel Berkins had spoken as though a match between them was to be expected. Perhaps an offer would be coming soon. The thought was exciting, but she kept her focus on Timothy. "Why do you feel as though you betrayed me?"

"Because now he knows of your money, and so his motivations can't be trusted."

Can't they? "You assume that his interest in my fortune will supersede his interest in me, then?"

Timothy considered for a moment, then shook his head. "Not at all."

She raised her eyebrows and cocked her head. "Are you certain of that?"

Timothy took a breath. "Please let us not dissolve into argument yet again. I do not think he is interested *only* in your fortune. I just wanted to make sure that you knew that *he* knew. Just in case."

Maryann felt as though she held the flint and steel capable of starting another fire between them. She was angry that he would assume her money would replace her appeal. Yet she recognized that—though offensive as it was—his assumption was the result of Timothy's concern for her. She allowed herself to remember the afternoon they'd spent together this week, the way they had teased one another, the footraces in the park—she could still hardly believe she'd done it. If she wanted that ease to continue, she had to put the flint and steel away, even if she had cause to use it. She took a breath and softened her expression.

"You once told me, Timothy, that you could never marry just for purse. I feel the same, but I also accept the reality that my fortune will be a boon to my future husband all the same. Colonel Berkins is the first man who has made me *forget* that I am an heiress, and that has been wonderful. His situation is secure, and I have no reason to doubt that his *primary* interest is in my character." It felt good to say the words. Better yet, to believe them. Timothy still looked concerned, and she placed a hand on his arm and smiled. "But I thank you for telling me how he learned it and appreciate your concern for me."

Her releasing him from responsibility did not seem to reassure him very much, but after some mental argument with himself, he nodded. "I do want your happiness, Maryann."

"Thank you," Maryann said. She stepped to his side and slid her arm into his. "Now you may escort me to my carriage and tell me how things are between you and Miss Shaw."

He took her up on her offer and recounted his time with Miss Shaw from earlier that morning on a walk and at that evening's event. Maryann wished she could hear it without the twinge of envy, but she did believe that twinge was lessening.

"She is quite remarkable," Timothy said.

"Are you convinced she is your perfect woman?"

"Not yet," he said after a moment's hesitation.

They bade farewell to the hosts before continuing to the foyer where the footman fetched her cloak as well as Timothy's coat and hat.

"The two of you seem to get on very well," Maryann said.

She'd seen them a number of times this evening, and Timothy had always been attentive and Miss Shaw had always been adoring. By the looks of things, he was as besotted as Mr. Fetich was with Miss Callifour. Yet he continued to have this hesitation. Why did some part of her like his caution?

"We do get along," Timothy said. "And since you are the keeper of so many of my imperfections, perhaps I can confess this one additional thing to you and ask if you might advise me."

Timothy helped Maryann with her cloak before putting on his own coat and extending his arm to lead her down the front steps where they would wait for her carriage.

"I am always happy to offer advice to a friend, Timothy," Maryann said.

"Yes, well, as I've spent more time with Miss Shaw and considered making an offer to her, I've realized that it is not *just* making an offer. It is rising from my place as a penniless bachelor to a man of land and family. In a sense, making an offer will change everything I have known regarding life as a grown man. It is rather overwhelming."

"Indeed it is," Maryann said with a nod. "As a woman, I suppose I have always taken it for granted that a man knows how to establish such things, but it does sound quite intimidating."

A woman's responsibilities were demanding as well, but Maryann had been raised to her place, and when her mother became ill, she and Deborah had shared their mother's work until Deborah and Lucas married, and then Maryann had taken the whole of it.

"I've never seen it done," he said so quietly that she did not know if she'd heard him correctly.

"What do you mean?"

He looked embarrassed as he faced her. "My father died before I was born, as you know."

She nodded for him to continue.

Timothy glanced down the path as if looking for the carriage. "My mother wouldn't keep servants; she'd been a maid and was uncomfortable managing other people. Because of that, our home was . . . unkempt and rather chaotic. Though we were children, we learned to manage many things—especially my sister—but only enough to get by.

"For instance, I remember one year after a spring storm, the ceiling began to leak. We placed a pan beneath the leak, and it became my job to manage that pan . . . for the next three years. It didn't occur to any of us that the roof needed to be fixed, and it wasn't until Uncle Elliott came to see us during one of his visits from India to England that he had it fixed. He instructed our steward to do monthly checks inside the house, even if my mother tried to refuse it.

"My clothes were all hand-me-downs from Peter, and to this day I am not sure where he got *his* clothes, as mother did not sew and no one came to see us save the vicar and his wife a few times a year.

"Mother simply did not have the capacity to function the way normal women did, and she had no one she trusted enough to rely on. She died when I was ten, and I went off to school, where I learned from other boys how to better manage myself. After school, I moved into rented rooms befitting a London bachelor.

"I've never lived in a managed household, never instructed staff or spoken with solicitors or men of business or stewards or such—save for an appointment I had with my uncle last week regarding my upcoming inheritance. Yet, as a married man with holdings of my own, I will be expected to take on all such things and more, and I've not the first clue how to do it."

"Oh, Timothy," Maryann whispered, placing a hand on his arm. "I had never considered this."

He smiled. "Obviously, neither have I until recently. It is therefore difficult for me to separate my being ready to make Miss Shaw an offer and being ready to step into all this responsibility."

"What of your brother? Did you not tell me that he had restored your childhood home?"

"Yes," Timothy said. "I barely recognize the house when I visit, which I shall be doing next week, by the way." He brightened, his countenance lifting. "He is having an engagement party. I can only imagine it's her idea as Peter is not one to entertain."

"I imagine he would be glad to give you advice, especially as he understands your situation better than anyone. He had as little example as you did."

The Landsing carriage pulled up in front of them, and Timothy signaled to both the driver and the footman that he would assist her inside.

"That is an excellent idea, Maryann. Once again you have come to my rescue."

She laughed without thinking and then banked it quickly, though the echo seemed to ring through the night air.

Timothy took both of her hands in his and stared at her intently, suddenly serious. "I should never have said what I said about your laugh, not only because it was cruel but because your laugh is sincere and bold and . . . just like you."

"I think you mean brash and—"

"Real," he cut in. "Promise me you will never contain it again."

"You are not the only one put off by it, and I've no wish to make anyone uncomfortable."

He shook his head before she even finished speaking. "Promise me," he said. "It is everything it should be and everything you are. Never hold it back again. Promise?"

How could she say no to him when he held both her hands between them and stared into her eyes with such sincerity and regret? "I promise."

He grinned that boyish grin that made her heart skip a beat, and then released her hands and opened the door of the carriage so he might hold her hand while she stepped inside.

"Have a good night, Maryann," he said as she settled onto the bench.

"Would you like a ride?"

"No, thank you." He pulled his hat down low over his eyes but lifted his chin so she was all but looking up his nose. "I fancy a run tonight."

She nearly held back her laugh, but then remembered her promise and laughed loud and bold. It made him grin even wider.

It was nearly midnight before Maryann returned home. Lucas was reading in the drawing room as he often did on the nights she attended events alone. They talked of who was there, who wasn't, the latest gossip, and how Deborah was feeling—tired, as had become her usual disposition.

"I spoke with Timothy tonight," Maryann said, hoping her voice sounded casual. She straightened the lace doily on the side table to avoid his eyes. "I think he'll be making an offer to Miss Shaw."

"Miss Shaw?"

She met his eye. "Miss Rachel Shaw. I introduced them a week ago." Had it only been a week? "She is . . . perfect for him."

Lucas's expression was intent enough that she shifted in her chair but pushed forward. Her thoughts had been filled with Timothy through the journey home. "I wonder, Lucas, what you know of Timothy's childhood and, uh, family." She was troubled by all he'd gone through and wanted to discuss it with someone she knew cared for Timothy as she did.

"His childhood? Norfolk, I think, or possibly Nottingham. I know he has an older brother and sister. His uncle is a viscount, and he supports Timothy, I believe."

Was that all he knew? "What of his mother? Has he ever talked to you about her?"

"I believe his mother was a bit reclusive."

Isolated, Maryann corrected silently in her mind. *A former maid.*

"She died before he came to school, and I think his father died when he was young."

Before he was born, Maryann corrected once more.

"Timothy's sister was caught up in some sort of scandal—I've never embarrassed him enough to ask details—and his cousin, Harry Stillman, is a bit of a scamp here in London. Were it not for Timothy's excellent character, I think he would suffer more for Harry's actions and the lack of family consequence. But, well, Timothy seems to outshine such things, a remarkable thing for a society so quick to draw out the worst."

Maryann nodded her agreement, wondering if she knew more about Timothy's family than anyone else did. Though Timothy had a great many friends, none were closer than Lucas, and if Lucas did not know the details, she did not imagine anyone else would. The possibility that she could be the sole keeper of his history made her feel a combination of gratitude and responsibility.

"Why all the questions, Maryann?"

She stood and smiled in case any of her thoughts had shown on her face. "Just curious. Miss Shaw seems to be a good match for him." It was true, wasn't it? Did Miss Shaw know anything about Timothy's family? Was that part of Timothy's confession tonight, testing out the things he would need to tell his intended wife?

"I played cards with him last night, and he said nothing about a new woman of interest."

"I imagine he doesn't keep you up-to-date on the women he is attentive to, though, does he?"

Lucas considered that. "Well, no. But he talked about your shopping trip in Piccadilly." He grinned, as though he wanted her to draw some conclusion from his comment. She refused to do so.

"We had a nice afternoon," Maryann said before turning to leave. "Good night, Lucas. You really don't have to wait up for me."

"Except that if I don't, Deborah can't sleep."

She looked back. "You're a good husband, Lucas."

His smile softened. "I am trying to be."

She said good night once more and then made her way up the stairs, humming to herself as she reviewed the evening, which had been one of the best she'd had in a long time. The bedchamber was lit, and when she entered, Lucy stood from where she'd been waiting in the window seat.

"Oh, Lucy," she said in a sweet and dreamy voice. "What a lovely evening I have had this night."

She crossed to the vanity, but stopped when she realized the maid had not said anything. She turned to Lucy, whose eyes did not reflect Maryann's happiness. Maryann felt her smile fall. "Lucy, whatever is the matter?"

"Oh, miss, I am so sorry," she said in a tight voice.

Maryann took hold of her arm. "What is it? Deborah? The baby? Has something happened?" She looked to the door of her bedchamber. Lucas would have said something if—

"It is not your sister, miss, or anyone of the household."

Maryann held onto Lucy, potential relief frozen because, though the problem was not Deborah, there was obviously still a problem. "Then what is it?"

"It is Colonel Berkins. I am so sorry. He is not what he has worked so hard to seem, and he has managed to fool everyone."

Chapter Twenty-Three

The shock and hurt of Lucy's discovery only lasted a short time, then Maryann transitioned into the woman she'd been at home at Orchard House—the one who managed the household and her mother's care and thanked people who asked after the family's well-being without dropping a shred of evidence toward the toll it all took. Like then, this situation wasn't different because she knew the truth. The decision to *not* let this situation linger and fester was the easy part, but she was awake for hours considering the best way to confront Colonel Berkins. Her first priority was to protect her and her family from embarrassment and scandal. The second consideration was to protect Colonel Berkins from the same.

Sunday moved forward at a snail's pace, and she felt trapped in the confines of the town house with no sea to escape to. She could not go anywhere in London without an escort, but all she wanted was to be truly, totally alone. She feigned a headache in order to claim some sense of privacy for her thoughts, and spent the day in her bedchamber reviewing her options.

She could not call on the colonel, and to invite him to come to her house would require that Deborah attend them. She considered trying to meet him unattended, but she was more mindful of her reputation than ever. Finally, amid the heaviness of a second sleepless night, she wrote him a request that he take her on another carriage ride Monday afternoon. It was the only real option for them to have a private conversation.

She tiptoed downstairs in her nightdress and left the note on the tray for outgoing messages; there were some invitation responses already set there, waiting for the footman to deliver them at decent hours. Then she moved silently back to her room, crawled beneath the covers, and willed herself to sleep with the knowledge that she would be all right. She had not been in love with him. Not yet.

She slept until eleven o'clock—bless Lucy for informing the household that she would not be receiving visits that morning—and then dragged herself through her morning routine. Near noon, she received Colonel Berkins's response of excited acceptance, and at a quarter past two, he lifted her into the carriage. She'd have used a ladder if one had been available in order to avoid the intimacy, but she did not have the option. The feel of his hands on her waist did not excite her this time. She wouldn't let it.

She only waited until they had turned off Holland Street before she spoke, hoping that once she said the words out loud they would stop looping through her mind.

"I have some questions about Spain," she said.

"Ah, one of my favorite topics," he said with a grin. "What would you like to know?"

"Why did you not stay there?"

"The war all but ruined the country, and my land is here in England. My mother and sisters are here too. I have been gone a long time."

"But to leave something you love so much, is that not difficult?"

He nodded, and his expression fell while his eyes got a faraway look. "Of course."

"You once said you wanted to bring the best parts of Spain back to England."

"Yes," he said, smiling again, but she sensed some nervousness there. Or perhaps she only wanted to see nervousness so he would seem less a cad and more the desperate man she preferred to believe he was. They turned a corner, but she had already braced herself by gripping the edges of her seat so she would not fall against him.

"Did you specifically mean that the best parts of Spain were your woman and child and that you actually brought them to England with you?"

He froze completely, and all color drained from his face, but he did not turn to look at her. A few moments passed, and he steered the horses to the right to avoid another carriage.

Maryann took advantage of his speechlessness. "I certainly cannot know more about Spain than you, a man who has lived there," she said, impressed with herself for speaking so evenly. Lucy's revelation had shocked her Saturday night, and yet she'd felt more foolish than betrayed. Confronting him did not hurt. "But aren't there areas of Spain that have been less affected by the war than others? I know the country does not run as England does, but it seems a man with military training and English manners—and who speaks the language and has a vested interest in the people—could do quite well there. Why did you not marry this woman and live in Spain as an honest man rather than pretending she is a servant with a dead husband?"

He swallowed. "I don't know what you are talking about, Maryann—"

"It would be best if you called me Miss Morrington," she said, her tone remaining calm. "And better still for you to be honest with me. I am trying to help you, Colonel Berkins, if I can."

He was silent for several long seconds.

Maryann waited him out. Maybe it *would* have been better to have met him in secret, where one of them could turn and run from this. Why should she have any concern for his situation after what he'd done? But she was worn out and did not have the energy to make this about her, when it was *not* about her. At all.

Finally, he cleared his throat. "I had hoped that you and I would be able to make an arrangement," he said in a voice she could barely hear above the noise of the carriage and the crowds.

"You *had* planned to tell me, then." She didn't necessarily believe him, but it was nice to think he would not have lured her into such a torrid arrangement without her knowledge. *What a gentleman*, she thought sarcastically. For the briefest moment it crossed her mind that if it were not herself involved in this situation and if Timothy had not been the one to have introduced the colonel to her, Timothy and she could have talked about this for hours. She pushed the thought away. It was taking all her focus to keep her confidence for the tasks she had to execute today. There was no room for anything but the business of it.

"Yes," he said, regret heavy in the single word. "I'm sorry."

She wondered if he were sorry for not having told her yet or for thinking she would have agreed to his arrogant and asinine plan. "I would never marry a man who kept a woman."

"She is not my *woman*," he said quickly. "Not in the degrading sense you are using it."

"You love her, then?" If he didn't love her, it would be nothing for him to have left her and his illegitimate child in Spain. But the information Lucy had found was very different than that of a military man bidding adieu to the distraction encountered within his service. It had not come to the surface of the gossip earlier because much of his staff had come from Spain with him. They spoke a different language and worked hard to protect the true identify of his "maid," who did not know how to make a bed. A member of the English staff had sniffed out the truth and brought it to Lucy, who had been asking questions two weeks earlier.

Maryann spoke to fill the silence. "You wanted to make a life for her here and . . . be with her when you could. That is why you made such a point of all this travel for business your wife would need to expect."

He swallowed. "There is nothing like this in Spain." He waved his hand through the air to indicate all of London. Streets. Parks. Laws. Security.

"And how do you imagine she will manage in a country so different from her own? And with a child you cannot claim?"

"They are safe here," he said resolutely. "That is my priority."

The fact that the words sounded almost sweet proved to Maryann that her heart had never been engaged upon Colonel Berkins. But she could not grant him immunity from the consequences of his actions.

"My prospects are not so low that I would share my husband, and I suspect you will have a very difficult time finding any Englishwoman who would. If you are sincere in your goal to be upfront about your situation, I believe you shall find yourself run out of this city entirely, and what will become of her and your child then? A better choice, I believe, is to find a way to return to Spain."

"Spain is a disaster," he said miserably. "Ferdinand has compounded the nightmare begun by Napoleon. It is not safe."

"Then perhaps Naples, or even Spanish Florida. My father has a friend who has settled there. You could raise your family in a place new to all of you."

"It is not that simple," he said. "We cannot marry because she is Catholic and I am not."

"Convert, then."

He paused, as though he'd not considered that. She did not imagine he was particularly devout to the Church of England. Never mind that it was ridiculous to choose an immoral and illegitimate relationship over religious differences. Surely no church would sanction that.

"You can hire someone to manage your affairs in England so that you have a livelihood to support you elsewhere. Or sell your land completely and invest wherever you go. I better understand why you were so amenable for me to live in Somerset, and so determined that I understood that you would be gone so much." She shook her head, pushing down her embarrassment and anger. "You ought to solve your own situation before you attempt to pull someone else in to cover your tracks, Colonel."

He was quiet, the carriage barely moving though the park entrance was coming closer. "I am sorry, Miss Morrington."

She appreciated that for what it was and reached into her reticule to extract a piece of paper. "I have listed the names and addresses of a few contacts of my father who have international business experience, including the solicitor who helped his friend immigrate to America. I suggest you speak with one or all of them and see what arrangements you might be able to make."

She did not think her father would mind her sharing the information, but she hoped to never need to tell him she'd done it.

She held out the card, and he transferred the reins to one hand as he took it, holding her eyes as best he could in the process.

"Why are you doing this?" he whispered.

"People deserve to be happy." It seemed that her lot in life was to help everyone else find happiness while her own lay just out of reach.

He slid the note into his coat pocket, then slowed the horses to allow another carriage to cross in front of them. The park entrance was just across the road. "I should take you home."

"If you do, my family will be suspicious, and I would prefer that no one know what your intentions with me were. To be the woman you believed would stand for this leaves me terribly embarrassed." She had kept her poise until now, but stating her embarrassment made her cheeks flush. She swallowed and reminded herself that she was doing the right thing. She was being kind and forgiving and helpful. Everything would be all right.

"When I learned of your fortune, I began to lose hope of having your compliance, but by then I had come to enjoy your company and thought that—"

"Do not insult me further by trying to explain yourself," she cut in, her chest getting hot. If he hadn't known of her inheritance until Timothy told him, then he'd based his whole plan on her age and plainness making her willing to enter any match. "You were wrong in a hundred different ways, let us leave it at that."

They entered the park in silence. She forced a smile as she passed Lydia Henry walking with her sister. Maryann had taken pride in the first carriage ride she had enjoyed with Colonel Berkins, feeling triumphant and validated in being seen with him. This drive was sheer torture.

"You are not going to tell anyone, then?" Mr. Berkins asked after a few silent minutes.

"Unless I learn that you are courting another woman, no. Should I hear that you are attempting to make an arrangement with someone else, however, I will tell *everyone*." She held his eyes a moment to make sure he knew she was serious. He nodded, and they both faced forward again.

When they returned to the house, Colonel Berkins produced a short ladder from beneath the seat of the carriage, and though it was not as efficient a descent as him lifting her down, it was a welcome option. He walked her to the door, thanked her, and promised her an update after he had sought out the contacts she'd given him.

She entered the house while mentally crossing off "Confront Colonel Berkins" from her list of unpleasant tasks she had to do today. It wasn't her last task, however.

"Milton," she asked the footman as she took off her gloves. "Is Mr. Landsing at home?" Lucas had been staying closer to home since Deborah had begun feeling so poorly.

"In your father's study, miss."

"Thank you."

Lucas had his feet on the desk and was reading a letter when she entered. He quickly corrected his position, his feet thumping to the ground as he sat up straight. "Oh, uh, good afternoon, Maryann."

"I wondered if I might have a word," she said, smoothing back the hair that had been mussed from her bonnet.

"Of course," he said.

She sat in a chair across from him and insisted to her emotions that she would stay strong. If she could confront Colonel Berkins on his situation, she could talk to her brother-in-law about this one.

"I feel that Deborah would benefit by removing to Somerset before her pregnancy becomes more advanced and your mother convinces her to not to go to Orchard House at all—you know that is where Deborah wishes the child to be born." Lucas opened his mouth, but she put out a hand, not yet finished. "Additionally, I have had my fill of London and would like to attend her back to our home. I'm wondering how you and I might manage to make an exit happen without upsetting her about my leaving before the season is finished. What are your thoughts?"

Chapter Twenty-Four

When Maryann appeared at the entryway into the Thornocks' drawing room Thursday evening, Timothy nearly went to her before remembering that he was in the middle of a conversation with Miss Shaw, Mr. Hawthorne, and the two Miss Callifours. He forced his attention back to the group but kept glancing her way, his eagerness to talk to her making it difficult to be attentive. He had not seen Maryann since the ball last Saturday—no one had—but he'd heard a rumor just this evening that she was leaving London. Miss Shaw had told him, and then seemed to watch his expression closely for a reaction, which he tried not to show. Timothy had worried he'd not have the chance to speak with her before *he* left London for Peter's engagement party.

Once Maryann finished greeting the hosts, she turned to face the room. He smiled brightly at her and nodded toward his group so she might know she was invited. She seemed to hesitate until the elder Miss Callifour excused herself and met Maryann partway. The women linked arms and spoke quietly with their heads together as they crossed the remainder of the room. The circle opened to admit Maryann, and she greeted everyone in turn. Mr. Hawthorne complimented her dress before Timothy thought to do it himself.

She *did* look elegant in a rich blue gown with black lace across the bottom and a sheer ruffle that brushed the floor. She wore diamond earbobs, a blue and diamond pendant that rested at the base of her throat, and elbow-length silver gloves that caught the light.

Amid his notice, Miss Shaw stepped closer to him, and he felt her shoulder brush across his arm. He looked at her, and she smiled back. She looked very well tonight, too. He had already told her as much, and she'd ducked her head and blushed demurely. He couldn't take his attention from Maryann for long, however.

"Miss Morrington," Timothy said as soon as there was an adequate lull in the conversation. "How are you this evening? We haven't had the pleasure of your company this week."

She smiled politely but did not hold his eyes. "I am well, Mr. Mayfield, thank you."

"You have not been about society. We feared you were ill."

"No, I am quite well, thank you."

The elder Miss Callifour spoke, drawing everyone's attention. "Mr. Hawthorne was just telling us of the opening night for *Macbeth* at the Royal Theatre. Who played the lead roles?"

Mr. Hawthorne continued his report, and the Callifour sisters announced they would be attending the play next week. Miss Shaw confirmed that she was awaiting her mother's arrival in London before making plans to see the play.

"What of you, Mayfield?" Mr. Fetich said. "You are a great lover of the theater, are you not?"

"Indeed," Timothy said. "I hope to see the production, but

have not yet decided when." Mostly, he was out of additional funds until his next quarterly allowance that would come at the end of June. He had enough to meet his needs, of course, but he had already spent through the portion dedicated to entertainment this quarter.

"Perhaps your schedule shall become better secured once Mrs. Shaw arrives in London," the younger Miss Callifour said, sharing a glance with Miss Shaw.

Timothy noted the slight flush in Miss Shaw's cheeks and knew she hoped he would attend the play with her and her mother. Though he'd been very attentive to Miss Shaw of late, he was uncomfortable with the idea that his attention had not only been noticed but dissected. And yet, he *was* interested in furthering his connection with Miss Shaw, wasn't he?

"And you, Miss Morrington?" Miss Shaw said, rather more boldly than Timothy was used to from her. "Have you plans to attend? I understand it will be the last production of the Parliamentary season."

"Sadly, I will not be attending," she said. "I'm afraid my sister and I will be returning to Somerset sooner than we'd planned."

Even though he'd heard the whispers, Timothy was shocked to hear her confirm it. Why had he not been informed of this ahead of everyone else?

"You are returning to Somerset?" Timothy said without hiding his surprise. "The season is not yet finished."

"I miss the sea," she said with a shrug.

"But, I had thought you and Colonel Berkins were getting on." Timothy wasn't sure he liked Colonel Berkins and had not sought him out since having let slip that Maryann was an heiress.

Maryann wouldn't meet his eye. "The colonel had some unfinished business in Spain, I'm afraid. I have wished him well."

Timothy opened his mouth to say more, then stopped himself at the uncomfortable looks on the faces of the other people in their group, specifically Miss Shaw, who was looking up at him with as close to a scowl as he'd ever seen on her face. He'd already been more eager than was polite. He felt his neck heat up as he fumbled through his regrets.

Mr. Hawthorne drew out the topic. "I am also surprised to hear you are leaving so early in the season, Miss Morrington. I hope it is not anything any of us have done to send you away."

The group chuckled, except for Timothy, who stared at her and kept his teeth clamped tightly together to keep from saying more than he should. He would have a private conversation with her later and ask then what he could not ask in front of all these people.

"My sister is, ah . . ." She shared a look with the elder Miss Callifour, who nodded her encouragement. "She is entering her confinement soon and will benefit from the country air."

Timothy startled. Deborah was expecting? How had he not known that either? It irritated him to be left out of such important happenings in the lives of people he cared so much about. Miss Shaw slipped her hand into the crook of his elbow, bent as he held his drink. It embarrassed rather than thrilled him to have her attention, but he only mildly wondered at it. His mind was too scattered with everything else he'd learned tonight.

"You will return next season, of course," the younger miss Callifour said.

Maryann smiled with polite regret. "No, actually, I do not expect I will."

"Whyever not?" Timothy blurted.

She looked at him, holding his eyes but clearly ill at ease. "Perhaps I *am* being hasty to say I shan't return. Only I shouldn't want to leave my sister at that time; the baby shall only be a few months old. We shall see."

She didn't mean it. He could tell by her *tight ears*. What had happened between her and Colonel Berkins? She'd been sneaking out of ballrooms with him last week and now . . . Timothy felt heat rush through him. Had the colonel compromised her in some way? Was she leaving in shame and regret? Timothy had never called out another man, but if the colonel had taken advantage . . . He clamped his lips tighter to keep the words from spewing forth.

Maryann shifted her attention to Miss Shaw, still on his elbow. "How are you enjoying London, Miss Shaw?"

"Oh, I am enjoying it very much," she said, casting a featherlight look of adoration at Timothy that made him swallow. "Everyone has been so kind and attentive, and there is so much to do in the city."

"I am glad to hear you've settled in well," Maryann said, a sincere smile on her face. "What have been the favorite events you have attended so far?"

The party continued, and in time, Maryann moved on to converse with other groups. Timothy tried to find distraction in cards, music from the young ladies, a light supper, but he could not keep his thoughts away from Maryann and what had changed in the last five days.

Miss Shaw was everywhere he turned, which only added to his irritation, and then made him feel guilty for being irritated. He had paid her a great deal of attention, and he should be flattered she was returning it. Still, he was planning how he might have a private conversation with Maryann when Mr. Fetich stood to make an announcement regarding his engagement to the elder Miss Callifour. The room lifted with polite applause, and the guests took turns congratulating the happy couple. Maryann did not seem surprised by the announcement, which made Timothy wonder if the announcement was why she'd come tonight. She was so removed from him, as though she'd erected a wall between them. It made him more eager than usual for her attention.

Timothy was talking with Miss Shaw and her aunt when he saw Maryann slip through the doorway toward the entry of the house.

"Would you please excuse me, ladies?" he said with a smile. They agreed, but he was aware of Miss Shaw watching him as he left the room on Maryann's heels.

She was standing in the foyer, waiting for her cloak when he approached her.

"You are leaving early."

"Not so early," she said lightly. "The engagement has been announced, and I ordered the carriage to return for me at ten thirty."

Ten thirty *was* early, but since their time was limited, he jumped to the heart of the matter. "Why are you leaving London?" It was sharp and too direct, but he did not need to tiptoe about things with her as he would with someone else.

"As I said, Deborah is expecting and anxious after what happened last time. I am doing all I can to support her."

"That is not the only reason," he said. "Is it Colonel Berkins? Did something happen that—"

She laughed, but it did not bother him anymore. She sobered quickly and fixed her golden-brown eyes on him, her jaw tight. "It is all of it, Timothy." She waved her hand to indicate the foyer, the street, the city as a whole. "Save for Colonel Berkins, who did not want me after all, I have found no men interested in anything more than my money, and I am exhausted by it. I am out of prospects and out of patience."

Colonel Berkins had rejected *her*? Timothy wanted every detail but could not ask it. "Perhaps if—"

"I am finished with London, Timothy," she said with finality. "And Deborah needs my help in Somerset."

Deborah had lost a child shortly before her mother died, but Timothy could not shake the feeling that Maryann was using Deborah's happy news as an excuse to hide her own feelings.

"Why will you not come back next season? You make it sound as though you have given up on finding a match entirely."

The footman arrived with her cloak, and Timothy took it from the man so he might put it on Maryann himself. He sensed a strange energy between them as he settled the fabric upon her shoulders. Was the tension due to his frustration with her leaving? Her sadness at losing Colonel Berkins? He stepped around to face her and attempted to tie the strings of her cloak, but she shook her head and took them in hand, turning away. At the same time, Timothy realized they were no longer alone. Miss Shaw and her aunt had entered the foyer with Mr. and Mrs. Clauson. Had they arrived in time to see him helping with Maryann's cloak? He didn't like that it made him feel guilty.

"Your carriage is ready," the footman informed Mr. Clauson. Timothy proceeded to help Miss Shaw with her cloak so he would not seem to have paid particular attention to Maryann. When he finished, he realized Maryann had slipped out. The footman handed him his hat. Timothy had had no need for an additional coat on such a warm night.

As he walked down the steps with Miss Shaw, he saw Maryann step into the Landsing carriage ahead of them. Timothy helped the ladies into the Clauson carriage, complimenting their company and agreeing that it had been a fine evening.

"Are you sure we cannot offer you a ride, Mr. Mayfield?" Mr. Clauson said a final time.

"No, thank you," Timothy said with a shake of his head. "I appreciate the offer, but my rooms are not far. I shall see all of you at Lady Dominique's ball Saturday night, I believe. Tonight has been great fun."

"It was a lovely evening," Miss Shaw said last, holding his gaze as he began to close the door.

"It was, thank you."

He wished them a safe ride, then stepped back so the carriage could pull away. Ahead of them, the Landsing carriage turned right at the end of the street. He turned and walked the other direction until he could round a corner, out of view. Then he removed his jacket, leaving himself in only his waistcoat and shirt-sleeves, and pushed his hat low over his face. He took off in a run, utilizing his familiarity with London and a half a dozen shortcuts he knew of to put himself ahead of the Landsing carriage. Thank goodness he'd had his boots stretched, otherwise he could not have made it half a block.

Chapter Twenty-Five

Running at full speed, Timothy reached Holland Street just as the carriage turned the opposite corner. He could barely breathe and was sweating through his shirt in the muggy night air. He summoned a final burst of speed and arrived in time to wave off the footman who was reaching for the carriage door. Good thing he practiced such exertion every Sunday.

He opened the door while sucking for air.

Maryann had already leaned forward to exit the carriage and jumped back into her seat when she saw him. "Timothy!" she said in half surprise, half reprimand. "What on earth are you doing?"

"We . . . are . . ." He braced his hands on his thighs and took another deep breath. "Not finished . . . talking."

She looked at him through the carriage doorway with wide eyes. "You chased me here?"

"Not . . . exactly." Another breath. "Can . . . we talk?"

She pursed her lips, and then shooed him forward so she could step out of the carriage. He was late extending his hand to help her down but put it out once she was on the sidewalk. She raised her eyebrows and walked ahead of him to the front door where the footman waited. The carriage rolled away, heading for the stables.

She led Timothy directly to the well-lit parlor. Lucas was reading near the fire and looked up when they entered. He stood quickly, apparently surprised to see Timothy so late at night. "Uh, good evening, Mayfield."

"Might I talk to Maryann for . . . a few minutes, Lucas?" Timothy asked. He was still breathing hard and had his coat over his arm, but at least he could speak in full sentences. Or nearly full sentences.

For a moment, Lucas looked as though he might protest, then he turned to Maryann.

"It's fine," she said, taking off her bracelets as she crossed the room. "There is a fireplace poker handy if it becomes necessary to defend myself."

Lucas looked as unimpressed with this comment as Timothy felt. What had he done to deserve that?

"It is fine," she repeated when she reached the side table where she deposited her jewelry and began peeling off one of her silver gloves.

Lucas looked between the two of them, a hundred unasked questions behind his eyes. "I shall be in the study."

He left them, leaving the door open a few inches. Timothy did not think Lucas would eavesdrop from the hallway but there wasn't much he could do about it either way.

Focus.

He turned to Maryann, who was pulling off her remaining glove by loosening each finger in turn. He looked away as though she were undressing, which she wasn't, but it was a strangely intimate action, and the sensation it evoked reminded him of the feeling of her hand on his knee. He waited a few seconds longer to be sure that she would be finished when he looked up at her again.

She stood, waiting expectantly, her ungloved hands clasped in front of her.

"Why would you not return to London next season?"

She lifted her hands and began fiddling with one of her earbobs. "Honestly, Timothy, why does this matter to you?"

"Because we are friends, and I feel that . . . I feel that you are hiding something from me. If Colonel Berkins is part of your decision, I hope you will accept my apology for having facilitated the introduction."

"Apology accepted," she said simply as she put one of her earbobs—a round sparkly thing—on the table beside her bracelets.

"He hurt you, then?" Timothy *would* call the man out!

She shook her head. "No, but his happiness was not mine. At least I learned of it before I was much compromised."

"*Much* compromised?"

She worked on the other earbob. "Do not worry yourself. It was only a few kisses, and not very good ones."

"Just a kiss?" Fire lit within his chest. "You *kissed* him?" Before she could answer, he made another realization. "And what do you mean 'not very good'? What have you to compare it with?"

She smiled at him, more sincere than polite, and placed the second earbob next to the first. "I don't think that is any of your business," she said, lifting her eyebrows. "Do you think you are the only man to steal kisses from gentlemen's daughters?"

Timothy's face caught fire to match the heat in his chest. "Wh-what are you talking about?" *How could she know?*

That bark of her laugh set his back up even more. She undid the necklace from her neck—her lovely, smooth neck. *Focus,* he ordered himself again.

"What do you think we women talk about when we turn a room or giggle behind our hands? I have spoken with and learned of many of your conquests, Timothy, which is why your reaction to *my* conquests surprises me."

"Dear heavens, do not say 'your conquests' ever again." He rubbed a hand over his face, appalled. He imagined the women of the *ton* talking about the intimacies he'd shared with, well, some. Nothing salacious, just a quick kiss when no one was watching. He felt it a necessary tool for measuring physical compatibility. He never imagined they would speak of it to anyone. Certainly not Maryann.

Timothy straightened and stared at her. "I promise, Maryann, never to share this with anyone. Your reputation will not be affected."

She smirked as she transferred the necklace from one ungloved hand to the other and back again. "As you wish. Is there something else you wanted to speak about? I've explained why I am leaving London and assured you that I bear you no ill will regarding Colonel Berkins. How else may I help temper this fettle you find yourself in? A footrace perhaps?"

He straightened his waistcoat, wondering if she would take him more seriously if he was wearing his coat rather than being in his shirtsleeves. "If you leave London and do not return next season, how shall you make a match?" Every year counted against her.

She smiled and added the necklace to the small pile of jewelry she'd been making. "The lovely thing about being an heiress with an older brother and sister is that there is no requirement that I marry at all. When I am thirty, my money becomes mine, so why should I want to give it to a man who cares not a whit for me?" She gave him a teasing grin. "After all, I shall have to kiss the man who marries me and bear his children. I could never accept such actions with someone who does not make my blood run warm through my veins."

He allowed her words to take center stage and ignored the increased warmth of his own blood when she spoke of intimacies. He was beginning to understand why men and women did not form friendships like this.

"Maryann," he said, keeping his tone as even as he could manage. "Are you saying that you may not pursue marriage *at all*?"

"Yes, that is what I am saying."

"But that would be such a . . . waste."

"A waste of what?" She sat down on one of the striped chairs and put her hands daintily in her lap. He was too worked up to sit and began to pace back and forth.

"It would be a waste of your talents and gifts," he said, turning on his heel to retrace his steps. "You will make some man a very good wife, and you deserve the blessings of children and security—not money, I understand you have that. You deserve a man to care for your heart and for your person."

"I thank you for such beautiful compliments, but London does not seem to be the place where I will find such a man. I must matter for my own sake, Timothy. And I have yet to meet a man who seems to see *me* at all."

He stopped and found her eyes. *I see you*, he thought. "I shall miss you, Maryann. The city will lose some of its joy without you in it."

She looked toward the fireplace. "It is kind of you to say so, but I am sure you will hardly notice." She said the words with a laugh, lighter than her usual, which led him not to trust it as genuine. "It is time for you to begin officially courting your paragon so that you might not lose her to the interests of another man. I believe she was rather put out with your attention to me tonight."

He did not know why she'd brought Miss Shaw into this; the girl had nothing to do with it whatsoever. "I shall still miss you," Timothy said again, needing her to believe him. "You say you are leaving next week?"

"Wednesday, I think. Deborah is coming with me, and Lucas will come a week or so later, when he has finished his responsibilities in Parliament."

Timothy's shoulders slumped. "I shan't return from my brother's until Thursday next. You will already be gone. I may not see you again."

She smiled sadly at him. "As your friendship with Lucas is unchanging, I am sure we shall cross one another's paths again in the future. And are you not going to Lady Dominique's ball on Saturday? Deborah has been resting all week in anticipation of being able to attend. She's assisted in the planning. It shall be our last public event."

"I am attending," he said with a nod, not mentioning that he had offered to serve as Miss Shaw's escort—the first time he would serve in that official capacity.

"As am I, so I shall see you there." She stood but did not move toward him.

"And that will be our last opportunity to visit."

"For a time, but not forever." Her smile was false, and he hated it.

He held her eyes for several seconds. "Will you miss *me*, once you are in Somerset?"

"Very much," she said in a whisper soft enough he wanted to wrap it around his shoulders on a cold winter's night. She opened her mouth as though to say more, but then closed it and took a breath. Her expression turned mischievous. "But I am sure I shall find some local boy to distract me."

He scowled at her and resisted asking her how many men she had kissed and why she had kissed them, and then make her promise that she would never kiss another. He followed her lead in trying to keep things light. "I wish you were wearing a bonnet so I might pull its strings in retribution."

She laughed, loud and true, and he found himself filled by it. "Oh, you are such a child sometimes," she said.

He walked to her and tugged at one of the curls on the side of her face instead, but he did not release it, transfixed by her eyes. Finally, he let the sleek curl slide through his fingers and withdrew his hand. "Saturday night, then."

She nodded, without looking away. "Saturday night."

Chapter Twenty-Six

*M*aryann had not expected to be sad about leaving London, not after feeling so much relief when she'd made the decision to go. Though the season had brightened for a time beneath the sun of Colonel Berkins's attention, knowing that light was false had been enough to make the skies even gloomier now that she knew the truth. She wanted to get away from the pomp and ceremony, the gossip and posturing she could no longer tolerate. But mostly she'd wanted to get away from *him*. Timothy. Without anyone to distract her, the feelings she'd tried so hard to overcome had crawled out of hiding once again. And then he'd said that he would miss her.

Staying will not change what is, she told herself. It would not make the fortune hunters stop hunting, nor would it change the fact that she was so much older than the majority of the debutantes. It would not make her prettier or willing to settle for less than being loved for herself. And it would not make Miss Shaw less perfect for Timothy. It was inevitable that he would overcome his nerves and make an offer. What man wouldn't?

Tonight, Lady Dominque's annual birthday ball—always held

on June fifteenth—might be the last grand event she would ever attend. *Once I am back in Somerset, I will not miss such things*, she told herself. Her beloved sea and the familiar faces of people she'd known all her life would make up for anything she left behind here. She could put flowers on her mother's grave. She could sleep in the bed she'd slept in every night of her life before coming to London.

Deborah, standing beside her in a circle of women, suddenly drew a breath at the same moment she took hold of Maryann's elbow, tight. It was a signal they had decided upon before having left the house.

"Will you please excuse us," Maryann said to the women, interrupting Mrs. Whittaker's account of her trip to Ireland. Maryann quickly steered Deborah toward the woman's retiring room, which, thanks to Deborah's detailed knowledge of this event, was nearby. She'd been nervous about being too far away from it at any point in the evening so they had kept to the western side of the ballroom.

As soon they were out of the ballroom, Deborah lifted her skirts and quickened her pace, pushing past women dressed in lovely satins and organza gowns. There were shocked exclamations and squeaks as Maryann followed Deborah through the maze of women, throwing out apologies like coins at a wedding. She caught up just as her sister reached the retiring room, bent over a chamber pot behind one of the screens, and retched. At least her hair was pinned up and the retiring room was clean and well attended. A maid came to offer a wet towel. Maryann thanked her.

After much heaving on Deborah's part and soothing comfort on Maryann's, Deborah straightened and took the wet towel. She held the cool cloth to her mouth, folded it, and then pressed it against her sweaty forehead. She was crying, and Maryann led her to a small bench also behind the screen. They sat side by side, Deborah's head against Maryann's shoulder as she sobbed. The maid slipped behind the screen to remove the chamber pot and restore a clean one in its place. Maryann smiled at the girl, who nodded before disappearing. Quiet as a mouse. She thought of Timothy's mother, a maid in a household such as this.

"I am such a ninny," Deborah said as she finally caught her breath. "I have rested all week and I ate toast before we left and everything. I have not vomited for three whole days."

"You are not a ninny," Maryann said as she rearranged the soft curls around Deborah's face. Her sister's eyes were red and puffy, but her skin was gray, and she looked utterly exhausted. Her collarbones stood out more than they should. "I think it best that we go home."

Deborah shook her head. "It is your last London ball, and Lady Dominique will be so disappointed if we leave early."

"I do not care a fig for it being my last ball, and Lady Dominique will understand better than anyone. She knows how difficult it was for you to come at all, and we managed to stay a full hour." Maryann's only regret was a selfish and confusing one. This was her last time to see the man who may have ruined her for every other man in the world. Perhaps it was best that last night's conversation be the end of it between her and Timothy.

Deborah looked at her doubtfully, then her expression turned sad. "I was hoping Timothy would come and that you two would dance."

Maryann pulled back and laughed loudly to cover the tenderness she felt towards her sister; never mind that she had been hoping the same thing. "Oh, Deborah, you are hopeless." She kissed her sister on the forehead and then looked her in the eye.

"Timothy has made his choice, and I am glad for him. As I told you, all is well between us, and I wish him every happiness."

Deborah nodded glumly, and Maryann stood. "I shall find Lucas and have him order the carriage. Perhaps it would be best if you stay here until it is ready."

Deborah frowned. "Do I look that atrocious?"

Maryann did not answer but scrunched her face, which Deborah interpreted clearly enough.

"All right, no need to press the point. I shall wait here, though I'll free up the screen for someone else."

Maryann helped Deborah to her feet and into a satin-covered chair in another portion of the room, away from the screens. The doctor had said the sickness brought on by pregnancy often lasted only a few weeks, but some women continued to feel ill throughout. She sincerely hoped Deborah would not suffer too much longer; it drained her vibrancy and could not be good for the child.

Maryann found Lucas speaking to none other than Timothy, as well as some other men, outside the card room. She smiled easily enough and nodded a greeting to Timothy before pulling Lucas away. She whispered to him the situation, and he excused himself in order to fetch the carriage.

Maryann had taken a few steps back toward her sister when she felt a familiar hand on the back of her arm. She closed her eyes, wanting to remember the exact placement of each finger, how they pressed against her skin and spread warmth so completely through her. She opened her eyes and faced Timothy with a smile.

"What has happened?" His blue eyes were full of genuine concern.

"Deborah is not feeling well. Lucas has gone for the carriage so that we might take her home."

"You are leaving with them?"

"I cannot stay at a ball without a chaperone." Never mind that she'd been attending events unchaperoned for weeks.

"There is no one else you could go home with? Surely Lady Dominique can take your charge."

That was not a poor solution, but Lady Dominique had enough responsibility, and Maryann did not *want* to stay. That Timothy wanted her to stay would be something to take to Somerset with her. "I must attend to my sister," she said—an excuse no one could argue with.

Timothy looked toward the place Lucas had disappeared, then at the dance floor, then across the room at something, or someone. Maryann did not turn her head to see. Then he turned those lovely blue eyes back to her.

"I should like to dance with you before you leave," he said in a flurry of words. "It will take some time for the carriage to be ready, will it not?"

"I'm sure I don't know how long it takes to ready a carriage."

"Wait here, will you, Maryann?"

She realized then that he hadn't dropped his hand from where he'd initially placed it on her arm. They were standing very close to one another, and the warmth she'd felt before had taken over her entire person. She should pull away from him and restore the distance. Instead, she nodded. "I will wait here."

He smiled, dropped his hand, and left her. She tried to follow him with her eyes, but he'd worn his charcoal coat tonight, and it was difficult to track him among the other attendees similarly attired. Mrs. Forrester and her daughter approached, cutting off her view, and asked after Deborah; they had seen the quick exit. Maryann conversed with them quietly over the particulars.

News of Deborah's condition had spread through discreet

whispers rather than formal announcements, and the three of them discussed timing and travel arrangements until Timothy's touch at Maryann's shoulder drew her attention and seemed to mute every sound in the room. There was something about knowing this was their last interaction that added a vibrancy to every detail.

She excused herself from the Forresters and faced Timothy. He looked both anxious and excited. She would miss his boyish laughter and the hopeful way he encountered every day. She'd miss his teasing and his eagerness to be always moving.

"Miss Shaw has relinquished me, and Lucas will hold the carriage until you arrive."

Maryann's chest tightened. "Miss Shaw?"

"I was engaged with her for this next set, but when I explained, she graciously allowed me to dance with you in her place."

In her place, Maryann repeated in her mind. *In her place.* "I should not want to be the cause of any discord."

"You shan't," Timothy said, steering her to the edge of the floor. "She understands that when I return to London, you will not be here." As soon as he said the words, he turned to look at her, surprised as though just now realizing what Miss Shaw had meant.

Maryann smiled and nodded her understanding before looking ahead.

Miss Shaw was willing to forgo one dance in exchange for a Maryann-free future. There was nothing to feel but gracious acceptance of what was. And perhaps a bit of validation that though Timothy's attention to Maryann was not what she wished it was, he had made enough place for her that his beloved had noticed. Perhaps Miss Shaw was even jealous. It was nice to feel on the opposite side of that emotion for a moment.

The current set ended, and then Timothy escorted her to the floor. *Our last dance,* she said to herself, realizing they had shared only one other dance this whole season—her first dance after she had come out of mourning. *I shall make the most of it,* she decided as they moved through the crowd.

She was attuned to every step he took beside her, the feel of her hand resting on his arm, the smell of cologne that was so very *Timothy*—she could find no other way to describe it. He was breathing a bit fast, but then he'd made the arrangements with Lucas and Miss Shaw in a matter of minutes.

While passing between two other couples, he stepped closer to Maryann, and she relished the feel of his arm pressed against hers, his hip a few inches higher than her own. As they took their position for the set, he trailed his hand across her back. It was something she likely would not have noticed with any other man. With Timothy, here at their last dance, she imagined it as a trail of deep purple soaking into her skin.

They stood facing one another. Other couples smiled and nodded and interacted with one another as best they could with the space between them. She and Timothy only held one another's eyes. She could not muster a smile, and he had an uncharacteristic solemnity about him. It was too much to hope that he was trying to commit every moment to memory, as she was, but she chose to pretend that was the case. She'd been careful not to let her imagination run away from her in regard to Timothy these last months, but she was leaving. What was the harm in giving free rein now?

The music began, and they stepped forward to one another, paused, and then stepped back. Maryann executed her hopping steps, then changed places with the woman to her left. Timothy did the same until they were facing one another again. Forward, pause, back. All without breaking eye contact.

As the dance continued, the rest of the room seemed to fade away until it truly felt as though they were the only two people present. When the dance required that she step around him, she trailed her fingers across his back much as he'd done to her when they had taken their position. When he passed behind her a few steps later, she thought he was closer than was necessary, closer than the other men were to their partners. She swallowed as the warmth inside her turned hot.

And so they danced. Subtle touches, intense gazes, close proximity. The air crackled like oil in a fire, and she soaked it all in knowing this would never happen again. For the space of the dance, she let herself believe that she was the one he wanted.

They were facing one another when the dance ended, but as the other partners exited the floor, she and Timothy stood, holding on to the last whispers of intimacy the dance had woven just for them. Reality could not be held back for long, however, and the sounds of the room returned. Timothy led her from the floor along with the last of the other dancers. With the fading fantasy, Maryann deemed Miss Shaw a lucky woman.

Timothy stayed with her while her cloak was fetched, then led her into the night where Lucas's carriage was waiting. It wasn't until Timothy handed her into the carriage that she realized they had not spoken a single word since the dance had begun. She sat on the upholstered seat, across from Deborah and Lucas, who had been waiting. They did not speak either.

"Thank you, Timothy," Maryann said in a soft voice.

"Thank you, Maryann," he said from the open door. "I mean it when I say that London shall not be the same without you."

She could think of nothing to say that would not reveal too much. As it was, the fantasy was crumpling at the edges. He would go from the carriage to the ballroom and dance with Miss

Shaw—his perfect woman. Timothy may never think of this dance ever again.

She swallowed the rising lump in her throat as she nodded her thanks. He closed the door and hit the side of the carriage, signaling the driver to depart. For a moment, his face was framed in the square of the window that separated them. The carriage jolted forward, and a moment later, Timothy was gone.

Maryann leaned back against the cushions as Deborah moved from Lucas's side to sit next to Maryann. Deborah took her hand with her own and gave it a squeeze. Maryann squeezed back and closed her eyes. No one spoke for the ride home, and she did not wonder why her sister and brother-in-law did not ask after her mood. She inhaled and exhaled and focused on the bouncing of the carriage and her sister's hand in hers.

Upon arriving at the house, Maryann and Lucas helped Deborah to her room where Maryann first dismissed the maid, and then Lucas, so that she could take care of her sister by herself. She had given similar care to their mother when she was failing and found satisfaction in the ministrations. Purpose. Only when Deborah was in bed with a cool compress on her forehead did Maryann call Lucas back in.

Maryann returned to her room. Lucy was out for the night, but Maryann did not ring for another maid who could help her undress. Instead, she shut the door, trapping the silence inside and pulling her feelings of loss and abandonment close. She sat at her vanity, put her face in her hands, and gave into the heartache.

She would not miss London, but she would miss *him*. So much.

Chapter Twenty-Seven

Timothy arrived at his childhood home on Monday morning via a horse hired by Uncle Elliot for the journey. The weather was perfect, and the countryside could not have been more lovely. He met Julia Hollingsworth, Peter's soon-to-be-bride, at dinner that evening along with her mother, Mrs. Hollingsworth. Peter's two daughters, whom Timothy adored, and Uncle Elliott were there to complete the party.

Miss Hollingsworth was young, beautiful, and quiet, though he didn't mean the observation to be any kind of judgment. It had taken him by surprise when Uncle Elliott had told him in London that Peter was to be married, but it was even stranger to see his brother watching Julia. The joy that had gone out of him when Sybil had died was ignited again. He smiled, laughed, and engaged in conversation more than he had in years. It made Timothy think back to what Uncle Elliott had said in the pub that day, about the right woman lighting something within you. It seemed Julia Hollingsworth was that woman for Peter.

The girls were excused to bed after pudding, and the adults retired to the drawing room so they might continue to visit.

Timothy heard the story of how Peter and Julia had met, keeping to himself his surprise that Peter would fall for his daughters' *governess*. He also learned of Mrs. Hollingsworth and Uncle Elliott's connection thirty years prior and suspected that the hints his uncle had dropped that day in London were all about her.

If Maryann were here, she would sniff it out. She was attentive to details in ways he never thought to be. He wondered what she would make of his family and then shook the thought from his mind. What would *Miss Shaw* think? He was more anxious about the latter, but then he had known her for a shorter period of time.

Miss Hollingsworth was the first to say good night; she was living with the local vicar until the wedding, which was still two months away, and the carriage had arrived to take her home. Peter walked her out, and while he was gone, Mrs. Hollingsworth claimed herself also ready to retire. Uncle Elliott escorted her, supporting Timothy's suspicion that there was something between them.

Alone in the room he barely recognized from his childhood, Timothy took note of the many details that had changed. Telling Maryann some of his history had brought those memories to the forefront of his mind. He would not call his thoughts nostalgic—that implied some level of pining. He did not think much on his childhood because there was not a lot of joy to remember.

Timothy fingered the sheer blue drapes covering the windows, remembering that they had once been heavy red velvet curtains. There had been soot stains around the fireplace due to a clogged chimney that had gone too long without repair. Mother had kept a large chaise longue in this room and often used it as a bed in the later years, claiming that the upstairs rooms were too cold.

"They have gone up?" Peter asked.

Timothy turned from the painting on the wall, a flower garden he thought may have once hung in the upstairs hall but looked much better here. "Just now."

Peter nodded and checked his watch. "I suppose I ought to retire as well. Tomorrow shall be a busy day." He made a face that showed his enthusiasm, and Timothy laughed.

"I suspected this party was not your idea."

"Indeed not." Despite having said he was ready to retire for the night, Peter moved toward the fireplace. "Amelia is using it as a chance to teach Julia how to hostess a formal party, which is a fair reason."

"Amelia is Mrs. Hollingsworth, I presume?"

"Yes, my apologies. We are rather informal in this odd household."

"I like her," Timothy said, then clarified. "Well, I like both of them. Though they have very different temperaments." Julia was quiet where Amelia was forward; she was still when Amelia busied about.

"Thank goodness for that," Peter said with a slight shake of his head. "Amelia is remarkable, do not misunderstand, but a woman like her will require a great deal of . . . patience. I am grateful for Julia's more mild character."

Timothy laughed. "Our uncle seems rather . . . patient, though."

Peter grinned, looking like the boy Timothy had once caught frogs with. During a particularly bad stretch, they had learned how to roast frog's legs over this very fireplace.

"They will make a match, mark my words," Peter said. "But they are taking their time to be sure it is the right course."

Timothy smiled and returned to one of the velvet chairs.

"And you and Miss Hollingsworth? You have known each other a few months?" Compared to thirty years, it did not seem very long.

"Remarkable, isn't it?" He looked into the fire again with soft eyes.

Heart-to-heart conversations were rare between Timothy and his family members, but as Peter was here and Maryann's encouragement to ask his advice was still fresh in his mind, he seized the opportunity.

"I hope I don't offend you, Peter, but I did not expect you to marry again." In fact, Peter had told Timothy more than once he would *not* marry again and that Timothy ought to be prepared to provide Peter's heir the way their father had provided Uncle Elliott's.

"Neither did I." Peter picked up his pipe from the mantel and packed it with tobacco from a nearby metal box.

Would Timothy own a pipe one day? And a mantel upon which to store it? Would he walk around a house with as much ease as Peter walked around his? It truly was *his*. They had not been much of a family here, but Peter had changed everything about this home, inside and out. It was impressive.

"What made you change your mind? Wanting an heir after all?"

"I care nothing for an heir," Peter said as he put a taper into the fire and lit his pipe. "I am certainly not against having more children, and I would enjoy having a son, but that is not my motivation in marrying Julia." He sucked quickly on his pipe to draw the flame deeper into the leaves. A small tendril of smoke rose from the bowl, and he tossed the taper into the fireplace while continuing to work the pipe.

"Then what *is* your motivation?"

Peter blew out a puff of smoke, turned, and met Timothy's eyes. "I fell in love."

Timothy leaned forward, his elbows on his knees. "Really? This is a love match?"

Peter laughed, a rich sound that oddly enough reminded Timothy of Maryann's laugh. "You are so surprised." He sat on the settee, lounging against the back that put Timothy further at ease. They were brothers, discussing manly things.

"Well, I thought that perhaps you were lonely or wanted a mother for the girls. I did not think you of all people would find love before marriage." He smiled to soften what could sound like an insult. "It is so very modern of you."

Peter worked his pipe a few more seconds before he removed the stem from his mouth. "I had no idea you saw me as such an unfeeling stone of a man, Timothy. Let me assure you, however, that nothing but love—not even the loneliness you mention— could have induced me to marry again." He shrugged lightly. "Julia makes me better."

"She makes you better," Timothy repeated, a question in the tone. Did Miss Shaw make him better?

"She has guided me toward being a better father to my girls. She has given me hope and purpose and brought a sense of new- ness and fun into my life." He looked at Timothy, his eyebrows drawn together. "That sounds like a bunch of honeysuckle, but alas it is true." He inhaled deeply on his pipe, held the breath, and then blew out the smoke. "Julia and I enjoy the same things, share the same humor, love my girls, and love each other. I don't know how to explain it any differently, but, yes, she makes me want to be a better man, and I can think of nothing of greater value in a wife. She says I do the same for her, though that is hard to believe sometimes. I feel very much a rough stone in need of smoothing, not one to smooth out another."

Timothy pondered Peter's words. "Do you feel the same for Julia as you felt for Sybil?"

Peter's smile fell, or rather changed. "Similar, but different," he said evenly. "I am not able to fully explain that either. I love Sybil, and I will always love her, and I rejoice to see how she is reflected in our daughters. Somehow I know that she understands what is happening here and wishes me happy with Julia just as I would wish her happy were I the one to be gone."

"How can that be?" Timothy asked. "How could she want you to be happy in the arms of another woman?" It sounded very stark when he said it like that, and yet he wanted to understand these various facets of love and loving and marriage and loss. How did it all work between a man's head and his heart? He'd once felt so clear regarding what he wanted in a wife, but things had felt muddled of late. Especially since his last dance with Maryann.

"I could make myself mad pondering on it too much, but I believe Sybil is happy for us and that God wants Julia and me to find happiness together. For nothing less would I take this risk, I assure you."

"Risk?"

"Sybil died before my eyes, Timothy." His eyes became dark. "Living without her has been the hardest thing I've ever done. My daughters needing me was as far as my desire to live went. Loving Julia means I am risking loss all over again. It terrifies me." He paused, his pipe resting on the arm of the settee. "What if we lose a child? What if one of us falls ill? It is all well and good to expect life to be pudding and primroses forever, but that is not likely. It is a risk to love someone, and another risk to commit to them come what may. I am willing to risk the chance of hardship for the promise of joy and support and partnership that we are both committed to work toward. That is the true promise of marriage—to support and lift one another through all the circumstances of life."

"I have never thought of marriage in such dire ways," Timothy said. "You may have talked me out of it entirely." Loss of children? Illness? Struggle? Those were the opposite of what Timothy expected for his future. He imagined lively parties and happy children and always having someone to talk to. But that was not realistic, was it?

How would he and Miss Shaw face such challenges? He could picture her in his mind smiling and standing beside him, but she seemed to lack the fire or drive that would be necessary to make difficult decisions. She felt like such a fragile soul. How would she cope with loss? How would she stand against struggles or even tragedy?

Peter's words broke into his thoughts. "I can only guess that Uncle has extended his marriage campaign—and its weight—to you. Hence the reason for your questions."

Timothy looked up with surprise. Peter knew? But of course he did. Uncle said he'd created a gift for each of his nieces and nephews. "Is that another reason you are marrying again, Peter?" he asked it quietly, as though someone might overhear him.

"Not in the slightest." Peter spoke with crisp sincerity. "I have refused Uncle Elliott's gift for me. I told him I felt that the whole campaign was foolish and that it would twist motivations. Is that what troubles you? Are you feeling pressured to marry now that he's promised you material wealth when you do?"

"Not at all," Timothy said with the same sincerity. "I have always known I would have to marry for fortune, and that has been a great weight on my shoulders these last years. Not needing a woman to bring security has led me to seek the kind of woman I have ever only dreamed of."

"You have met someone, then?" Peter smiled and sat up.

"I have," Timothy said, thinking of Miss Shaw, but he could hear the hesitation in his voice. "Were I to make a list of what I want in a wife, she would match nearly every one of them." He was unwilling to admit that he *had* made a list and she fit every line. Peter would laugh.

On the journey to Norfolk, however, it had not been thoughts of Miss Shaw that filled him with warmth. It had been thinking of the dance with Maryann. He was not *attracted* to Maryann, was he? But if he wasn't, then why had that dance left him so . . . unsettled? Was that the right word? Because there was also something fulfilling about it. Desirable. He had not experienced the energy of that dance with any other woman. Not even with Miss Shaw.

"Except?" Peter pressed.

Timothy didn't understand. "Except?"

"You said she would match *nearly* every one of them. What aspects does she not fit that have put your decision in doubt?"

Timothy considered the question with all the gravity it deserved. "I don't know."

Peter lifted his eyebrows. "You don't know what it is she does not possess that you wish for?"

"No." Timothy realized that he sounded like an idiot and shook his head. "I have no quarrel with anything about her, and any man would be lucky to have her, but . . . there is another woman."

Peter gave Timothy a half-grin. "Really?"

"She is nothing of the woman on my list." It hurt to say it.

"How so?"

And so Timothy explained Miss Shaw—paragon of beauty and accomplishment—and Maryann—woman of grace and wit.

"Which is more interesting?"

"Maryann," Timothy said immediately, and then felt badly for Miss Shaw.

"Which is more attractive?"

Timothy thought and thought and thought some more. After a full minute, he shook his head. "I don't know. They both are, but in different ways. Miss Shaw is beautiful—striking and feminine and completely captivating. Maryann is . . . different. Her beauty comes from her confidence, and . . . I feel something with her that I do not feel with Miss Shaw. Or at least something I have not *yet* felt with Miss Shaw. There was this dance . . ."

He explained the dance, which led to explaining Maryann leaving London, and her fortune, and even Deborah and Lucas and how they fit into the whole of it.

"I hate to even think that I am choosing between them. It feels as though I am saying one is not as good at the other."

"Or is it simply saying that one is better *for you* than the other?"

Timothy let out a breath, wishing he felt better for this conversation. Instead he felt more confused. "And what if I choose wrong? What if I choose one, and down the road, I regret that choice."

"We are not our parents."

The insight startled Timothy since it was something he had thought so much about. Peter held Timothy's eyes, his expression firm. "I am marrying a woman who worked in my household. If anyone has considered the implications of repeating history, it is I. But Uncle Elliott has helped me understand that I am not our father. And Julia is not our mother. I understand your fear, but we are men of our own making, Timothy, and I do not see one thing in your character that makes me doubt your ability to be a good husband and father. If I could root that fear from your chest I would."

Timothy swallowed the lump in his throat, not realizing until now how much he needed to hear that. "It is still frightening."

"Yes, of course, it is. As I said, to love is risk. To commit is risk. But a worthwhile risk, I think. The question I think you need to ask yourself brings us back to the start. Which woman makes you better?"

Maryann. But as quick as he thought it, he reminded himself that he'd had months to get to know Maryann. He'd known Miss Shaw for only a few weeks.

When he said nothing out loud, Peter cleared his throat. "There is no such thing as a perfect woman, Timothy, nor a perfect man. But imperfections do not eclipse the whole."

"Julia is not perfect, then?"

Peter laughed, but only once before glancing toward the door. Then he leaned forward and lowered his voice. Timothy considered reminding him that Julia had gone to the vicar's, but then her mother was within these walls, so maybe the caution was warranted.

"Julia is better with some of the dogs than I am, which makes me crazy even as I admire her skill." He paused and glanced at the door again. "She prefers simple meals to the more elaborate ones I enjoy, and she likes the girls to sit at the table with us for dinner. I've never had children at the table before." He sat back, and his manner relaxed. "Her mother has been teaching her the responsibilities of the household, and things are improving, but Julia is uncomfortable taking charge with the staff."

He paused a moment and took a puff off his pipe while Timothy tried to keep himself in his chair and not take to pacing.

"But those *imperfections* go both ways. I like fancier meals than she, I prefer not to have children at the table, and I want her to manage the staff as a woman of the house is supposed to. Additionally, she feels I spend too much time with the dogs, and she wishes I would buy a new suit for the wedding, which I am opposed to because I already own a perfectly acceptable one.

"We have both made compromises to accommodate each other. It isn't always easy, but the reward outweighs the difficulties. I would suggest that you look for a woman who both captivates your senses *and* can weather the storms that will inevitably come, rather than a wife who answers an advertisement."

Timothy considered all of this information. "You have given me a great deal to think about, Peter."

"I hope the excessive thinking will be to your benefit," Peter said. He took another few puffs of his pipe, then stood and dumped the bowl in the fireplace. He turned to face Timothy. "I think you will make the right choice. You're a steady sort, Timothy, and have proven yourself a good man. You'll know the right course."

"Thank you. Your confidence means a great deal to me." Timothy wished he felt the same confidence in his ability to make the right choice.

Timothy stood, feeling stuffed to the brim with all that he'd learned, when he remembered something else—something Maryann had specifically encouraged him to do. "Uh, Peter?"

Peter looked up, his eyebrows raised. "Yes?"

"I have also come to realize how ignorant I am of what it takes to manage a home and family. Marriage will change so many things for me in day-to-day living that it makes my head spin. I wonder if I might stay an extra day or two and perhaps you could tutor me on what I am to do with myself once I am a man of home and family."

Peter smiled widely. "I would consider it a great honor, little brother."

Timothy scowled. "You need not say it like that."

Peter laughed heartily, then began walking toward the doorway. Timothy caught up with him in a few strides. "The first thing you must do," Peter said as they reached the stairs, "is get a dog. No man is complete without a dog."

Chapter Twenty-Eight

Timothy stayed in Norfolk two days following the engagement party. He enjoyed visiting with some of his cousins who had attended—Harry had not come, still put out with Uncle Elliott, it seemed—and playing with his nieces.

Peter made good on his promise to offer the foundations of Timothy's education on matters of estate and home and family, and Timothy felt the relief of not being alone in this. Peter had had no more example than Timothy had, yet it was hard for Timothy to look at his brother now and imagine he'd once dug out the privy himself because there was no one else to do it. He'd come a long distance from their childhood, and Timothy took confidence in his own ability to do the same.

Amid the instructions of how to manage time and tasks of home and family, Timothy watched Peter and Julia. They tended to the dogs together each morning, spent time with the girls together, and often took evening walks together. She insisted the girls join them for dinner each night, raising her eyebrow when Peter protested. He tickled his children and chased Julia around a hedge during a game on the lawn. She made him better. Timothy could see it, and her whole face lit up when she looked at Peter.

Seeing their interaction caused an ache in Timothy's chest—he wanted *this*. Belonging. Family. Comfort with someone else. Each time he thought of a similar future, it was Maryann not Miss Shaw in the images. By the time he said his farewells to Peter and his family, Timothy knew the choice he needed to make. He only hoped he could make it without causing pain for anyone.

Timothy returned to London on Thursday in time to wash off the travel and attend the Middletons' dinner party. He arrived fashionably late, as usual, and was not seated near Miss Shaw for dinner. At one point, he smiled at her from across the table. She smiled back, then ducked her head as though his attention made her feel shy.

After the men returned to the dining room following their port, Timothy found his way into Miss Shaw's company where she was talking with two other ladies and her mother. He had forgotten that Miss Shaw's mother had arrived in London while he had been gone. One of the items on his list was that his perfect woman's mother would adore him; ironically, he did not even have to try to earn her approval. She warmed up to him immediately. He listened to her talk of her family and her husband and the lovely home they kept in Nottinghamshire.

Miss Shaw engaged in the conversation as would be expected of a debutante. When talk moved to the theater and questions were directed to her, she spoke of a few plays she'd seen in her own county, though she could not pick a favorite. Eventually, Mrs. Shaw excused herself to speak with an old friend, and Timothy took the opportunity to ask that he and Miss Shaw look out on the gardens.

The veranda doors were open, and the night was quite

temperate. She looked lovely in a pale green dress with gold stripes on the underskirt. Her hair was done up in large, looping golden curls, save for the smaller curls at the side of her face. Dozens of small green flowers had been artfully included in the arrangement of her hair. She wore a simple cross at her throat, reminding him that one of the items on his list had been limited jewelry.

Maryann wore limited jewelry most of the time but also looked lovely when she displayed her more elaborate pieces. The condition suddenly seemed a very silly stipulation to have in a life partner.

During their walk, she named a few of the flowers in the garden that Timothy did not know. When they had taken the path all the way back to the veranda, Timothy leaned against the stone railing and attempted a transition into more serious conversation. If he could help her see that they were not right for one another, it would be easier on them both. "Do you like London, Miss Shaw?"

"Yes. The people are lovely."

"Well, some of them are," he said with a grin.

She smiled, but politely. Not as though they were sharing a joke.

"Would you like to live in London?"

She met his eye and then ducked her chin. He had found that coy action engaging once. Now he found it irritating, and felt terrible about that. He did not want to stand in judgment of her, but then had he not been standing in judgment of every young woman he'd met this season? Gauging them? Wondering how they might make *him* happy? The realization embarrassed him.

Before his circumstances had changed, Timothy had looked for a woman he could love—who was also wealthy. Now he looked for a woman who would measure up to the aspects that pleased him. As though he were ordering a coat or a dog. The realization brought unexpected shame.

"I will live wherever my husband lives," Miss Shaw said quietly, interrupting his thoughts.

"Yes, but do you like London? Would you be happy living in the city?"

"If my husband is happy here, I shall be happy here."

Timothy laughed, but it was not genuine. Would Miss Shaw notice? "Come now, Miss Shaw, that is no kind of answer. What would *you* like?"

Her cheeks flushed, and she didn't answer, instead she looked back over the city. He had not meant to be harsh, but obviously he had not been careful in his commentary. He cleared his throat. "Say that you married a man with a house in London and a house in the country—which would you prefer to keep as your primary residence?"

"Whichever he chose," she said softly and with just a hint of a question in her tone.

They lapsed into silence, which weighed heavily on him, but he counted backward from ten to one and then from one to ten while he waited for her to ask him something—anything. After a full thirty seconds, Timothy felt he had no choice but to speak.

"I shall be leaving town next week," he said.

She frowned, rather prettily, and looked at the floor.

I have made my choice, he told himself. *Why am I still here?*

"I haven't seen my sister for some time. My uncle created a parcel for her and asked that I deliver it."

His visit to Donna would be the first he'd seen of her in a long while, and he was nervous about the reunion. Not because they did not share accord, but because so much had happened in his sister's life these last two years.

Timothy wondered what Miss Shaw would think of his stories from his childhood, or what she might say about his exiled sister.

Maryann would likely share an honest and well-thought-out opinion with him, ask questions, and show sympathy. He did not even want to tell Miss Shaw as he suspected she would be put off by it. She was so young and naive. Yet she'd been threatened by Maryann. Had she seen what he himself hadn't?

Miss Shaw nodded and finally lifted her eyes. "I shall look forward to your return, Mr. Mayfield."

Timothy smiled a little sadly. She had not asked after his sister or opened the door in any way for him to confide in her.

They returned to the party, and Timothy allowed distance between him and Miss Shaw, suggesting to Mr. Hawthorne that he discuss the play with her again as she and her mother would be going that week. Mr. Hawthorne hurried to their circle, and once Timothy could see that Miss Shaw was engaged in conversation, he gave his regard to the Middletons and exited the party.

He ran home through the streets of London, the air moving in and out of his lungs, and he felt . . . free.

When he reached his rooms, there was a note under his door informing him that he had a parcel at the front desk. He woke up the clerk to get it; he received so few packages. The crate of goods Uncle Elliott had made up for Donna was already in the corner of his room.

The bleary-eyed man went into the locked storeroom and returned with a small wooden box that he set on the counter between them. Timothy stared at the box adorned with clasps and a handle, then gingerly undid the trappings. He lifted the top to reveal a dozen tiny jars of paint, fitted to the sides of the case, along with a box of brushes and a folded rag. On top of everything was a paper, folded in half.

Timothy,

May your world always be filled with color. Thank you for your friendship and escort about London. I shall always cherish it.

Your friend,
Maryann

Timothy read the note through twice, smiling to himself and wishing he were already in Somerset. Everything was suddenly so very clear.

Chapter Twenty-Nine

*M*aryann had been fifteen years old when she'd assumed charge of some of the household tasks of Orchard Hall so that Deborah could go to London for her season. Mother had been ill back then, but not failing.

By the time Maryann was nineteen, she was running the entire household. Mother was confined to her bed, her hands curling into themselves and her mind sputtering. Deborah had divided her time between Somerset and Sussex, where she visited their Aunt Bridget, Papa's sister, who lived closer to Lucas's family estate. Deborah and Lucas were waiting for Mother to improve before they married, but Deborah had wanted to become familiar with the society there too. Maryann was well suited for the household responsibilities and content to stay at home.

Now she was home again, mistress of her castle, as it were, and trying to remind herself that this was what she wanted. Would she really live out her life here? Alone? Childless? She knew she was being dramatic. She was only twenty-two years old, and just because she had not found her future in London did not mean there was not a future to be found. Only the future she wanted was so very specific, and she could not have it. She hoped that in time, she could make room in her imaginings for something else.

James, his sour wife, Adele, and their three wild children, had come to dinner last night. Their family lived in Orchard Cottage, a smaller house on the west side of the estate. If Maryann was not married by the time James inherited, she would likely trade places with them and live out her life in the smaller home. Because of her pending dependence on them, she had not asked after the missing furniture and artwork she'd noticed upon her return to the house nor did she refuse when they asked if she could entertain the children Wednesday afternoon.

Maryann did not mind having time with her niece and nephews, but the two hours would often become four, and maybe even six. In the past, Adele had more than once sent a note hours after leaving the children with her to ask that they stay the night as she had a headache, or stomach ailment, or a last-minute invitation to a friend's entertainment and would be out late. Wednesdays were the governess's day off, and Adele worked very hard to avoid being a mother on those days.

Today was not Wednesday, however, it was Monday, and Mondays at Orchard Hall were busy. Maryann welcomed the work. When her thoughts were humming with the details of household management, they were not reliving her dance with Timothy, or worrying about Deborah, or missing her friends in London. The contrast between a city full of friends and entertainment and an estate devoid of both was stark.

Maryann met with the housekeeper to go over the week's menu, discuss staff, list household materials in need of replacement or repair, and half a dozen other items of household business.

Seeing as how this was her first Monday back, there was more to be discussed than usual.

After meeting with the housekeeper, Maryann asked for tea to be brought to her father's study where she reviewed the household accounts for the months she'd been away and made notes about those things she would need to discuss with Mrs. Sheils. Why was the amount paid to the butcher the same when the family had not been in residence? It should have decreased by at least half.

Maryann had lost track of time when there was a knock at her door. "Mr. Mayfield to see you, miss," Mr. Barrett said from the doorway.

She blinked, sure the butler had said a different name than what she'd actually heard. The vicar was Mr. Morrley; perhaps that was what Barrett had said. "Who?"

"Mr. Timothy Mayfield. He claims to be a friend from London. I put him in the drawing room."

Timothy is here? All the warmth and excitement she'd been trying to forget after Lady Dominque's ball hit her square in the chest, and she hurried from the room while smoothing her hair and . . . her steps slowed as fear and insecurity pushed in. Why was he here? Though the feelings from the dance were still fresh, so was the heartbreak of accepting both their fates. His destiny was Miss Shaw. Hers was not Timothy; perhaps no one at all.

"Mr. Mayfield," she said when she entered the room. He was standing near the fireplace and looked up at her with his usual smile in place. She turned toward Barrett, who had trailed behind her. "Would you bring us tea? Perhaps a sandwich for Mr. Mayfield as he's traveled a long way to visit."

Barrett nodded and left the door open behind him. She considered sending for Deborah but wanted to know for herself why

Timothy had come before she bothered her sister. The journey home had been difficult for Deborah, and she was still recovering.

Maryann crossed to one of two matching settees that faced one another and sat down while waving him to the other. He remained standing.

"I did not expect to see you here in Somerset, Mr. Mayfield." She did not know how to act and the role of "London hostess" seemed the safest default. "You look tired," she added.

"Why are you not calling me Timothy?"

Because you are in love with someone else, and I need to protect my feelings toward you so they can return to what they should be. "I can call you Timothy if you would prefer."

"I would prefer that, thank you," he said and finally sat down on the settee opposite her. They sat in silence for several seconds, as though waiting for the other to speak.

"Thank you for the paints, Maryann," he said, finally. "It was a very thoughtful and unexpected gift."

"You are welcome." That was not what had brought him here, was it? She'd thought of the paints only the day before leaving London, feeling the need to leave him with some token of the color he'd brought into her life. Or had she been creating one more opportunity for them to communicate with one another? Through a note, of course, not his presence in her family home.

"I have not used them yet," he said. "I'm unsure where to start, but it may be the kindest gift anyone has ever given me. I no longer have any excuse not to paint." His smiled widened.

She was terribly pleased by the compliment but did not want to give so much away. "I assumed Miss Shaw would be the one to teach you. She is a remarkable artist."

"Yes, she is," Timothy said. "But I did not ask her—did not even consider it, actually."

That was strange, but it also felt like he wanted Maryann to ask why he hadn't considered asking an accomplished water-colorist who was everything he'd ever wanted in a woman to teach him.

Because she knew he wanted her to ask, she took a different approach. "Is everything all right, Timothy? Why have you come?"

"Why have I come," he repeated. He stared at the floor, took a deep breath, let it out, and then looked up to meet her eyes. "I am not in love with Miss Shaw."

She blinked and stared and held herself tightly. Controlled. "You came all the way to Somerset to tell me you are not in love with Miss Shaw?"

He suddenly smiled, as though something had just occurred to him. He sat up straighter, and when he spoke, his tone was light, almost playful. "Actually, I need help sorting it all out, and you are so very good at helping me to do that."

The knot inside her that was anxious and unprepared for this visit became even tighter. "I helped you sort out tight boots and how to match a waistcoat. That is not worth a hundred and fifty miles distance."

"*You* are worth that distance, Maryann," Timothy said with as much seriousness as he'd ever said anything before. "And that is why I have come. I am not in love with Miss Shaw, but . . . I *am* in love with you." He grinned, wide and proud and quite pleased with himself.

Was this a game? She took a breath and remained calm despite the fact that he seemed to be watching her for a reaction. "I believe the woman who will make you happy is blonde, green-eyed, has a mother who loves you, plays the piano—"

"Not so," Timothy interrupted, shaking his head. He jumped

up and began walking the perimeter of the room. "I *thought* that was what I wanted, but I should have listened to you when you told me that list was foolish. It *was* foolish, and I have come to know that for myself."

She continued to hold her feelings close and stood in front of her chair. "What is this, Timothy? Miss Shaw will not have you? Is that it?"

Cat. Mouse. Games. Players. Win. Lose.

Timothy's smile faded, and he shook his head. "Miss Shaw is not the woman for me, Maryann."

"Because . . . Did she not like babies after all? Was her appetite not as hearty as you would like?"

"Forget the list, I beg of you. The list was folly. Miss Shaw is not the woman I want. You are. Have you not heard that?"

"What I have heard are excitable thoughts from an excitable man who sounds a bit panicked." She considered a few moments and cocked her head to the side. "You are tired of living in rented rooms and can't stop thinking of the house in London and the land in, where was it, Kettering? You need a wife after all, and anyone will do."

"No," Timothy said rather sternly, if a bit desperately. "If all I wanted was a wife, I could find one easily enough. But I want you, Maryann. Have you not heard me say that any of the three times I've spoken it out loud? I am in love with you." He walked toward her, a new smile teasing his lips.

She crossed her arms in front of her and stepped behind her chair. He stopped, pulling his eyebrows together.

"Why are you saying these things?" she whispered, every part of her body throbbing with caution and warning. She knew he'd expected her to run into his arms, but after all these months of trying to ignore and forget her feelings for him, and after the dance that had ignited them all over again, she could not risk the pain of rejection again.

"Because I am speaking from my heart," he said, putting a hand to his chest.

"When I left London, you were courting Miss Shaw. She was your heart's choice."

Timothy shook his head. "I was never *courting* her. I did think she might be the woman I had always dreamed of—she fit the list—but I believe a great deal of the anxiety I confided to you was due to my knowing she wasn't the right woman for me."

Maryann said nothing, and Timothy dropped his hands to his side, his shoulders slumping. "I have no desire to speak poorly of her, but . . ."

He paused, then continued. "She did not know which course at dinner she liked the best. Honestly, she lacks opinions about most things, simply either agreeing with me or stating she has no preference. I pressed her on where she would want to live, and she could not give me an answer. She would only say that she would be happy living wherever her husband lives."

"Any woman would give the same answer, Timothy."

He gave her a challenging look. "You would not."

She lifted her chin in defiance. "How would you know?"

He moved toward her, stopping on the other side of the chair so that it was all that separated them. He cocked his head to the side and smiled again. His smiles were his undoing, as they only made Maryann more cautious. She'd been a fool for those smiles too many times already.

"All right, where would you like to live, Miss Morrington? Assuming you could have your pick of the country or the city—which would you choose?"

"I will live wherever my husband chooses."

He narrowed his eyes. "And if he left the choice to you?"

"He wouldn't."

He let out a harrumph of a laugh and crossed his arms over his chest. "All right, what is your favorite play?"

"I'm not sure. What is *your* favorite play?"

"*Hamlet.*"

She batted her eyes and gave a false smile. "That is my favorite play, too."

He dropped his arms and his smile. "Stop that. Tell me what you really think. Be . . . *you.*"

She did not dare. Things were too vulnerable. "Miss Shaw told you what every girl is taught to tell prospective husbands. 'My will is your will, dear husband.' That is what we do."

"But that is not what *you* did. Not with me. You told me to change my coat and trim my hair and stop bouncing my knee beneath the table and get advice from my brother. You told me I was an idiot to think that the woman I could find lasting happiness with could be found by matching up a list of requirements." He paused. "And you were right. Miss Shaw is exactly what I thought I wanted, but I did not miss her when we were apart. She does not make me a better man. *You* do that."

"Just because you do not want Miss Shaw does not mean you want *me.* And you do not *need* me now that you have a fortune of your own. That need was the only reason you pursued me in the first place. There are several weeks left in this season, and then next season or the one after that. You are tired and—"

"I am not tired, Maryann," he interrupted her sharply. "I am in love with you."

The words fell like stones at her feet. He did not understand what he was saying.

"No, you do not," she said evenly as she blinked away the

tears rising in her eyes. "And if you were any friend to me, you would not spout off such things in your frustration and fear."

She headed for the open door before she lost control. When she felt his hand on the back of her arm, she pulled away and faced him. She did not meet his eyes or give him time to speak. "Change out of your traveling clothes. Have a bath and a good meal. You can sleep here tonight, and I shall have Barrett arrange for you to return to London first thing tomorrow."

The feel of his gaze on her face was heavy. She walked past the doorway in order to get away from him and to reach the bell-pull to summon assistance. "The east guest chamber has a balcony that overlooks the sea. Perhaps the sea breezes can help you to repair your emotions more quickly. I find that it always seems to do the trick for me when I am out of sorts."

His voice was soft when he spoke. Sad. Tired. Tempting her to believe him. "Have you not heard anything I've said, Maryann? I have professed my love quite boldly. And . . . that dance." He paused and seemed lost for a moment. His voice lowered a degree. "Surely you felt what I felt when we danced that night. I have scarce been able to get it out of my mind."

Pride or preservation, perhaps both, kept her from reacting to his admission. She wasn't ready to let down her guard. It was one dance, one moment. They had had a hundred other moments where she'd longed for more from him than he would offer.

"We have managed an odd but honest friendship these months, Timothy, but our comfort with one another does not mean you *love* me, nor that you can change your expectations so quickly. Your words today are unfounded and, quite frankly, unfair after you have been so determined against everything I am." She waved a hand in front of herself to indicate her figure, her face . . . everything.

Timothy's expression slackened, and she thought maybe he finally understood. Movement in the doorway behind him caught her eye, and she focused on the butler holding a tray with fresh tea and the sandwich she'd ordered for Timothy.

She put her lady-of-the-manor smile in place. "Thank you, Barrett. Please escort Mr. Mayfield to the dining room with the tray so that he might enjoy his food while the east guest room is readied for him. He will be staying the night. I have work to attend to this afternoon and shall take a separate tray in the study when you're able, please."

Barrett looked between them. "Shall we set a place for Mr. Mayfield at supper, then?"

She hadn't thought of that, but of course they would supper together. She would have to sit with him and behave as a hostess should. But Deborah would be there. Was it too late to invite James as well? Would he help dilute the tension or make it worse?

"Yes," she said. "And please arrange for a hired carriage to take Mr. Mayfield back to London in the morning."

She could tell that Timothy had more to say, but she would not allow him to say it. She stayed where she was until Barrett invited Timothy to follow him, and after a final look between them, Timothy followed.

Maryann inhaled slow and steady, and then exhaled slow and steady. She did not know how to even start thinking over what had just happened and so escaped to the study and the ledgers and work that would keep her mind off the man she wanted but did not dare believe wanted her.

Chapter Thirty

*L*ucy put what felt like a dozen more pins into the twist at the back of Maryann's head. "Are you not glad Mr. Mayfield has come?" she asked.

"No, Lucy, I am not." Maryann had not confessed her feelings for Timothy to anyone but Deborah, and certainly not to her maid who bartered in information. She had avoided Timothy all afternoon, but her anxiety had grown by the minute as supper approached.

Lucy took a step back and nodded that she was finished. Maryann stood and smoothed the skirt of the yellow dress she'd chosen—the one Timothy had said he did not like. He was right in that it washed out the natural pink of her cheeks and rendered her hair a flat brown. But it was not as though her looks had ever dazzled him.

Maryann smiled at her maid. "Thank you, Lucy."

She forced herself to take normal, steady steps toward the door, though her nervous energy made her want to . . . run. Out the door and to the beach if she could choose her destination. She had yet to reacquaint herself with the beach. She had too much to do at the house before she could indulge herself. Maybe if she'd made time for the waves she would not feel so tense now.

She heard the voices before she reached the parlor. Apparently Deborah was feeling well enough to come down. Thank goodness for that. Deborah had once wished for a match between Timothy and Maryann. Could Maryann find the words that could express to her sister how much she needed support *against* him now?

She entered the room, and Timothy rose to his feet, a drink in his hand and a smile on his face. She met his eyes briefly, then turned to look at Deborah, who had remained sitting. What had they been talking about? Her? Would Timothy have attempted to enlist Deborah's support?

He said he loved me, Maryann told herself, but even with hours between that confession and this moment, she did not believe it.

"Good evening, Timothy. Deborah." She kept her eyes on her sister as she crossed to her. She considered sitting on the settee across from Deborah, but feared Timothy would claim the place next to her, and she was not ready for that. She stood to the side of the settee, and Timothy stood opposite her. He would not sit unless she did. And she would not.

She looked pointedly at her sister. "How are you feeling?"

"Better," Deborah said with a relieved smile. "I think I have finally recovered from the travel, thank heavens." She looked from Maryann to Timothy. "And it is wonderful to have company."

"Yes," Maryann agreed, turning to the footman standing just inside the parlor door. "We are ready to move on to dinner."

He nodded, and Maryann followed him, leaving Timothy to escort Deborah.

Deborah sat at the head of the table, which Maryann took comfort in because it meant that she and Timothy would not be seated next to one another. Then she looked up and caught Timothy's eyes directly across from her. He smiled that teasing grin of his that made her insides soften. She looked away and wished she'd arranged for him to leave tonight instead of tomorrow. After a week, or maybe two, she could have written him a letter and asked him to clarify his confession of his muddled feelings. Perhaps they both needed time to understand what—if anything—was between them.

He does not love me.

He said that he does.

She imagined the petals of a daisy dropping to the ground one at a time as the phrases repeated one after another in her mind.

"I wish Lucas were here," Deborah said as leek soup was placed before her. "It feels odd to be entertaining you without him, Timothy."

"I am afraid I did not even stop to see him before I left London."

"Had you waited a few more days, you could have come with him," Deborah said. "He was hoping to finish his responsibilities by the first of next week, then close up the house."

"I'm afraid my purposes could not wait." He put his serviette in his lap.

Do not look up. Do not look up.

She looked up. Timothy's eyes met hers immediately. She could feel Deborah looking between them.

"And what *is* the purpose of your visit, Timothy?"

Don't say it, Maryann thought to herself. *Don't say it.*

"I have been visiting my sister in Trowbridge. My uncle asked me to deliver a parcel to her."

Maryann let out the breath she'd been holding and lifted a

spoonful of soup to her mouth. He would keep his feelings, or what he thought were feelings, between the two of them. That was a relief. She could make it through this meal after all. Then they would retire to the drawing room, Maryann would call it an early night for Deborah's sake, and she would not even have to see him in the morning. The traitorous, fantasy-filled part of herself regretted that he would be gone so soon. But London had forced her to grow up and see reality, which was that men were fickle, untrustworthy, and easily dazzled by a pretty face.

"I do not believe I know anything of your sister," Deborah asked. "Has she family in Trowbridge?"

"Yes, a daughter," Timothy said.

Maryann waited to see if Timothy would expound upon his sister, whom Lucas had said had been embroiled in some kind of scandal. Would Timothy tell Maryann if she asked? She banked the sudden desire to pose the question.

"It was fortunate for me that Trowbridge is somewhat on the way to Dunster. My sister helped boost my confidence in continuing my journey."

Maryann's hand tightened on the spoon.

"Boost your confidence, whatever for?" Deborah asked.

"Confessing myself to Maryann."

Maryann choked on her soup and quickly lifted her serviette to her mouth. Her eyes snapped up to meet his. His eyes were not laughing, rather they were serious and sincere.

Deborah froze with her spoon halfway to her mouth. "To . . ." She looked between them, then settled her eyes on her sister and lowered her spoon back to her bowl. "Maryann?"

Maryann placed her serviette in her lap, though she kept it clenched in her fist. "Miss Shaw will not have him, and so he has come to me because he thinks that I will." She shrugged to emphasize how little this affected her.

"That is not true," Timothy said, putting down his spoon. "I have come to Maryann because after all these months I have determined that I am in love with her."

Maryann looked at him but continued to speak as though she were addressing her sister. "He does not know his own mind."

"Yes, I do."

"No, you don't," she said sharply, embarrassment filling her cheeks with heat. "You are a silly man whose moods are as flighty as a sparrow!"

Timothy startled at her insult but didn't look away. "I *am* silly at times, I agree, but I am also very determined when I am certain of a thing. And I am certain of my feelings for you." He must have noticed that the sharpness in his tone was incongruent with his words because he took a breath and then spoke softer. "London lost its color once you left, and Miss Shaw's . . . mildness was the exact contrast I needed to see how invigorating it was to be in your company. My being here is not silliness, Maryann. It is determined devotion to . . . have you, I suppose."

Maryann's cheeks grew even hotter.

"For my wife," he quickly added. "For my partner and companion. To acknowledge it makes my heart soar like an eagle." He smiled a perfect, soft smile that brought tears to Maryann's eyes. It would be so easy to believe him. She looked at the tabletop between them.

Deborah cleared her throat. "I think this is excellent news. I have hoped for this from the very first introduction, and I am thrilled that Timothy has come to declare himself." She turned to Maryann. "Why are you so put out of this?"

"It is a game," Maryann said, her hands still in her lap. "He is desperate, and I am an easy choice."

"I am not desperate," Timothy corrected. "And coming to Somerset is not an easy choice."

"But *I* am," she said, looking up at him. "Because we have accord. Because we are friends. Because you know—" She barely held back the words *"because you know that I am in love with you."* She took a breath. "He is here because of fear," she said, glad that her voice was calm even though her emotions were not. "He is afraid he will not find a match."

He laughed, which only increased her fortitude. *A game*, she repeated to herself.

"I am not afraid," Timothy said. "I could quite likely have a match with Miss Shaw if I wanted it. I could also live the rest of my life without a wife. Nothing is forcing my hand save for the feelings that, now acknowledged, I cannot deny."

"See," Deborah said to Maryann, grinning so wide that the circles beneath her eyes were barely noticeable. "What have you to argue about that?"

The triumphant tone of Deborah's voice was equal to the frustration churning within Maryann's chest. She took another bite of soup, willing manners and decency to help her find her balance. After a few moments, Deborah and Timothy followed her example. The three of them made it through two more courses in silence, though Deborah only picked at her meal and occasionally put a hand on her stomach. Maryann hoped Deborah wasn't feeling ill, but if she were, she might excuse herself, which would give Maryann the chance to tend her. And leave Timothy behind.

"London can be a chaotic and confusing place to build a relationship," Deborah said as the main course was removed.

Maryann groaned at her sister's forced attempt to resurrect this topic. "Why don't we invite Timothy to stay a few days? He might like to take a break from the city and enjoy the sights of Somerset. He could stay until after Lucas arrives at least." She smiled at Timothy. "Maryann told me once that you have never seen the sea. You must stay long enough to experience it after coming all this way."

"Visiting the seashore would be the second-best reason for me to stay on," Timothy said, clearly delighted by the invitation. "Maryann gave me a set of paints, and I can think of no better place to try to capture on paper than here. From what I have seen already, it is a painter's dream."

"No," Maryann said, sitting back so the footman could take her plate. "Timothy will return to London in the morning."

"Oh, Maryann, don't be silly," Deborah chided.

She stared at the pudding placed before her. She felt ganged up on. Surrounded and . . . scared. She also knew she had lost. Deborah was the eldest and within her right to invite Timothy to stay until Lucas arrived. And Timothy would stay because it worked to his advantage. But she could not be a pawn in the game he was playing. Neither of them understood how fragile she felt.

She pushed away from the table, placed her serviette on the chair, and turned away without a word for fear anything she said would reveal her. She heard another chair push out behind her. She didn't have to turn to know it was *him*.

"This is not a game to me, Maryann." His tone was serious, which only said that he believed what he was saying. His belief did not make it true, however.

She kept walking.

He followed her from the dining room.

"It is not a game," he said again. She moved quickly down the hallway toward the stairs that would lead to her room. To safety. To solitude. She lifted her skirts when she reached the first step, wishing she could run. "Maryann, look at me."

She did not look or slow her momentum, but her heart rate increased as she heard his footfalls behind her. She lifted her skirts higher and took the steps faster. She was reminded of the time she'd challenged Timothy and Lucas to attempt to navigate a ladder in skirts and petticoats.

He took hold of her arm and turned her around. She spun on the step and brought up her hand to slap him for not letting her leave a room with dignity, for coming to Somerset after she'd finally gained the strength to leave him, for being a man of too many smiles and too much flippancy.

He caught her hand and pulled it toward him, causing her to stumble down the two steps that separated them. She fell against his chest, and he wrapped his hand around her waist, holding her against him, which ignited all the same feelings the dance had built between them. Her breath caught in her throat.

For a moment, she thought he would kiss her, but he let her go and took a step down. He opened his mouth to speak, but then said nothing and took another step down from her. They stared at one another while she blinked at the tears that said more than her words ever could.

"Give me a chance," he whispered.

Maryann turned and continued up the stairs, her skirts held high to keep her from tripping.

Her bedroom was empty. She paced, reviewing everything that was said during the meal all the way to his parting comment, which softened her heart too much to be trusted. She wished she had said *this* instead of *that*, pausing now and then to ask herself if she were being foolish, then pacing again with determination that she was being sensible.

She heard the door creak and turned in time to see Deborah step inside. Good, now she could convince her sister to send Timothy away. Couldn't she? Maryann folded her arms over her chest and lifted her chin. "He is playing a game, Deborah, and I am tired of losing to him."

"You are the only one who seems determined to see a winner and a loser here," Deborah said. She made her way to the bench at the foot of Maryann's bed and sat, resting her hand on the small rise of her belly. "You are acting like a child."

"I am acting like a woman who has been bruised before by this man and who is unwilling to be broken by him."

"Again, why do you insist on seeing only those two options? I have never met a gentler soul than Timothy Mayfield, and I cannot believe for even an instant that he would ever hurt you."

"He already has," Maryann said. "I can't bear it again, Deborah."

"Yes, you can."

Maryann frowned, and Deborah continued. "You are as strong as he is gentle, and if he were to hurt you again, you would lift your chin and continue on. But I think he is sincere in this, Maryann. I believe you have his heart and his devotion, and I do not understand why you are so set against his suit."

Maryann shook her head.

"I invited him to stay until Lucas returns," Deborah said, causing Maryann's eyes to snap back to her.

"Even though you know I do not want him here."

Deborah considered a moment, then shrugged. "Yes."

Maryann's fury built up equal to her fear, and she clenched her fists at her side as she tried to think of how to explain what was clanging in her chest. She'd hoped for her mother to get well, and she had died. She'd gone to London to make a match, only to find dozens of men willing to settle for her in exchange for her fortune. She'd thought she'd found reprieve in Colonel Berkins, and he'd seen her as a screen behind which to hide his true choice. She'd hoped to have Timothy's affection, and he'd chosen to seek out a woman of fiction without fault or blemish. Two weeks ago, he'd been making cow-eyes at Miss Shaw and spending every minute he could in her company.

But now Maryann was expected to rejoice in the blessing of him having changed his mind? Forget the hurts? Forget how often she had expected something better than reality had turned out to be? She felt tears rising and blinked them quickly away as she focused on her sister once more.

"You do not care that this hurts me?" she asked, her voice tremulous.

"Oh, Maryann," Deborah said, standing and walking toward her with her arms outstretched.

Maryann crossed her arms and backed up. She did not want her sister's embrace where she might dissolve into sobs. She needed to feel strong.

Deborah stopped, and both her arms and her expression fell. "I do not want you to dismiss a chance at happiness because you are afraid."

"You do not care that this hurts me," Maryann said again, this time as a statement. She turned away from her sister. "You issued the invitation," she said quietly. "You can serve as hostess for his visit."

"Very well," Deborah said, heading for the door, her voice sad rather than irritated. "Good night."

Chapter Thirty-One

$\mathcal{M}$aryann avoided both Timothy and Deborah all day Tuesday, though she watched from the window as Deborah took him on a tour of the grounds. She felt betrayed by Deborah for being so nice to him, but also left out to see them enjoying each other's company without her. She rolled her eyes at herself and returned to the ledgers which, thanks to her studious attention, were nearly caught up. At supper, she let Timothy and Deborah talk about visiting Dunster the next day.

"Would you like to join us?" Timothy said, drawing her into the conversation for the first time.

"No, thank you," Maryann said, cutting her meat. "James is bringing his children in the afternoon, and I've work to do before they require my attention."

"James is your brother?" Timothy said, looking between Maryann and Deborah. "The path you indicated led to his house, did it not, Deborah?"

"Yes," Deborah said with a nod. "He is the eldest."

"Right, and he lives in a house on the property with his wife and three children," Timothy nodded as he remembered the details. "What time will the children arrive?" he asked Maryann. When she did not answer him, he turned toward Deborah. "We should make sure to return in time to be of assistance."

"You don't need to assist," Maryann said. "You are a guest."

"As a guest, then, might I choose to assist with the children? I love children—spending time with my nieces is pure joy. We have such fun."

Deborah laughed. "Of course, you can. I shall warn you, however, that they are very energetic children."

"That is the best kind," Timothy said.

The next day, Deborah and Timothy took the carriage to Dunster.

Maryann had run out of accounts to settle and lists to make but felt obligated to remain busy as that was her reason for not going with them. She was beginning to feel foolish for her stubbornness, but she didn't trust herself to soften. Each time she was tempted to let Timothy's words into her heart, she remembered how delighted he'd been when he met Miss Shaw. She'd remember the list and how it felt to not meet any of those expectations. Yet he'd said the list was folly, which it was. Could he truly feel what he believed he felt for Maryann? Could the time they'd spent together really have made a difference?

Determined to be productive, she made sure each book in Father's library was in its proper place—a very important task, she told herself. Keeping her hands busy was not enough to occupy her thoughts, however, and she continually had to pull her mind away from wondering if Deborah would show Timothy the huge oak tree on the far side of town that was decorated with ribbons each spring. Or Mr. Greyson's bookshop where the man ran a lending library to rival those in London.

What if they go to the sea without me? Her stomach tightened at the thought that she *could* be the one to take Timothy to the sea for his very first time . . . if she were not so set against his company. Deborah thought she was being ridiculous. Her own arguments were feeling more threadbare with each repetition to herself.

He said he loves me. Why must I have so much doubt?

The children arrived at one o'clock, an hour earlier than expected. Timothy and Deborah had yet to return, so Maryann suggested a walk through the woods. Anna stayed close to Maryann's side, holding her hand, as the boys—Frank and Claude—ran back and forth from the stream to the trail. She felt calm in their company and enjoyed the summer sunshine as she exclaimed over the treasures the boys brought her—a stick in the shape of the letter Y, a rock, a leaf the size of Claude's hand. The boys were running back to her on the path when they both came to a stop, looking past her in a way that sparked her protective instincts.

She tightened her hold on Anna's hand and turned to see none other than Timothy coming toward her with long strides, his coat billowing out behind him. Her heart skipped, and she swallowed the nervousness that sprang into her belly. She would need to welcome him as a friend to cue the children not to be afraid of this stranger. She smiled as he came closer.

"Good afternoon, Timothy." Gracious, but he cut a fine figure in the dappled sunshine.

The boys came to stand behind her, cautious but curious.

Anna pulled in closer, hiding in the folds of her skirt. Maryann bent down and picked her up. Anna curled into Maryann's side and put her fingers in her mouth. So much for Deborah's warning to Timothy that they were wild children.

"Boys, this is my friend, Timothy Mayfield. He's visiting from London and is a good friend of Uncle Lucas." She gave each boy an encouraging smile. "Timothy, these are my nephews, Frank and Claude." She nodded to each boy in turn, then bounced the hip holding her niece. "And this is Anna."

Timothy bowed deeply and then offered his usual smile and sparkling eyes. "A pleasure to meet you all. Deborah thought you might have taken this route, and I fairly ran to catch up. I love nothing more than to be out-of-doors on days with such exceptional weather."

"The boys like to play in the stream," Maryann said.

"As do I," Timothy said with a nod, looking to the boys. "My brother and I would make boats out of sticks and leaves and such. Have you ever done that?"

The boys nodded, though neither spoke up. Timothy was not dissuaded by their hesitation, and within minutes, the boys were sitting on their haunches watching as he crafted a vessel from leaves, cinched together with sticks speared through the layers like toggles.

When they had made four vessels—one for Anna and for each of the "boys"—they headed toward the stream and set them to floating. Within minutes, Maryann was alone on the path while Timothy held Anna on one hip and the boys ran ahead, cheering for their individual boat to win. One would think they had known Timothy all their lives, they were so easy in his company. Her heart asked who would not want a man who was so good with children? But wanting him had never been the issue. Trusting him had.

The boys were completely soaked by the time they returned to the garden. They'd insisted on saving their boats, and Maryann had not argued fast enough to keep them out of the stream. She helped them remove their muddy shoes so that the mud might dry and the shoes could be cleaned before James and Adele returned.

The children were the perfect bridge between Maryann and Timothy, and she was grateful not to have the tension, but the lack of it also made her feel vulnerable. The more time she spent in his company, the more her refusals to accept what she'd dreamed for so long to hear him say faded away.

Timothy suggested they play tag while waiting for the shoes to dry. "The running shall dry your clothes as well so long as you run very, very fast," he said as he tapped Frank on the shoulder and took off on a run. Anna was on the ground, and she ran after Timothy with a happy shriek. The man was magic.

"Tag Aunt Maryann," Timothy called over his shoulder.

"Oh, no," Maryann said with a laugh. The children were well tended enough that she could make her escape. "I shall order tea." She managed to run through the kitchen door before anyone caught up with her. A quick peek through the kitchen window assured her that boys had turned their attention to Timothy. She watched for a few more seconds and then ordered a tea tray for the children before making her way to the parlor.

When she saw Deborah there, she paused. Deborah merely glanced at her, however, then went back to the book she was reading. Maryann came into the room, glanced out the window, and then settled onto the settee where she'd left her sewing basket.

She'd not made a single stitch since returning home. There had been too much work to do.

"Did you have a good time in Dunster?" she finally asked when the silence had chipped away at her resolve.

"We did," Deborah said and gave a short summary of what they'd done: driven around town, mostly, had tea at Geary's Inn, and visited the dry-goods store where Deborah had purchased some lavender candles. She said nothing about the oak tree or Mr. Greyson's lending library. Or the sea.

"I'm glad you had a nice afternoon," Maryann said when Deborah finished.

"I'm glad that you're glad we had a nice afternoon." She gave Maryann a sardonic smile and then went back to her book.

Maryann couldn't sit still—which was very Timothy of her. She put down her sewing and went to the window, then leaned forward when she couldn't see the children on the grass. A sound behind her caused her to turn.

Timothy held Anna on one hip in the doorway and the boys, still barefoot, ran forward. Frank had a vase half filled with water, and Claude held a handful of daisies. The boys handed their items to Maryann, looked to Timothy, who nodded his approval, and then they both scampered out of the room. Timothy caught her eye before leaving the room and winked.

She blushed despite herself.

With Deborah watching, Maryann put the flowers in the vase and set it on the table in front of the window. She stared at them until the boys racing back onto the lawn caught her eye again.

"Oh, yes," Deborah said, an exaggerated evenness in her tone. "A man like *that* should be avoided at all costs."

Maryann turned from the window to face her sister. "You told him my preference for daisies."

"No," Deborah said, turning another page. "You asked me about that the first time he sent you daisies, and my answer is the same now as it was then. No one is trying to manipulate you, Maryann."

Maryann stared at the flowers again. Timothy had only ever given her daisies, but it couldn't be a coincidence. He knew, somehow. "Two weeks ago, he was completely dazzled by Miss Shaw."

"And now he is here. Confessing his love for you." Deborah sighed, a touch of irritation in the sound. "He realized that he wanted you, not her, Maryann. He came from London to say it."

"You speak as though I should believe his confession despite his shallow fickleness. His feelings toward me are not trustworthy."

Deborah set her book aside, not even taking the time to mark the page. "And *you* speak as though he should be shackled to that silly list forever. What of becoming wiser through the experience life has given him? His choices were limited, then they were not, and through that, he learned what he truly wanted. He doesn't even need your money now, and yet you continue to paint him with the ugliest brush you can find and hold him in the smallness of one poor choice. Why won't you allow yourself to see more than that?"

Maryann said nothing, her gaze fixed on the flowers picked from the same woods where she had picked daisies all her life. Many were missing a petal or two, one had browned edges, and another's stem had been broken so that the flower hung down like the head of a dejected child.

"You won't answer me?" Deborah asked.

Marianne looked up, not understanding the reprimand.

Deborah repeated the question. "Why won't you let him in,

Maryann? Is it because of Colonel Berkins? Is that what has shut you off?"

"No," Maryann said. She could be honest about that much. "I simply do not believe that Timothy feels what he thinks he feels."

"And what of *your* feelings?"

"My feelings are irrelevant." Maryann turned away from the flowers and her sister.

"He will keep you warmer than your pride ever could."

"Deborah!" Maryann said, whipping her head to look at her sister, her cheeks hot.

Deborah smirked and stood, holding Maryann's eyes as she stepped closer. "Have you ever known Timothy to be insincere?"

"Yes," Maryann said without hesitation.

Deborah cocked her head to the side. "When?"

Maryann opened her mouth to reply but then could not think of an example. He'd been sincere in the drawing room the day he confessed himself in need of a rich wife but determined to marry a woman he could love as well. He'd been sincere when he ticked off the items of his list. He'd given her honest feedback regarding the women he'd met and found lacking, and he'd shared the insecurities of his childhood and his fears of taking on the responsibilities of a married man.

"You cannot think of a single instance?" Deborah pressed.

Maryann's shoulders fell. "He is not false," she finally said. He never had been. "But he feels things one moment and then feels differently the next. There is no way of knowing that what he thinks he feels right now will last."

Deborah put a hand on her belly, which did not yet push against her dress, though Maryann could see the outline when she emphasized it. "If you are determined to know his heart better than he does, then I suppose no one can talk you out of it." She rubbed her hand over the mound beneath which her child grew.

Maryann knew what she was doing. She'd lost a child already. It had broken her in hundred pieces, but despite the fear of another loss, she was trying again. Her hope was greater than her fear.

Deborah began to walk toward the door. "He has come from London to tell you he loves you, yet despite him always being upfront and honest and sincere, you refuse to believe him. Is that not shallowness on your part?"

Then she left Maryann to her thoughts, from which Maryann could no longer hide.

Chapter Thirty-Two

They had tea—or rather, lemonade—outside. Maryann forced herself to stay even though she wanted very much to lock herself in the study. She watched Timothy with the children and found herself wanting to cry. Was her fear, or pride, or both so much stronger than the feelings she'd had for him all these months? Yet, how did she simply step over those stumbling blocks when they felt like the only protection against her heart being broken?

After tea, they retrieved brushes and helped the children clean their shoes. They went inside and put together a wooden puzzle Maryann had done as a child. When James and Adele arrived—surprisingly on time—to pick up the children, Maryann invited them to stay for an early dinner, then watched as Timothy asked James about estate management, and Adele about where she'd grown up. Her mother had died when she was a child, a detail Maryann had always known, but it sounded different when she talked about the solitude that had followed her mother's death. And the way she'd felt put away when her father remarried a year later.

After dinner, James took his family home, leaving Maryann, Deborah, and Timothy alone for the third evening in a row. They entered the drawing room together, and Maryann gazed out the window that overlooked the woods separating the estate from the part of the seashore she had always thought of as theirs. The evening light was bright gold, foretelling a beautiful sunset.

Deborah and Timothy conversed behind her as she took a deep breath, pulling every bit of courage she possessed tightly to her.

"Would you like to come to the seashore with me?" she asked, still staring out the window.

The conversation behind her stopped. She hadn't said his name, but they would know who she meant. She could not look at him, not after all but ignoring him these last two days. As it was, her heart thumped like a drum against her chest.

"I would like nothing better than to go to the seashore with you, Maryann."

His words rolled over her like waves onto the shore. She nodded, then turned. "Let me change my shoes," she said.

They met in the foyer a quarter of an hour later. Deborah did not see them off, but as they made their way toward the path that would lead to the small bay, Maryann knew her sister stood by the parlor window, watching them, smiling hopefully and wishing them well. Maryann did not know what she was expecting from this excursion and tried to keep her mind from creating a dozen possible ways it might go.

"Does your father's land extend all the way to the sea?" Timothy asked.

"No, but this particular bit of shoreline has limited access, so I've always felt as though it belonged to our family," she said.

"Do you ever swim?"

"The current is too strong," Maryann said. "Though we wade in to our knees when the tide is out."

He continued to ask questions, and she continued to answer, feeling more and more comfortable. As the sound of the sea drew closer—breaking waves and the calls of seabirds—she felt herself relaxing. When they stepped out from the tree line, she took a deep breath, held it, and then let it out. She turned to smile at Timothy, meeting his gaze and holding it. "Here we are."

Maryann sat on a rock in order to remove her shoes. She had taken off her stockings at Orchard House, knowing she would not be able to resist walking in the shallows. As soon as she could, she walked past Timothy, lifting her skirts a few inches—not as far as she would have if she were unattended—and waded into the water.

The chill of the water took her breath away, but when the wave pulled back, she could swear it took some of her tension with it. Ebb and flow. In and out. Inhale. Exhale.

Timothy stepped beside her, inhaling sharply when the wave came in and washed over his bare feet. She looked down to see his feet also bare, his trousers rolled up to the knee. She laughed, and he grinned back at her. His face was filled with a pure and rapturous joy. After a moment, they both looked out to sea again. Timothy ventured forward, and Maryann wished she could join him, but it would require her holding her skirts up even higher than was already appropriate.

The splash of water in her face made her gasp even as she realized she should have expected it. Without thinking twice, she kicked water back at him. Her years of practice left him wide-eyed and dripping. She turned to run, which did not spare her from his retaliation, but the water only splashed the back of her dress. He chased her from the water and caught her arm. She spun around to face him, laughing, and they both froze. Stared.

Maryann swallowed as his smile softened. He did not take his hand from her arm, but the grip loosened while the breeze stirred her hair that had escaped the pins.

"Maryann."

Did her name ever sound as lovely as when he said it? Her heart was caught, and she didn't know what to do.

"I owe you an apology," he said. "When I first came here and declared myself, I was not very considerate of your feelings. I'm sorry."

"I forgive you, Timothy." She made to take a step back, but his grip on her arm tightened, then loosened. Then let go. She looked at him standing there with the sun at his back and his arms at his sides. Was she disappointed that he had not restrained her? *Be still*, a voice said in her mind. It sounded like her mother, and she felt herself relax enough to let this moment, whatever it might be, happen.

"I spoke with my brother," he said, his voice as soft as the waves behind him. She stared at the trees that separated her from the safety of her father's house. "He advised me to seek a woman who made me a better man. That was you. He told me to seek a woman who made me feel things—body and soul—that I didn't feel with another woman. That was also you. He told me that nothing would be more important in a partner than someone who would weather the storms beside you. He told me that imperfections did not eclipse the whole."

She turned away and braced herself to hear him say that he'd decided he could accept her imperfections.

He continued. "I am hoping with all my heart that you can see past mine." He put his hand on her arm again.

She closed her eyes, and when he pulled her gently toward him, she walked backward until she stepped on his feet, pushing them further into the sand. She could feel his breath on the back of her neck. She waited. For what?

"I am not a perfect man, Maryann. I am excitable, and I talk too much. I am not good at sitting still, and I am, as you have repeatedly said, silly. I am so eager to see the good in a thing that I don't always grasp the gravity of a situation or understand how other people feel, but I never intend to hurt anyone. When I realize I have, I am sincere in my apology. I know that I've hurt you. I have made you feel diminished. I am so sorry for that, Maryann."

"I already said I forgive you," she whispered.

"Thank you," Timothy said.

He ran his hand down her arm until his fingers wove between her own. "You do not trust me when I say that I love you. You do not think that I know my own heart in this."

Ah, there was the rub. "I'm not anything you want in a woman, Timothy."

"*Thought* I wanted."

She looked over her shoulder, and her eyes had to travel up until they met his. They were the same color as the sea behind him. The sun stretched toward the horizon, emphasizing the gold of his hair as the sea breezes swept across her skin. "And what if you change your mind, again?"

"I won't," he said, smiling. He brushed his fingers along the back of her neck, evoking a delicious shiver.

"How do you know?"

"Because I danced with and walked out with and flirted with a hundred women, and not one of them lit the room the way you did every time you entered. I never craved their company the way I did yours, even though I did not understand why."

She couldn't look at him and closed her eyes. *Did* he know his heart in this? Could either of them trust it?

"And then, Maryann, that dance . . ."

He released her hand and put both his hands on her waist, moving forward until she could feel his chin against the side of her face, his breath in her hair.

She inhaled slowly to prevent herself from gasping at the sensation of being this close to him. Timothy and the sea at the same time? Mercy.

"If you did not feel what I felt that night, then tell me to stop."

She swallowed and spoke in a whisper back to him. "I don't know what you felt, Timothy."

His hands tightened at her waist. "I felt as though you and I were the only people in that room," he said then dipped his chin and pressed his lips along the curve between her neck and her shoulder.

She did gasp that time.

"I felt as though we were moving in the same steps, connected through an energy granted by heaven itself. Everything about us in those minutes was so very right, and I felt as though it had always been there, only I had not known what to look for." He trailed kisses from her shoulder to the base of her neck, and she feared her knees might give way.

He reached out his hand and took hold of her shoulder in order to turn her smoothly in the sand to face him. She was completely captured by those eyes. She no longer cared that he would see all she felt within hers. His hands slipped back to her waist; his eyes did not leave her face.

"That was the dance for me," he said. "That is what *this* moment is for me as well."

She thought he would kiss her, and her hands came up to his shoulders, but he made no movement toward her, only continued to hold her in the power of his gaze. "Am I the only one who felt those sensations, Maryann? Because I think you felt them, too."

"I did," she said and with those words went the last of her hesitation to believe him. "But I had known that I would."

He pulled his eyebrows together, and she resisted the urge to press her finger on the worry line that formed between them. He didn't understand.

"I tried for months to see you as a friend because that was all you wanted from me." She blinked at the tears she could not hold back. "I tried not to compare myself to the women you pursued, I tried not to despise the parts of me that did not measure up to your paragon, and I tried, so very hard, to feel with another man what I felt for you."

"I am sorry."

She shook her head. She didn't want an apology. What she *did* want was harder to determine. "I let down my guard with you in ways I can't seem to do with anyone else. You listened when I spoke, you asked after me when our paths did not cross, you told me the truth when I asked for it. But even then, I was not what you wanted."

"What I *thought* I wanted," Timothy said again. His expression softened, and he brushed the tendrils of hair from her forehead. "I want you, Maryann. Now and forever. You have made me a better man already. Imagine what you could do with me in a lifetime." He smiled, wide and free. The waves crashed and the birds called and the sun gilded the moment in dripping gold. "Trust the feelings that you've had all along and that I've only recently realized. Let us be happy together."

Let us, she repeated in her mind. It was her choice, wasn't it?

He was not justifying his past decisions or making light of her pain. He was not insisting she see something his way. He was only asking that she be honest about the feelings she had. What she could say swirled through her mind, but none of the words felt right. Instead, she smiled at him and nodded, once.

It was all he needed, and when his lips met hers, the richness and warmth and power that had sizzled between them in Lady Dominque's ballroom descended like a summer rain, soaking through her dress and skin. When he pulled her closer, she went up on her toes and wrapped her arms around his neck. Her mouth burned beneath his.

When he pulled back, they both had to take a moment to catch their breath.

"Tell me you do not kiss every man this way," Timothy said.

She laughed, throaty and too loud for the circumstances. "I have *never* kissed any man this way, Timothy."

He kissed her again. "And you will never kiss another. Never."

"Never," she agreed, pulling him to her once more.

Again, he broke off the kiss before she was ready. "You love me?"

The soft wanting of those words made her want to cry. She thought of what she knew of his mother, his childhood, and what it must mean to him to belong somewhere. "Oh, Timothy, I do love you, and if you will have me, flaws and all, I will spend the rest of my life showing you just how much."

He smiled his wide, beautiful, boyish smile. "I shall hold you to such a proclamation, you know."

She went up on her toes again, feeling starved and drunk all at the same time. "I am counting on it."

Chapter Thirty-Three

imothy held his chin between his thumb and finger as he surveyed the remaining flower arrangements—elaborate displays of pink roses and peach-colored gardenias and, her favorite, daisies. A simple flower with deep meaning. "Set these last two on either side of the door," he finally said.

"You're sure?" Maryann asked, eyebrows raised. He'd already chosen three other locations before this one. Between Timothy, who loved any excuse for a party, and Deborah, whose own wedding had been simple due to their mother's illness at the time, Maryann had stepped aside and let them create the wedding party of their dreams. For her part, she'd have married Timothy over an anvil once she finally accepted that, when all was said and done, *she* was his perfect woman.

He paused, but then nodded. "Yes, by the door. I am sure."

Maryann nodded at the workmen who were waiting for her confirmation, and they each lifted one of the heavy vases. There was only so much decoration appropriate for a church wedding, but Timothy and Deborah had conspired to push the boundaries. A peach-colored cloth hung over the pulpit, and a garland of evergreens and daisies was draped across the balustrade. Timothy's eyes were wide and bright as he surveyed the room.

"Are you pleased, Timothy?"

He nodded but did not look completely at ease as he gave the room another once over. She placed a hand on his arm and leaned toward him. "It is nearly ten o'clock. We are to be married in less than twelve hours. Can we agree that this is good enough?"

"I do not want 'good enough.' I want it to be perfect."

"It *is* perfect," Maryann said, using her free hand to turn his face to hers. "And do you know why?"

He smiled, the tension finally leaving his face as he reached up and tapped her nose. "Because you will be there, and I will be there, and together we shall promise each other the very moon?"

She laughed. He was such a romantic. "Exactly. So, can we return home? Your family is waiting for us."

Peter and Julia would not be married for another month, and Maryann considered it generous of them to have made the trip so close to their own marriage.

Maryann and Timothy would live at her father's estate until they were ready to build upon the land that would become Timothy's upon their marriage. It might be years, she had warned Timothy when he agreed to the plan. He didn't mind. Like her, he had fallen in love with the sea.

His hand suddenly slid around her waist. They were hardly ever in a room together where he was not touching her. A hand on her back, his leg against hers. And when they were alone . . . even closer contact.

"You know," he said as he pulled her to him. "This is the last night we shall ever spend apart."

"So we had best get some sleep, as I imagine we shan't rest much come tomorrow."

His grin turned wicked, and he winked at her before releasing her waist, but kept hold of her hand as he led her from the church.

Father's carriage waited outside, and they climbed in, sitting side-by-side on one bench.

"I was thinking the other day," he said as the carriage rolled forward, "that had I simply married you right away for your money, we could have been just as happy as we are now."

She laughed, loud as always. He no longer winced at it. "What a strange thought," she said. She was still wealthier than he was, though tomorrow her fortune would become his as well.

"Not so strange," he said. "But I wonder if I would have known the choice was fully mine if not for my uncle's generosity."

"I'm not sure I understand."

He shifted on the bench so he could look her in the eyes. "If not for the campaign, I think I still would have pursued you, and I believe I would have fallen in love with you, but I think I would always wonder if my feelings were truly my feelings or if it was your money I wanted more."

"And I would wonder the same."

He nodded. "Yes, you would. What a terrible burden that would have been."

She snuggled into his chest and enjoyed the way he put his arm around her shoulders. On the surface, Timothy was fun-loving, perpetually cheerful, and at times even silly. But there was something deep and endearing and so very, very good about him. "Well, I am quite glad to have been the woman to put you in your place."

He kissed the top of her head and then rested his cheek against it. "In a few hours' time, my place will forever be right here, beside you."

She smiled and wove her fingers through his. He lifted their joined hands and kissed the back of hers before returning it to rest upon his knee, no longer off-limits.

"I just hope," he said, a hint of worry in his tone, "that everything will go perfectly tomorrow."

"We've talked about this," she reminded him. "Nothing is perfect."

"We may have talked about it, but I am not convinced." He kissed her on the top of her head again and gave her a squeeze. "Despite myself, it seems I have found it."

Acknowledgments

This story was a joy to write. Thank you to Jennifer Moore (*The Shipbuilder's Wife*, Covenant 2018) and Nancy Campbell Allen (*The Lady in the Coppergate Tower*, Shadow Mountain 2019) for helping me brainstorm it into life and to Jenny Proctor (*Wrong for You*, Covenant 2017) for reading the full manuscript.

Thank you to Lisa Mangum, my editor, and Heidi Taylor Gordon for championing the story, and Lane Heymont, my agent, for doing all the business work that goes into a published book. Thank you to Richard Erickson and Heather Ward for the lovely cover, Malina Grigg for typesetting, and Jill Schaugaard and Callie Hansen for marketing and promotions. I am so blessed to have this kind of team.

Thank you to my family for giving me purpose and readers for giving me encouragement and God for giving me a chance.

Discussion Questions

1. In this story, Timothy tends to look past the difficulties he experiences in life. How is this a strength? How is it a weakness?
2. Did you ever make a list of the aspects you wanted in a partner?
3. Did you have requirements that you later found not to be so important?
4. Who was your favorite character in this story?
5. Was there a particular scene that stood out to you in this story?
6. At the end, when Timothy confesses his feelings to Maryann, do you feel she was too hard on him? Too easy? Just right?

About the Author

JOSI S. KILPACK is the author of several novels and one cookbook and a participant in several coauthored projects and anthologies. She is a four-time Whitney Award winner—*Sheep's Clothing* (2007), *Wedding Cake* (2014), and *Lord Fenton's Folly* (2015) for Best Romance and Best Novel of the Year—and the Utah Best in State winner for fiction in 2012. She and her husband, Lee, are the parents of four children.

You can find more information about Josi and her writing at josiskilpack.com.

MAYFIELD FAMILY SERIES
Promises and Primroses: Book 1

*Hearts and history collide as two couples
risk it all for a second chance at love.*

"Kilpack smoothly introduces the Mayfield clan and sets
the stage for the series while making plenty of room for
developing this volume's central characters. The narrative
flows smoothly. Regency fans will be eager for more
Mayfield romances."—PUBLISHERS WEEKLY

"Kilpack [adds] refreshing twists to her latest sweetly
charming romance, the enticing launch of the Mayfield
Family series. Teen fans of Austen-era romances will
adore this novel's spunky heroine." —BOOKLIST